Daughter's Revenge

To Dolly,
A wonderful friend.
Love you,
Margy Millet

Margy Millet

Copyright © 2014 Margy Millet
All rights reserved.

ISBN: 1500810002
ISBN 13: 9781500810009
Library of Congress Control Number: 2014914517
CreateSpace Independent Publishing Platform
North Charleston, South Carolina

Contents

Chapter 1	1
Chapter 2	13
Chapter 3	23
Chapter 4	31
Chapter 5	43
Chapter 6	52
Chapter 7	58
Chapter 8	65
Chapter 9	75
Chapter 10	82
Chapter 11	92
Chapter 12	106
Chapter 13	120
Chapter 14	127
Chapter 15	134
Chapter 16	148
Chapter 17	160
Chapter 18	179
Chapter 19	187
Chapter 20	205
Chapter 21	214
Chapter 22	222
Chapter 23	234
Chapter 24	245

Chapter 1

Caroline didn't understand what was going on; all she knew was that her geometry teacher told her that her mother was at the school office waiting for her and wanted to dismiss her from school. Caroline grabbed her backpack and notebook from the desk. As she was leaving the room, she looked toward Greg to see if he knew what was going on, but he just shrugged his shoulders at her and shook his head. She quickly looked at Livy and got the same result.

Caroline walked out of the room and toward the office. This was the first time in her eleven years of school that her mother came to the school during school hours. She had come for parents' night, but she had never come for her before. Caroline was seriously concerned, but there was no one to talk to——the halls were empty and everyone was in class. She walked faster toward the office. When she got there, she went directly to the front desk and the office secretary gave her a dismissal slip. Lina, which was what her two best friends called her, took the slip and turned to where her mother was sitting waiting for her.

Lina could see the stress on her Marcia's face as she stood up and met Lina in the middle of the office. Lina tried to speak to her, but Marcia immediately took her arm and started walking, pulling her gently out of the office. She remained silent while they walked out of the school.

As soon as they got in the car, Lina turned to Marcia, "Mom, what's going on? Why are you taking me out of school?" she asked, her voice coming out a bit rough.

"We'll talk when we get home," Marcia whispered firmly, close to her ear.

Lina stayed quiet as her mother started the car and drove out of the school parking lot. The drive home usually was short, but this time it felt like they were driving at a snail's pace and it seemed to take forever. Marcia parked the car in front of the house, got out, and walked toward the front door. Lina stayed in the car for a few extra seconds, then opened the car door and followed her mother, still not saying anything to her.

Marcia went to the study and left the door open, inviting Lina to follow. Lina walked over to her mother and gave her a big hug. "Mom what's wrong?" she asked as her mother held her.

"Caroline sit," said her mother letting her go and sitting on the sofa. Lina hesitated for a few seconds just staring at her mother, "please."

She could hear the strain in her Marcia's voice; she quickly sat next to her.

"Caroline, your father is in trouble," said Marcia.

"What kind of trouble?" asked Lina.

"He's been charged with embezzlement of a very large of amount of money from the company," Marcia replied.

"What? That's crazy!" said Lina jumping up from the sofa and pacing in front of her mother.

"Caroline, stop. Please just listen to me, okay?"

Lina sat back on the sofa as she said, "Okay."

"While auditing the books, they found several financial discrepancies and, according to the authorities, all the evidence points to your father," said Marcia, now with tears in her eyes.

Her mother could no longer hold the tears back and started to cry harder. Lina moved closer to her mother and hugged her. She held her mother for several minutes until her crying began to slow down. "Mom, Dad would never do something like this, you know that. Don't you?" she said hoping her mother agreed with her.

"I know honey, but they have proof of everything."

"How do you know this? Who told you?"

"Tim called me. He explained everything and suggested that I should go get you before you heard it from someone else or on the news."

"Mom, where is Dad now?" she asked.

"He's being held at the police station. Tim said that he's being questioned."

Lina got up and again started to pace the floor, "Did Mr. Barnes say anything else? How about a lawyer?"

"No, he couldn't go into any detail with me. Yes, I called our lawyer already and sent him to the police station."

"Good, we should go see him."

At that moment, Marcia stood up from the sofa. She went to Lina and stopped her from pacing, turning her so they were face-to-face.

"I spoke to your father. He doesn't want us to go to the police station. He said to wait for him at home."

"Mom, this could take hours, even days. We have to do everything possible to get him out."

"I know. We have a good lawyer. Let's just wait, okay. Caroline, please?"

"Okay, Mom. But…," before she could finish, Marcia stopped her from talking.

"Just go to your room, I'll call you down when it's dinner time, okay?"

"Fine," said Lina, upset; she hated it when her mother treated her like a child.

As she walked out of the study, she could hear her mother crying again. Lina was not ready to cry yet. She knew her father was being framed. He was one of the most honest people she knew. He always told her that the path of honesty and truth was the only way. She walked up the stairs and into her room. As she put her bag down, her cell phone rang. She saw that it was Greg calling. "Hi"

"Hi, are you okay?" he asked.

"No, do you know anything about what's going on?"

"Not much, just pieces here and there from my mom and the news."

"It's already in the news?"

"Yes, it's all over the local and national news."

She walked to her nightstand and picked up the remote control for the TV and turned on the news.

"We're just around the corner, going thru the back. We'll see you in a few minutes."

"We? Who's with you?"

"Livy is with me."

"Greg, I don't think this is a good idea. You two could get in trouble."

"Don't worry about us. We're at the back already; open the sliding door for us," he said.

Lina walked to the door and just as she opened it, she saw Greg and Livy on the porch. They both rushed to her and gave her a hug. "Everything is going to be okay, you'll see," said Livy.

"My father didn't do it," she said looking at them.

She needed to hear it out loud, even if she had never doubted it. Livy and Greg looked at each other, then at her, "We know," said Greg.

They stayed with her in her room, surfing channels for news about her father. After a couple of hours, someone knocked at the door and announced that dinner was ready.

"I have to go down. My mom is very upset and I think she needs all this routine stuff so she doesn't lose it."

"Okay, will we see you in school?"

"I don't know, I'll call you both. Let me know if you hear anything else, okay?"

"Okay," said Livy as she gave Lina a hug and kiss. Then Greg did the same. They said goodbye to her and left the same way they came in. She closed the door and went downstairs to the dining room where Marcia was already sitting at the table. Lina sat down next to her mother.

Marcia tried to smile at Lina but failed miserably. Even though Lina wanted to ask her mother more questions, she didn't. She ate quietly and noticed that her mother was playing with the food just like she was. Lina took a few more bites and stopped; she couldn't choke down another bite.

"I have homework to do. Let me know when Dad gets home, okay?" she said.

Her mother didn't answer her right away. "Mom?"

"Yes honey, I will."

She went back to her room and tried to do her homework, but she couldn't concentrate at all. She tried a couple of times to do other homework, but finally stopped trying and put her books away. She lay on her bed with the TV on, listening to the news.

Everyone seemed to believe that her father was guilty. The news made him look like a despicable executive with no scruples or honor. They also mentioned his wife and fifteen-year-old daughter. She was so angry at the news that she shut off the TV. She lay with her eyes open, just staring at the ceiling. After what seemed like an eternity, she turned to look at the clock on her nightstand; it was just a little after midnight and her father still wasn't home.

Lina got up and grabbed some underwear from the bureau and went to the bathroom. She took a quick shower and put her pajamas on. She got into bed and continued to stare at the ceiling. She couldn't stop asking herself who could possibly have done this to her father. She turned it over and over in her mind, but not one person came to mind. After another hour, she fell asleep, exhausted.

Lina woke to the sounds of music coming from her radio alarm. She shut off the alarm, got up and went to the bathroom. After brushing her teeth and getting dressed for school, she grabbed her bag and went downstairs to the kitchen where Anna was making coffee, just like she did every morning.

Anna and Len (short for Leonard) were drinking coffee and talking. When they saw her enter the room, they reached out to her and gave her a hug. No one said anything for a few seconds. They let go of her and looked at her. "Anna, I need coffee this morning, I didn't sleep much last night," she said as she put her bag on the counter.

"Okay," said Anna.

"Are you sure you're supposed to go to school? Maybe you should stay home today," said Len.

"What for? Any news about my father?" she asked.

"No," answered Anna.

She took the mug from Anna and sat on one of the stools at the counter, slowly sipping her coffee. She stopped when she felt she had enough. She left the mug on the counter, grabbed her bag and went out to catch the school bus. As she walked to the stop, she noticed that all the kids she passed stared at her. She ignored their stares and continued walking, and at the next turn, Greg and Livy were waiting for her, like always.

They greeted one another with a hug and kiss, then walked together another block to the bus stop. They only had to wait a few minutes before the bus came. They got on and sat in their usual seats. No one said anything to her, but they continued to stare and whisper behind her back. Lina was content just talking to Greg and Livy about their classes.

When the bus arrived at school, they stayed seated and let everyone else exit the bus before they got up and left themselves. They entered the school and made their way down to the cafeteria. As they pushed open the cafeteria doors, everyone in the room stopped talking and turned to look at them.

Lina started to turn around to go back out when Greg took her arm and pulled her to the line for breakfast. Livy moved in front of her and Greg went behind her. Most of the students turned back to their conversations except for a few curious faces who continued to stare. Livy grabbed a tray and they went through the line.

Livy and Greg added food to the tray while Lina pushed it along. When they got to the cashier, Greg paid for the food and picked up the tray for them. Livy led her to an empty table while Greg stayed behind her. They sat down and Greg divided the food between the three of them. "Lina, eat. You're going to need it," said Greg touching her forearm to get her attention.

"I'm not hungry," she said.

"Just take a few bites, okay?" pleaded Livy.

She heard the concern in Livy's voice as she turned to look at her two best friends since preschool. Only Lina called them Greg and Livy; everyone else called them by their given names, Gregory and Olivia, just like they were the only ones who called her Lina. She took a few bites of the scrambled eggs and sausage. Livy and Greg followed her lead and ate.

"Are you sure you're going to be okay?" asked Livy.

"Yes, besides, you two are in all my classes. I'll have someone to talk to."

"That's true," said Greg.

When they heard the homeroom bell, they stopped eating and grabbed their bags. They emptied the tray in the trash and brought it to the counter. The cafeteria emptied out quickly as the three friends walked leisurely to their homeroom. The school day went on in a daze for Lina. Even though some students stared at her, no one came over and asked her about her father.

When the last class bell rang, Lina got up and left the room with Greg and Livy close behind. They went to their lockers and put away the books they didn't need for the next day, and then went out and got on the bus. The ride back home was quiet. Lina just stared out the window wondering if she would see her father that day. She didn't understand why he was not out of jail. "Lina, our stop is coming up," Greg said.

"What?" she asked.

"Our stop," he said again.

"Oh, yea," she said, still not completely taking in what he said.

The bus stopped and they got out, and Lina started to walk quickly towards home. Greg and Livy walked next to her quietly; she knew they were trying to give her space. Lina stopped at the corner where Greg and Livy usually left her to go to their own homes, but they just stood there and looked at her.

"We're going with you," Greg said as Livy nodded her head.

She smiled at them and started to walk again. When they got to her house, she got her keys out and opened the door.

"Mom," she called.

They all put their bags on the floor in the corner next to the stairs. She walked towards the study and called for her mother again. "Mom."

"Over here, Caroline," Marcia said.

The voice came from the study. Lina knocked on the closed door and opened it. They all walked in where Marcia was with Greg's father, Tim, and a man who definitely looked like a lawyer. Marcia walked over to Lina and gave her a kiss on the cheek. "Caroline, this is Mr. Campbell, your father's lawyer."

"Hi," said Mr. Campbell.

All three said hi at the same time.

"Where's Dad?" she asked.

"Honey, he's still at the police station," answered her mother with a soft voice.

"Why?"

"They haven't arraigned him yet."

"Why? When?"

"Please stop asking questions," said her mother, frustrated with her.

"Mom," said Lina, irritated with her mother, too.

Lina looked at Greg and Livy who were standing a bit away from the group.

"Marcia, if I may explain to her," said Tim.

Marcia nodded her head in approval and sat down.

"Caroline, the police are still doing their investigation and compiling the charges as we speak. They're going to arraign him tomorrow morning, then he'll be able to come home."

"Do you think he did this?" she asked him with no hesitation.

"No, I don't, but I have no say in the matter. The charges were brought by the auditors," Tim answered.

"I have to go Marcia. I'll see you tomorrow morning," the lawyer said.

"Okay, thanks. I'll show you the way out. I'll be right back Tim."

The lawyer left the room with Marcia behind him. Lina was aggravated with all this waiting. She wanted to see her father. Greg and Livy followed her as she and walked out of the study, grabbed her bag from the floor and went up to her room.

She threw the bag on her bed; she was very upset but didn't want to show it. She needed to stay strong for her mother's sake. As Greg and Livy both went to her and gave her a hug, she realized that her whole body was shaking uncontrollably. She was angry that no one would tell her anything more about her dad.

They hugged her until her body stopped shaking. Greg lifted her up, went and sat on the couch in her room, and settled her on his lap; Livy sat next to him holding her hand.

"I need to see my father. If they don't let me see him tomorrow, I'll need your help to get in. Livy, will you talk to your uncle the policeman for me?" asked Lina.

"I will," said Livy.

Livy leaned her head on Greg's other shoulder and brought all three closer. They looked towards door as they heard a soft knock. "Gregory, I'm on my way home. I'll give you a ride. Livy, I spoke with your father and he wants you home, too. I'll wait for you two downstairs," said Tim from the hallway.

"Okay, Dad."

"Okay, Mr. Barnes. I'm coming."

"Thanks. You're the best friends anyone could have. I love you two, you know that, right?" said Lina.

"We know," said Greg. He gave her a kiss on the cheek as he got up and put her back on the couch. Livy leaned toward her and gave her another hug and a kiss, too.

"Call us with any news, okay?"

"Okay."

She felt so alone after they had gone. She took a quick shower to clear her head. There was so much she wanted to ask her father when she saw him.

She put on a sweat suit and went downstairs. She looked for her mother in the living room but she wasn't there. As she approached the study, she could hear her mother crying.

Lina opened the door and saw her mother sitting on the couch with her hands over her face crying hysterically. Lina sat down next to her and took her mother's head and laid it on her lap, softly stroking her hair. After an hour or so, Lina heard a knock on the door. Anna walked in and announced that dinner was ready. "Okay, thanks," said Lina.

Marcia lifted her head from her daughter's lap and gave her a smile. "Thanks."

"I'm going to the bathroom to refresh my face, I'll meet you at the table," said her mother as she got up and walked out of the study.

"Mom, are you gonna be okay?" asked Lina.

"Yes, thanks honey."

Marcia ducked into the bathroom and Lina walked slowly into the dining room where Anna was finishing setting the table for them. She nodded to her and sat down. She just sat there with her mind reeling as she tried to think of ways she could help her father.

She and her mother ate silently, both extremely deep in thought. They ate very little before Marcia excused herself and left Lina alone again. She forced herself to take a couple more bites and then left the dining room, too.

She went to the terrace, feeling the need for some fresh air. She stayed out for only a few minutes before going up to her room. She opened her books and tried to finish some homework, but was able to complete only two assignments before losing interest in her studies.

She put the TV on the news. She dropped her sneakers on the floor and lay on her bed and listened to all the shit they were saying about her father. As she was about to lose her temper and throw something at the TV, her cell phone rang.

It was Greg," Hi," she said angrily. Greg sensed that she was upset.

"Hey, we're outside. Open the sliding door." She got up and went to the door and opened the slide. She moved back to the bed and sat up in the middle, leaving space for them. Greg sat to her right and Livy to her left.

"What's up?" asked Greg.

"The news is making my father look like this awful villain. They don't even give him the chance to prove his innocence and they're already judging him."

"Lina, you know reporters are just vultures and people love to believe the worst about people, even if they don't know the person. Everything will be fine, you'll see," said Livy.

"I know. It's just awful to hear them talk. What are you two doing here? Your parents are going to get mad."

"Let me handle my parents. You need me now and that's all that matters."

"Me too, besides you know how much me and my parents don't get along," said Livy.

Lina felt bad for her best friend. Telling her parents that she was a lesbian didn't go very well. Instead of supporting her, they distanced themselves from her. Livy was hoping to tell them about her girlfriend, but they didn't want to know. As long as she was discreet, they didn't care who she saw. Livy was the sister Lina never had and she would do anything for her.

"Let's find a movie," said Greg changing the channel.

When he finally found something they all agreed on he stopped. Within a few minutes, Lina was asleep. Greg lifted her gently while Livy pulled the blanket from under her. They got her comfortable under the blanket, and both gave her a soft kiss on her forehead. Greg shut off the TV and Livy shut off the light. They left the same way they came in and closed the sliding door as they left.

Chapter 2

Lina woke up agitated—her dream about her father was awful. She got up and took a quick shower and got dressed. When she got downstairs, she heard her mother and Greg's father talking in the living room. They stopped talking when she came in the room. She went and sat next to her mother who wrapped an arm around her waist. Lina was already taller than her mother.

As Marcia pulled Lina in for a hug she said, "You're up early."

"You, too. I'm going with you to court," stated Lina, not giving her mother a chance to object or maybe ask her to go to school.

"I know, honey. You want to see your father," said Marcia in a low voice.

"Yes," affirmed Lina.

Tim looked at her and gave her a big smile, "Did you let Gregory and Olivia know you won't be going to school?"

"Yes, I did. They wanted to come too, but I told them it wasn't a good idea."

"Yes, thanks. Those two would follow you to hell if you asked them."

"I would do the same for them," she said.

"Honey, go get something for breakfast. We still have an hour before we have to leave," said her mother as she gave her a gentle push at her back.

"Okay, did you eat already?" she asked.

Marcia hesitated for a moment before answering, "Yes, I did."

Lina could tell she was lying, but didn't want to start an argument with her. She knew she hadn't been eating well these past two days. Lina gave her mother a kiss on the cheek and went directly to the kitchen where Len and his wife were sitting at the counter drinking coffee.

They saw her coming and both stopped drinking. Lina sat on the stool next to Len, who put an arm around her shoulders and pulled her close. "How are you holding up, baby?" he asked.

"So-so. I'm having a hard time sleeping. I just want to see him."

"I know. You will."

"What do you want for breakfast?" asked Anna.

"Just toast and coffee. I don't think my stomach will hold anything else."

"Okay, honey," she said getting off her stool to make Lina some toast. Anna knew how Lina liked her coffee so she prepared her a mug and brought it to her.

Lina rested her head for a few minutes on Len's shoulder. He brought the other hand up and caressed her hair. Len and Anna had no children, so Lina was like their own child. They had been with the family since she was born. The love they had for her was totally unconditional. Lina took the mug that Anna gave her and took a few sips of the coffee. Anna put butter and jelly on her toast and put it on a plate for her.

As Lina ate her toast and drank her coffee, Len and Anna stayed with her, happy just watching her eat. After Lina finished her breakfast, Anna brought her a half a glass of orange juice. Lina smiled at her and drank the juice.

She put the glass down, got off the stool and gave a hug to Len and then one to Anna. She went to her room and grabbed her bag and her cell phone, which had been charging on the nightstand. She went back to the living room where Tim and her mother were still talking.

Lina sat next to her mother again. She only had to wait a few minutes before it was time to go. Marcia got up and grabbed her purse from the table and left the room.

"Don't mind her, she hasn't been herself," Tim said as he walked out of the living room.

"I know," she said following him out of the room.

The drive to the courthouse was quiet; her mother just looked out the window while Tim made several calls. When they got there, the place was like a zoo with reporters and TV cameras everywhere.

Tim got out of the car and helped her mother and her out. He ushered them both quickly into the courtroom, where they had to stop for security. Tim brought them to the courtroom where her father would be arraigned. Her father's lawyer was already there, and he directed them where to sit and sat down next to them.

Tim sat beside the lawyer. They whispered so no one could hear what they were saying, including her. In a matter of half an hour, the courtroom was completely full. They went quickly through two other cases before her father's. Lina was so nervous; the waiting was driving her crazy.

They called her father's case. He walked into the courtroom in handcuffs and looked up at Lina and her mother. The lawyer moved to the front of the court as his father came in. Her father winked at her and Lina's heart skipped a beat when she saw how disheveled and rough he looked. She gave him a big smile and winked back at him. The courtroom was suddenly all abuzz, and the judge had to call the court to order. The prosecutor and her father's lawyer each presented his case.

Lina was in a daze in the courtroom as the judge denied the lawyer's request to release her father on bail. Her father would be held at the police station until they transferred him to jail to await trial. Her mother was trying very hard not to cry. Lina was so angry that she couldn't look anyone in the face. She would have blown up at the slightest provocation. The judge said his piece and they moved on to the next case.

Lina didn't remember how she got home; all she knew was that her mother fell apart as soon as they got in the house. Lina rushed to her mother who was sitting on the couch, embracing her and holding her tight while her mother cried it out. After a long while, Anna came over with a drink for Marcia. Her mother couldn't hold the glass so Lina helped her.

"This will help her relax," said Anna in Lina's ear.

Lina nodded at her and gave the glass back to Anna. She brought her mother's head to her lap just like the night before and slowly caressed her back. After a few minutes, she could tell by her breathing that her mother was asleep.

Tim had been watching the whole time. When he saw that Marcia was asleep, he lifted her from Lina's lap and brought her up to her room. Lina opened the door to her mother's bedroom and threw the covers back on the bed as Tim carefully brought Marcia through and laid her carefully on the bed. Lina took her mother's shoes off and covered her with the blanket. They left the room and went downstairs.

Tim reached for her and gave her hug, "You're a good daughter," he said kissing her on the forehead. He let go of her, "I have to go talk with the lawyer. When Marcia wakes up, tell her I'll call her as soon as I find out anything. Okay?"

"Okay, thanks."

Line was finally alone, but she couldn't afford to cry; she needed to make plans to see her father. She went to the living room where she left her bag. She pulled her cell phone out and called both Greg and Livy and made plans to get together that night. She went to the kitchen and grabbed an apple from the fruit bowl and went out to the terrace and sat down.

As Lina ate the apple, she made plans in her head for tonight. After a half hour or so, she knew exactly what they would need to do.

Back in her room, Lina sat by the sliding door waiting for Greg's call. She put the TV on the news channel; she didn't have to wait too long to hear the segment about her father's case. The news reporter delivered a special report that laid out the story of the embezzlement and a description of her father's business life.

The news was so degrading. After listening for an hour or so, Lina was so disgusted that she shut off the TV. She was desperate to see her father and would do anything necessary to make that happen tonight, no matter what.

She closed her eyes and rested her head on the armrest. Even though she really wasn't relaxed it still helped her to get her head clear. After another hour with her eyes closed she opened them when she heard someone outside her porch. She pulled herself from the chair and went to meet Greg and Livy by the door. As they opened the slide, she grabbed her bag.

"Ready?" asked Livy.

"Yes," she answered.

"Let's go then," said Greg, "Stacie is in the car waiting with her older sister Lisa."

They walked out of the room and onto the porch and climbed down using the wall trellis. They went straight to the car and got into the back seat. As soon as they were settled in, the car took off. Lisa parked in a parking lot a block away from the police department. She made a plan to meet them back at the car in two hours. All four started walking towards the station. They got to the station and went in the front door and right up to the division where Livy's uncle worked. As they walked through the doors, one of the officers approached them.

"How can I help you?" he asked.

"Hi, I would like to see my uncle, Sergeant Wright," said Livy.

The officer instructed them to sit down and wait while he went to get him. They sat down on some chairs by the wall. Lina was very nervous and hoped their plan would work. After only a few minutes, Livy's uncle walked towards them.

"Olivia, what are you doing here?" he asked.

"Hi Uncle Phil," she said.

"Gregory, Stacie, Caroline. What are you all doing here?"

"Uncle Phil, can we talk to you?" Livy asked.

"Sure."

"Can we go somewhere else, please?" she suggested.

He pointed them to a room at the far side of the station. As they made their way to it, he stayed toward the back with Lina.

"Caroline, I'm so sorry about your father. No one believes he's guilty," he said.

"Thank you, Sergeant Wright, it means a lot to hear that from a police officer."

He opened the door to the room and everyone walked in. They all took seats around the table. Lina sat next to Greg and Livy.

"Olivia what's this all about?"

"Uncle Phil, you need to help Lina. She wants to see her father. All she hears from her mother, Tim, and the lawyer is that it's best for her not to see him."

"Olivia, there are specific orders for no one to see Joshua," said her uncle.

"Uncle, what can possibly happen if she sees him? We're talking about her father."

Lina moved closer to the sergeant, "This is my father. It's been two days since I've seen him. No one will tell me anything. I only know what I hear from the news on TV. Please let me see him."

The sergeant looked around the room and all of them were staring at him. He felt so bad, but if he disobeyed orders he could get fired. He paced in front of them, rubbing his hand on his chin. "I don't know…" he started to say but Lina stopped him.

"We have a plan that will keep everyone from suspecting it was you that helped me," offered Lina.

"Really?"

"Really," they all said together.

"Let's hear it," he said.

He sat in the empty chair next to Lina as she gave him the details of the plan. He was surprised that three teenagers had come up with such a sophisticated strategy, but it would work if everything went as planned. After they all were clear on the part each of them would play, they walked out of the room.

The sergeant went to the front desk and let his colleagues know that he would be doing a small tour to a group of high school kids for a school project, and that he would be gone for about an hour. No one questioned what he said.

He walked the group to the back of the station and directly to the holding cells. He opened the door of the cell where they were holding her father. Lina looked at the man lying on the bench. He didn't even turn around to see who was there.

"Dad," she said softly with a shaky voice.

Joshua turned around and instantly jumped off the bench and put his arms around Lina. "Caroline, my love, I knew you'd come. Phil, thank you."

"Don't thank me yet, let's wait until we pull off this plan. You have an hour; use it wisely," he said.

Lina smiled at him. The sergeant took the rest of the group to the far side of the station to one of the interview rooms. Each of them took a notebook out and started to take notes on his lecture.

Lina leaned closer to her father, not wanting to let go. He brought her to the cot and sat down with her next to him. "Sweetie, I'm so sorry you're going through all this…" Lina stopped him with a finger on his lips.

"Dad, there's nothing to be sorry about. I know you didn't do this," she said.

"Oh, honey. I love you so much. Now listen, we don't have a lot of time."

He told her when he first realized that something was off with the quarterly report numbers. He explained to her all the research and investigating he did, and that he had narrowed his suspicion down to three executives. He related the circumstances that got him into this situation, and figured that he had gotten too close to the guilty person.

"Baby, I have all this information on a flash drive. I printed some of the reports and there's also a notebook with my notes. I put everything in our special hiding place. Find everything and bring it to Tim. He'll know what to do," he said.

"Dad, are you sure we can trust Tim?" she asked.

"Yes, absolutely," he answered with no doubt in his mind.

"Oh Dad, I miss you so much."

"Me too, sweetie."

"You should go. You don't want Phil to get in trouble. I love you. We'll see each other soon. Okay, honey?"

"Dad, I don't want to go," she said holding him tight.

Joshua held her for a few minutes longer, then got up from the cot and pulled her up, too. He lifted her chin up and gave her a kiss on her forehead.

"I need you to get those things to Tim. I'm counting on you, honey."

Joshua walked her to the cell door that Uncle Phil had left open. He gently pushed her out and closed the door. Lina leaned on the cell bars and started to cry; she could no longer hold back the tears. Joshua moved towards her and captured a few of her tears with his fingers. "Don't cry sweetie. We'll be together soon, and we can put all this behind us. You'll see."

"Dad..."

"Phil," called Joshua, "Phil," he called a second time. After a couple of seconds, Phil and the group appeared again. Greg and Livy moved next to her and hugged her.

"It's time for her to go——for all of them to go," said Joshua, "again, thanks. Love you, sweetie."

He moved away from her and went back to the cot. She blew a kiss to him as they left. They walked quietly down the hall, and as soon as they got back to Uncle Phil's department, he escorted them to the front lobby and said goodnight.

They took the stairs down to the main floor, and left the police station building, walking quickly back to the car. When they approached the car, they saw that Stacie's sister was there waiting for them. They all climbed into the car and Lisa hastily drove off.

"Are you okay?" asked Livy.

Lina didn't answer right away. "Yes," was all she finally said. Her hands were shaking; she had this sick feeling in her stomach and her instincts warned her that something was wrong. Everyone saw how upset she was, so they all kept quiet, not wanting to upset her more. Lina sat back in her seat and turned her head to look outside.

Lisa drove toward Lina's house, stopping a few houses away. The group got out of the car and they all walked in the direction of Lina's house. Greg wrapped an arm around her shoulders and brought her closer to him as they continued to walk. Livy and Stacie stayed close to each other behind them. In about five minutes they made it to Lina's house.

"You don't have to come up," she started to say, but the other three just walked by her and climbed up the trellis. She followed them up to find them waiting for her on the porch. She opened the door and they all walked into her room. She sat on the couch and the others sat next to her. With Greg being the closest, she leaned her head on his shoulder and closed her eyes.

"He looks so tired," she said with a sad voice.

"Those cots at the police station look very uncomfortable," said Livy.

"He probably hasn't had a full night's sleep since he's been there," said Stacie.

"And probably hasn't had a shower either," said Greg.

"It's awful. It broke my heart to see him there."

She opened her eyes and sat up straight. She stood up and moved to the middle of the room, turning to face them, "It's late and we have school tomorrow," she said.

The three got up from the couch.

"You want me to stay with you?" asked Greg standing next to her.

"No, really. I'm fine."

They all gave her a hug and kiss and left the room. Lina closed the sliding door and leaned her head on it. She couldn't hold the tears back any longer and let them roll freely down her face. She stayed there crying for several minutes. When her tears slowed down, she moved to the bathroom.

At an unhurried pace, Lina turned the shower on, took her clothes off and got in. She let the water run down her body. After a while, she soaped up and rinsed off. She shut off the water, dried herself, wrapped the towel around her body and left the bathroom. She put on her pajamas, turned off the light and climbed into bed.

Chapter 3

Lina was startled awake by the alarm clock. She felt an emptiness in her heart as she reached for the nightstand and shut off the alarm. She quickly brushed her teeth, took a shower and got dressed.

She did her hair, looking in the wall mirror, and feeling that she was ready, she grabbed her school bag and cell phone and left her room. She went directly down to the kitchen where Len and Anna were. Right away, Anna got up from her stool and prepared a cup of coffee for her. Lina sat down next to Len as Anna brought her the coffee and sat back down.

"Thank you," said Lina.

They all quietly drank their coffee. Lina took a couple more sips, put the cup down on the counter and waved goodbye to Anna and Len. She walked straight to the front door and out of the house. She turned and looked back at her home——a home that right now was falling to pieces.

She shook her head and continued walking towards the street. She walked slowly with this odd feeling that she was leaving something behind. At the next street corner, Greg and Livy were waiting for her.

"Hi," said Livy giving her a hug and kiss. Greg did the same, keeping her in his arms for some seconds longer. He let go of her, slung an arm around her shoulders, and walked to the bus stop where there was already a group gathered waiting for the bus. The three friends kept their distance from the group.

When the bus arrived all the other kids rushed up the steps, but Lina, Greg and Livy took their time and waited for everyone else to go first. Greg found two empty seats next to each other, Lina took the window seat and Greg sat next to her, while Livy sat in the seat behind them. The whole ride to the school no one said anything. When they arrived at school, they went to their lockers and took out the books they needed for their first two classes and went to the cafeteria for breakfast. Greg took a tray and as the girls followed him, he picked the food. At the end of the line, he paid for everyone's food.

Greg found an empty table at the end and they sat down. They ate quietly, making small talk about the class that was coming up and about yesterday's assignment. As the first bell rang, they got up and threw the garbage away, leaving the tray on the counter. They got to the first classroom; they all sat together like always.

No one looked at her, not like yesterday when everyone stared, something had changed and she didn't know what it was. Class was over and she didn't even remember what the teacher discussed that day. She got up from her chair, put her book in the bag and walked out of the room. Just as they were going to the next class, Assistant Principal Meyers stopped her.

"Caroline, please come with me," said Mrs. Meyers.

Lina didn't react right away; she moved to the side and let the other kids enter the room. Greg and Livy stayed by her side.

"What's wrong? Why?" asked Lina.

"Please Caroline, just come. Your mother is at the office."

Lina took a step back from her; Greg and Livy moved closer to her.

"You two go in the room. Now," she said firmly to them.

Greg and Livy looked at Lina who didn't move.

"Go in, I'll be fine. I'll call you later," said Lina.

They both hugged her and went in the classroom; Lina followed Mrs. Meyers, staying a step or two behind. Mrs. Meyers didn't try to make conversation with her; as a matter of fact, she looked very nervous.

Lina's heart started to beat faster as they took the last corner towards the office. Mrs. Meyers walked into the office, and Lina saw her mother rushing towards her. She could see that her mother had been crying; her eyes were all red and swollen. Her mother stopped in front of her and pulled her into a hug. Lina heard her mother start to sob. Lina pushed away from her, "Mom, what's wrong?" she asked.

"Oh honey," was all Marcia could say before going back to crying.

"Mom, look at me," she said shaking her mother. "What's wrong with Dad?" she asked.

"I can't, let's go home. We can talk at home," said Marcia taking Lina's arm and pulling her forward.

"No, we can talk now," she said firmly as she pulled her mother to face her.

"I'm sorry honey," she said putting her hands on her face, "Your father is dead," just as she was going to say something else Tim showed up.

"Marcia, I'm so sorry," he said as he put his arms around her. Lina watched as her mother completely lost control and fell to pieces in his arms.

"Caroline," he said looking at her.

Lina didn't say anything.

"Let's get out of here," said Tim, holding Marcia.

Lina followed behind them. It all felt so surreal. She had just seen her father the night before and supposedly now he was dead? Lina wanted to scream, but looking at her mother she knew that it was up to her to keep control. They got in Tim's car and he drove off, but Lina noticed that they weren't heading to her house; her mother noticed, too. "Tim, this isn't the way to our home," said Marcia with a shaky voice.

"Marcia, you can't go back home. The police have confiscated all your assets until the investigation is complete," he said.

"What! But that's my home. It belongs to my family," said her mother.

"I know. As soon as they confirm everything, they'll let you go back home. For now you can come to my house."

Lina waited for her mother to argue back, but instead she put her head down and said nothing. Lina stayed quiet, too. As soon as they got to Tim's house, Lina got out of the car and walked around back to the gardens. She needed to be alone.

"Caroline," called Marcia.

"Let her be. She needs time to process all this."

When Tim opened the door, his wife Melissa rushed towards Marcia and took her in her arms. She walked with her to the living room. Melissa helped Marcia to the couch. "Can I get you something to drink? Coffee, juice?" she asked.

"No I'm fine, thanks Melissa," she answered as she stood back up.

After a few seconds, Marcia sat back on the couch and leaned her head back with her eyes closed. Tim motioned to his wife to follow him. She touched Marcia's shoulder softly and left the room behind him.

"Let her rest; just keep an eye on her. Caroline is outside in the gardens. She'll probably come in soon, but you should check on her, too."

"This is awful, Tim. How can this be possible?" she asked.

"I don't know Melissa. All we can do is to be here for them," he said.

"I know."

"I have phone calls to make; the police have a lot to explain."

Melissa nodded her head and walked back in the living room. Marcia was crying again. Melissa sat next to her and wrapped an arm around her shoulders.

After several minutes, Lina walked in the living room. She saw Melissa holding her mother while she cried. Lina walked to the couch and knelt in front her mother.

"Mom, I asked the cook to make you your favorite tea. It should be ready soon, okay?" she said.

"Caroline, I'm so sorry," said Melissa.

"Thank you, I'll stay with her."

Melissa let go of Marcia stood up and let Lina sit next to her mother. A few minutes later, a servant came in with the tea. Lina said thank you to the servant as she put the tray on the coffee table. She left the room and Lina went in her bag and took a small bottle out of it. She took a pill out of the bottle and put it back in the bag. She served her mother and herself some tea, handing her mother the pill and the cup of tea. Marcia didn't even question what she was giving her; she put the pill in her mouth and took a sip of tea.

Lina took her cup from the tray and settled herself back on the couch next to her mother. Slowly, they sipped their tea. Lina put her their cups on the tray and helped her mother settle her head on her lap. Lina started to caress her mother's hair and in a matter of seconds, her mother was asleep.

Lina had been caressing her mother for almost an hour when Melissa came back in the room. Melissa sat on the chair across from her.

"I gave her a sleeping pill. She'll be asleep for a few hours." As she was talking to Melissa, Tim walked in. He saw that Marcia was sleeping.

Lina looked up at him, "Can you please bring her to a room?" she asked him.

"Of course," he answered.

"I'll make the bed for her," said Melissa as she stood up from the chair.

Tim lifted Marcia in his arms. Her mother was a small woman, so it was easy for Tim to carry her. Lina followed them upstairs. After they settled her in bed, she took her mother's shoes off and covered her with the blanket.

"Let's talk," she said looking at Tim.

They followed Lina out of the room and went downstairs and back to the living room. Lina sat in one of the small chairs and Tim and Melissa sat on the couch across from her.

"What happened?" she asked.

"Caroline, maybe it's better if you hear it from your mother," Melissa started to say.

Lina shook her head, "No, she's not able to tell me anything in her condition. No Melissa, just tell me what happened. Tim, please," she said looking him in the eye.

"Caroline, the details are sketchy right now. They're still investigating."

"Fine, just tell me what you know," she said a bit distressed.

"According to the report, your father committed suicide sometime last night."

"What? No way! He was calm and well when I saw him last night," she said as she stood up from the chair and started to pace. She was very disturbed by what Tim said.

"You saw him last night! How? He wasn't allowed visitors?" exclaimed Tim.

"Yes. Tim, I saw him. Please just continue talking," she said trying very hard to stay in control of her temper.

"Like I said, the guards who were supposed to move him to the jail found him hanging by his own shirt from one of the ceiling beams," he said.

Lina sat back on her chair, remembering everything about last night. There was nothing that indicated that he was desperate or depressed. She looked up to see Tim and Melissa were staring at her. Melissa started to cry. Lina wanted to be sympathetic, but there were plans to be made for her and her mother; she didn't have time to grieve. "What now? When can we go back home? When do we get the body?" she asked.

"Caroline perhaps we should wait for your mother."

"Listen, my mother's whole life was my father. She isn't in any condition or mindset to take care of things right now."

"We know, but…," Tim began, but Lina interrupted him.

"Nothing is going to happen without her approval. I just want to take some of the burden from her, okay?"

"Okay. They're still investigating the charges against your father, so they're checking all his assets. As soon as they see that the house is in your mother's name, they'll let you back in. As for your father, they said his body will be available tomorrow."

"Okay," she said as she went into her bag and pulled out her daily planner. She opened the planner and pulled out several folded papers. "Here is the information you need for the burial preparation. You have the funeral parlor and cemetery phone numbers and names. Also, the number for the caterer for the reception after the funeral," she said trying very hard not let her hands shake when she gave Tim the papers.

Tim took the papers with a puzzled face. "Dad, gave me those papers about three months ago. He said if anything happened to him, he already had made arrangements. All I had to do was to call them. If you don't mind, I'll let you make the calls."

"Yes, I think it will be better if I do," he said, "I'll make the calls now." He stood up from the couch and left the living room.

"I need more fresh air," said Lina as she started to leave the room. Melissa nodded in her direction and said nothing. Lina knew the house very well; she spent plenty of time here with Greg. She opened the door to the terrace and walked out. She continued walking away from the house and to the gardens again. She sat on a bench and covered her face with her hands.

She wanted to cry, but tears didn't come. She was so angry with herself; she should have been there to help her father.

"I'm so sorry Dad, I failed you. But I'll avenge your death. I'll find the person who killed you, I promise," she said out loud.

Lina knew she had to get back home and find the information her father had hidden. She closed her eyes and all she saw was her father smiling at her like he always did. Lina laid her head back. After a few minutes, she got up from the bench and walked back into the house. After talking to Tim for a while, the rest of the day passed in a daze. She remembered flashes of talking to Greg and Livy, then having dinner with Greg's family. Her mother didn't come down to eat, so Lina brought her food up to her and helped her eat a little bit. Then she remembered saying goodnight to everyone and going right up to the bedroom they had prepared for her. She just took her shoes off and lay on the bed with her head on the pillow. She lay awake, staring at the ceiling with a heavy heart, wondering if she should tell Greg and Livy what her father had told her.

What if it's Greg's father or Livy's father? **she thought to herself.** *They're both executives in the company.*

After an hour of thinking through the situation, she came to the decision to tell them. After another hour of working out the plans for her father's burial, she finally fell asleep.

Chapter 4

Lina heard a soft knocking at her door; she opened her eyes and looked around feeling a little bit lost. Then she realized where she was. "Wait a minute," she said as she got up and went to open the door.

Greg and Livy walked into the room. Greg brought her closer for a hug, then Livy.

"I wanted to see you before I left for school, Livy too. Our fathers won't let us stay home," said Greg.

"Good, I wanted to see you guys, too. I want to talk you two, but not now. When you come home from school, we'll talk, okay?"

"Okay," they both said at once.

Greg and Livy hugged and kissed her goodbye and left the room. Lina closed the door and leaned her head against it. Her life had drastically changed since three days ago, and it was up to her to straighten it up again and prove that her father was innocent.

She went to the bathroom, took a quick shower and put on the clothes that Melissa had given her last night. As she made her way down to the foyer, she heard the voices of her mother and Melissa talking. She followed the voices and found them in the study together with Tim. The door was open so she walked in the room. Her mother turned to look at her, then got up from the chair and pulled her into an embrace.

"Mom, how are you doing?" she asked her.

"Okay…" her mother paused, "better."

"Great," she said as she turned to Tim, "How are the arrangements going?" she asked him.

Tim looked at her with concern on his face. She looked away and she could see sadness in Melissa's eyes.

"Well?" she said.

"Good. As of last night the funeral parlor has your father's body," he said.

"Okay, please call them this morning; have them prepare everything right away."

"Caroline!" said her Mother.

"Mom, I don't want to give the police the time to change their minds and ask for the body back. Tim please, ask them to get him ready for tomorrow."

"Caroline we need time to post the obituary in the newspaper, set up the wake," said Melissa.

Lina looked at her mother who was sitting quietly back in her chair. "No, there's no time. No wake. Dad wanted to be cremated. We'll do a small memorial service, that's all," she paused for a moment, "I need coffee," she said as she walked out of the room.

As she left the room, everyone remained quiet. She walked to the kitchen and sat at the table. One of the servants brought her coffee. They all knew her well because she spent a great deal of time here with Greg.

She slowly sipped her coffee and sat back in the chair, deep in thought. After a few minutes passed, she felt someone's hands on her shoulders.

"Caroline," said Melissa giving her shake.

"Ah, I'm sorry," she said, "What did you say?" she asked.

"I said Tim wants to see you."

"Okay." She put the empty coffee cup down on the table and walked out of the kitchen, noticing that Melissa stayed behind. As Lina walked into the study, Tim immediately started talking.

"I spoke with the funeral parlor; they will have everything ready for tomorrow, early evening. They will call with the exact time later on today," he said.

"Great, thanks Tim. Mom, we have to get ready to go back home," she said turning to her mother.

Tim jumped up and spoke to Marcia, "You can't go home yet. I spoke with the police captain; he said they're still investigating. The house is off limits."

"Damn it!" said Lina slamming her hand on the back of the chair.

"Caroline, that's no way for a lady to talk," said her mother.

"Sorry," she said.

Lina found the persistence of the police department infuriating. It was almost like they were doing it on purpose.

What can they possibly want in the house? she thought.

"Caroline, are you okay?" asked Tim.

Lina must have been showing that she was upset for Tim to be concerned. She had to stay calm. None of them could know about her father's secret, not yet.

"I'm fine, my apologies for my outburst," she said.

She turned to her mother, "I'm going to ask the driver to bring me shopping for some personal stuff we both need, okay?" she said putting an arm around her mother's shoulders.

Her mother looked up at her, "You're sure? I can go with you."

"No need, I'll be quicker alone. I'll be back soon," she said.

"Okay honey," her mother said giving her a kiss on the cheek. Lina kissed her back, said goodbye to Tim, and walked out of the study. As she made her way to the foyer, she saw Melissa coming with a food tray.

Lina smiled at her, "Thanks," she said as she continued to walk out of the house.

She went around to the side where she found the driver cleaning the car. "Hey, Tom. Can you please drive me to the mall?" she asked.

"Sure, give me two minutes; I'll meet you out front."

"Great," she said.

She went back upstairs to grab her bag and phone and out to meet the car in front of the house. Tom opened the car door for her and she got in. She told him which mall she wanted to go to. The drive was short; she was there in no time. She asked Tom to stay in the car, and said she would call him when she was ready to be picked up.

She walked into the mall, hoping there wouldn't be many people this early in the day. She quickly went to the stores and picked up the toiletries first, then to a clothing store for dresses and accessories for herself and Marcia. She found everything she needed with no problem.

She left the mall, took out her phone and called Tom. She knew she had at least five minutes to wait, so she went to the food court and bought a juice. As she stood in front of the mall waiting for the car, she had a strong urge to scream. She never thought she would find herself in this situation, but here she was.

Lina knew that proving everything her father told her would be difficult, but not impossible. She owed it to her father to try her hardest. After a few minutes of waiting, the car pulled up in front of her, and she got in and settled herself in the seat as the car pulled away from the curb. She had so much in her head, and everything depended on her getting into her home and retrieving the documents and flash drive her father had told her about. As they drove back to Greg's house, she came up with a way to sneak out and go to her house that night.

When they got back to Greg's house, she went in and directly to her room. She opened all the packages and put everything away. She went to the room where Marcia was staying and put her things away, too. She went back to her room, grabbed her phone, and checked for any phone calls or text messages.

She put her phone on the nightstand and went downstairs. She found everyone in the living room, sitting around making small talk. She went in and sat next to her mother. She put her arm around her shoulders and her mother leaned her head on Lina's shoulder. The conversation continued as Lina just listened. "Honey, have you eaten anything today?" asked her mother.

"No, but I'm not hungry. I can wait for dinner," she said.

"Are you sure?" asked her mother.

"Yes. I bought you a dress for tomorrow and shoes. Also some personal items. I put everything away in your room, okay?"

"Thanks honey."

"I'm going out to the gardens for some fresh air. Let me know when it's time for dinner," she said as she stood up. She walked out of the room and went through the kitchen, out to the terrace and on to the gardens. She strolled through the gardens, which were quite large, until she needed to sit down and rest. She sat down on one of the benches closer to the pond, where she saw some ducks and geese. As she looked around, she noticed the flowers were starting to bloom and she breathed in the many beautiful fragrances.

She settled on the bench and her mind went back to the night she talked to her father and how collected and calm he was. He was so sure he could get out of the trouble he was in, but someone stopped him before he could reveal the real criminal. Now it was up to her to do it. She hoped that Greg and Livy would understand the situation and help her.

"They will," she affirmed out loud.

She stood up and decided to take a walk into the back woods where she could really release her feelings without anyone seeing her. She walked for what seemed like miles and found a nice tree trunk and sat down. When Lina closed her eyes, all she could see was her father's face. She brought her hands to her face and started to cry, letting go of all the anger and sadness inside her. She gave herself permission to cry for a long time. This would be the last time she cried. After this, she knew she would need to be strong for her mother.

She brought out the tissues from her pocket and blew her nose and wiped the tears from her face. She stood up, brushed a couple of twigs from her pants and got herself straightened out.

She didn't know how long she had been in the woods, but it had certainly been a long time. She forgot that Greg and Livy should be waiting for her to talk to them. She began her long trek back to the house.

When she got closer to the gardens, she saw Greg and Livy walking towards her. She picked up the pace and met up with them.

"Hi," said Greg giving her a hug and kiss. He let her go and Livy did the same.

"Hi," she said.

"How was school?" she asked.

"Boring without you," said Livy smiling at her.

"The usual, you know," said Greg.

"Let's go to my room. I need to talk to you," she said looking around.

They silently went in the house through the living room and directly to her room. Lina sat in a chair while Greg and Livy sat across from her on the couch. Lina was not sure where to start. She looked at Livy's face, then at Greg's as they patiently waited. "My father didn't commit suicide. He was killed," it was the first time she had said or heard it out loud.

Greg looked at Livy, "We know."

"You do?"

"It's not like your father. He would have fought to the end to clear his name. There's no way he would kill himself," said Livy.

"Thank you," she said giving them a small smile.

"So what do you think happened?" asked Greg.

"When I spoke to my father last night, he mentioned he had been investigating the financial discrepancies. He also talked about some documents and a flash drive he was hiding with the information he had found so far. He believed he was close to finding out who was embezzling funds, but before he could be sure who it was, he was arrested for the crime. He knows he was set up to take the fall. He told me he had narrowed the search down to three executives, but he didn't have the time to tell me who they were. He told me where he hid the documents and flash drive," she stopped to look at their reaction.

Greg and Livy quietly listened to her story. She didn't see any sign on their faces that they didn't believe what she was saying. "What now?" asked Greg.

"We find the information my father gathered and start our own investigation," she said.

"Where do we start?" asked Livy.

"I need to get to my house and find the information," she said.

"That's going to be hard. I heard a conversation between my dad and uncle. There's a lot of police searching your house as we speak. My uncle was pushing my dad to tell him what they were looking for. He never got an answer from him."

Lina stood up pacing in front of them, "I think they're looking for my dad's papers. They must be nervous," Lina sat back down.

"Okay, when are we going?" asked Greg.

"Tonight, after everyone goes to bed," answered Lina.

"Okay, let's meet at the back of the coffee shop. What time?" asked Livy.

"Good, how about eleven o'clock? I know my mom will be in bed early, and your parents always go to bed early, too," said Lina.

They discussed their plan a bit longer until someone knocked on her door. Lina got up to open the door. Greg's mother walked into the room.

"It's dinner time. You all should clean up," she said.

"Okay," they all answered together.

Greg's mother left the room and closed the door. They all looked at each other, and out of nowhere all three embraced in a big hug. Lina leaned her head on Greg's shoulder while Livy gently touched her face. Lina didn't cry. She had promised herself she wouldn't cry again until she cleared her father's name.

Greg went to his own room while Lina and Livy went to the bathroom to wash their hands and make sure they looked presentable. They met up with Greg on their way downstairs, and they went directly to the dining room where Greg's parents and Lina's mother were already sitting at the table.

As each of them took a chair, the servants brought out the food. Dinner passed almost in silence, with the exception of Tim making small talk to Marcia and his wife. None of the adults directed any conversation to the three teenagers. As dinner came to an end, Lina, Greg, and Livy made their excuses and left the dining room. Instead of going back to the room, because it was early evening and the weather was nice, they went out to the terrace. They sat down and tried to enjoy the weather.

They continued talking in very low voices about Lina's father. They talked about the executives they knew from the company, and speculated about who had the knowledge and skills to pull off the embezzlement. When Tim came out to the terrace, they quickly changed the subject to school and classes. Tim watched over them for a few minutes. "Olivia, it's getting late. Don't you think it's time for you to go home?" he asked.

"Yes of course. I'll see you two tomorrow," she said as she gave Greg and Lina each a kiss on the cheek. "Good night Mr. Barnes," she said as she walked into the house and out the front door. Livy only lived a couple of blocks from Greg's house so there was no need to call anyone to pick her up. She walked home alone all the time.

"You two should get ready for bed. Tomorrow is going to be a hard day for everyone."

Greg didn't like that his father was treating them like little kids. He started to say something when Lina stopped him.

"Yes, goodnight Tim," she said pulling Greg by his hand. Greg didn't resist and went in the house with her.

"What's that all about?" he asked her.

"You were about to argue with your father. We don't need this right now, okay? Let's go say goodnight to our mothers," she said still holding his hand, which he didn't mind at all.

As they were walking into the living room, Lina's mother was just walking out.

"Caroline, I was just about to look for you so I could say goodnight," her mother said.

"Me, too. I just came to say goodnight."

She hugged her mother and gave her a kiss on the cheek. Her mother held on to her for a few minutes, almost in desperation. "Mom," she said.

Marcia looked at her, "Goodnight honey," she said.

On the other side of the living room, Greg was saying goodnight to his mother.

"Goodnight, Mom," said Lina.

Marcia let go of her and walked out of the living room. Lina watched her go; her mother had always walked tall and straight, but now her shoulders were slumped and her head drooped forward. Lina hated what this was doing to her. She turned back to the living where she saw Melissa and Greg staring at her. "Goodnight Melissa, Greg," she said quickly and moved away, not giving them a chance to say anything.

She went back to her room and took a quick shower. She got dressed in dark clothes and put her hair up in a bun. She shut the lights off, sat on the couch, and put the TV on very low volume so she could have some light in the room.

She leaned her head back on the couch and closed her eyes for a few minutes. She could hear her mother crying in the next room. About an hour later, she could hear Tim and Melissa going to their room. She waited until she didn't hear any more sounds from their room, then she shut off the TV, took her bag and phone, and went very stealthily to Greg's room.

Greg was sitting on his bed waiting for her. It was only ten o'clock, so they still had an hour. He tapped the bed and she went and sat next to him. He wrapped an arm around her shoulders and brought her close to his body. She closed her eyes and inhaled his essence. She loved the way he smelled———a mix of musk deodorant and his own male essence. She would never forget his smell—it was imprinted on her inner senses. She liked to feel his body heat, too. He was always so comfortable to lean into, even though he had a muscular body for his age. They stayed like that for half an hour. He moved his arm away and got up from the bed. Having her so close was making his body feel things that he couldn't allow right now.

"Time to go," he said.

She slid off of the bed as he took her hand in his and they walked very quietly out of his room. They took the stairs one at a time so as not to make any noise. When they made it to the bottom, instead of going to the front door, they went to the living room and out to the terrace. Slowly, they made their way to the side of the house and into the street.

They paced their steps so as not to attract anyone's attention. They got to the coffee shop and only waited for five minutes before Livy showed up. Lina looked around to see if anyone noticed them.

"Let's get going," said Lina as she started to walk.

Lina's house was about two blocks from the coffee shop in the opposite direction from Greg and Livy's houses. They kept a steady pace, walking casually so they wouldn't attract any attention from the occasional dog walker or runner they passed on their way.

They made it to her house in no time. The first thing they saw was a police car parked in front of the driveway entrance. They approached the car very slowly from the back, and quietly sneaked by it to the side of the driveway behind the shrubs. As they slowly made their way up the driveway, they saw two more cops go by them.

As they were right under Lina's room, someone came towards them. They didn't have enough time to react as Livy's Uncle Phil approached them. "What the hell are you three doing here?" he whispered in a displeased voice.

"Uncle Phil, Lina wants to go in the house," said Livy.

"You're crazy. There are about twenty police officers and FBI agents in your house."

"What? Why?" said Lina, in shock.

"Exactly, I don't know what's going on but the captain got a court order from the judge to search your house," he said.

Lina looked at Greg and Livy and was calm again. She knew they would never find the hiding place, but someone knew about her father's papers, that was for sure. Sergeant Wright moved closer to her and gave her a hug.

"Caroline, I can't let you in. I don't think they know for sure that you were with Joshua last night, but I think the captain suspects something. He was mad as hell at me because of last night's tour. Go back to Greg's until this is resolved. You'll get your home back soon," he said letting her go.

Lina understood the position Livy's uncle was in. She didn't want to get him in trouble. "I understand, thanks Sergeant Wright," she said as she started to walk back the way they came.

Greg followed her while Livy gave her uncle a kiss on the cheek and caught up with them. Lina walked quietly, keeping away from the driveway. Greg and Livy stayed close to her. As soon as they were back in the street away from her house, Lina turned around and looked at them. "Thank you, you're the best friends anyone can have," she said.

Greg and Livy surrounded her in a big hug.

"Sorry we couldn't get in," said Livy.

"That's okay. They won't find the papers," she said.

"Are you sure?" asked Greg.

"Yes," she said stepping away from them. "Let's go before someone notices we're missing." She took them both by the hand and started to walk away.

They walked quickly back to Greg's place. Livy's house was on the way, so she they dropped her off and were back at Greg's in no time. They sneaked back into the house and upstairs. Lina gave Greg a hug and kiss on the cheek.

"Thank you," she whispered in his ear.

"You're welcome," he whispered back.

She let go of him and walked to her room.

Chapter 5

Lina woke up emotionally exhausted. Keeping her emotions in check while around her mother and everyone else was taking a toll on her, but she knew there was no other way. She sat at the edge of the bed, put her head in her hands, and took deep breaths. "Oh Dad, I miss you so much. I'll take care of Mom, I promise," she said out loud.

She went to the bathroom, took a shower, got dressed and went downstairs. She was not ready to see anyone, so she went straight to the kitchen for coffee. There was no one in the kitchen, but she saw that the coffee maker was on. She took a cup from the cabinet and poured herself some coffee. She found the sugar on the counter and stirred two teaspoons into her mug. She took a sip of the coffee.

She opened the sliding doors and went out to the terrace. She sat down on a chair overlooking the gardens. She just stared at the gardens for some time, not thinking of anything in particular until Melissa came out. "Hi, Marcia is looking for you," she said, then turned and walked back into the house.

"Oh, okay," Lina said as she watched Melissa leave.

She stood up and followed Melissa in, putting the empty coffee cup on the counter. She knew they were probably in the dining room having breakfast. She walked in and sat next to her mother. Marcia wrapped an arm over her shoulders, pulling her close and giving her a kiss on the forehead.

A servant brought a plate with food and put it in front of Lina. Her first reaction was to say no, but she knew that her mother was watching her, so she just said thank you to the servant.

Her mother turned to her own food and started to eat. Lina did the same. Lina moved the food around the plate and only took a few small bites.

"I spoke earlier with Mr. Jones from the funeral parlor. Everything is ready for tonight at six o'clock. I sent a note to several friends about it. Marcia, if you don't mind, I would like to say a few words at the memorial," Tim said.

"Not at all. Thanks Tim," her mother said.

Lina didn't say anything; she kept pretending to eat.

"Tim, anything about the house?" asked Marcia.

"Nothing new. The word from the police captain is that they're still investigating," he answered with an upset voice.

"Oh," was all Marcia said.

Lina took a sip of her orange juice then slowly got up from her chair. "I'll be in my room. What time will we be leaving for the funeral parlor?" she asked.

"Around 5:30? Marcia, what do you think?" he asked her mother.

"Yes, 5:30 will be good."

"I'll be ready," she said, moving from the table and walking out.

"Caroline," called Melissa, "if you need help with anything you let us know, okay."

Lina turned and looked at all three of them, then brought her attention to Melissa. "Yes, thanks," was all she was able to say without losing control.

She walked up to the room, closed the door, and she leaned her back against the door and closed her eyes. Lina's heart felt like someone was squeezing it hard. Going to the funeral parlor would make the death of her father real. Tears ran down her face. She brought a hand to her face and briskly wiped the tears from her cheeks. She went to the bathroom, washed her face and went back to the room.

Lina put the TV on a movie channel; one that would help her stop thinking about her father. The memories of her father flooded her mind, and her heart was breaking. She shook her head and focused on the movie. After it was over, she picked up one of the books she'd been putting aside to read for a rainy day and she started to read it.

She read for a while, until suddenly she heard her mother in the other room. Lina could hear that Marcia was crying, so she went to her room, opened the door without knocking, and walked in. "Mom," she said softly as she went to where Marcia was sitting.

Lina held her Mother in her arms and slowly massaged her back, then her head. Marcia cried for some time, then after several minutes she was able to speak. "I'm sorry, I tried so hard to not cry, but I can't help it. I loved your father so much," she said.

"I know Mom, me too."

Marcia lifted a hand and softly touched her face, "I can't live without him."

"Yes you can and you will. We have to remember him as he was: caring, loving, and funny. He wouldn't want you to destroy your life because of him. I'll be here to help you, okay?"

"Thanks honey. I'm fine. Go get ready," she said as she kissed Lina's cheek.

Lina went back to her room to get ready. In no time at all, she was showered, dressed, and downstairs. She went in the living, sat down on one of the small chairs and waited for the rest of the group. After a few minutes, everyone came down and was ready to go, including Greg. Greg sat next to her in the car, and her mother sat next to her on the other side.

Everyone was quiet on the way to the funeral parlor. When they got there, Lina followed everyone out of the car and waited for her mother. Marcia hesitated in front of the door. Lina moved next to her, took her arm, and slowly they both walked into the funeral parlor.

They entered the room where her father's urn was placed. Marcia and Lina sat in the front row, while Greg and his family sat behind them. Livy and her family sat behind them, too. Lina held her mother's hand tightly to stop it from shaking.

For about a half an hour, people steadily came up to them and offered condolences. After several minutes went by with no one else approaching them, Tim got off his chair and stood behind the podium next to where the urn was placed. He waited until everyone quieted down and was seated, then he started to speak.

Marcia lasted about five minutes into the speech before she started to cry. Lina gave her a tissue and threw her arm over her mother's shoulders, pulling her closer to her as Tim continued with his memorial speech. Lina looked around the room and saw that everyone was in tears. She noticed that her mother's doctor was trying to get her attention; she nodded to him and went back to listening to Tim.

She didn't need another person to tell her how great her father was; she knew better than anybody. He was a wonderful father to her. After another five minutes or so, Tim finished his speech. He walked toward Lina's mom. Lina let go of her, and Tim gave Marcia a hug and kiss. "I'm so sorry," he said to her mother with sadness in his voice and tears on his face.

He went to Lina and gave her a kiss on her forehead. Lina gave him a small smile. They stayed in the room for another few minutes until Melissa announced that there was coffee and pastries in the room down the hall. Melissa took Marcia's arm and helped her stand up. They walked to the urn and said their goodbyes; then they all walked out of the room together. One by one the people went by the urn and said some words.

Lina stayed behind at her seat, and Greg, Livy, and Stacie stayed with her. She just sat there staring at the urn for a few moments.

"You want us to go?" asked Stacie.

"No stay. I just don't know what to say," she said.

"Say what's in your heart," said Livy.

"Thanks," and without giving it a second thought, she stood and said," Dad, I will revenge your death, I promise."

She turned and looked at her friends.

"I'll help you," said Greg.

All three of them came to her and embraced her in a group hug. Lina took a hand from each between hers and smiled at them. They all walked out of the room and down the hall to where everyone was gathered. Lina walked into the room with her friends beside her. Slowly and methodically, she moved around the room, shaking hands with everyone there and listening to their sympathetic words. When she got to Dr. Webster, he pulled her to a corner away from the group.

"Caroline, how are you doing, darling?" he asked.

"I'm okay," she answered.

"Good. Your mother isn't. She called me yesterday to ask me for medication to help her sleep. I spoke with her for quite a while," he said.

"And?" said Lina.

"She's not doing well. You need to get her out of here; this entire police situation is upsetting her. The word that I hear from the police is that the investigation is ongoing. I don't think being around this place is doing her any good," he said firmly. She listened to what the doctor had to say. She knew her mother was very upset; she saw it in her eyes.

"Thank you, Dr. Webster. I will."

The doctor walked her back to her mother and left the room. After a few minutes, the group began to disperse and people started to leave. She moved closer to her mother; she saw her uncertainty and took her hand. They stayed together until the last of the people were gone, leaving them with just Greg and his parents. The funeral parlor attendant carried the urn over to her mother. He placed the urn in her hands, then gave her a hug and kiss on the cheek and left the room.

Her mother held the urn tightly to her chest and a small stream of tears rolled down her cheeks. Lina held her mother by her waist and they all moved towards the front of the funeral parlor. As they exited the building, they were approached by Captain Wright. She could feel her mother's body starting to shake when she saw him. "My sympathies," was all he said to her and walked away.

On the ride back to Greg's house, she sat next to her mother, not letting go of her. Everyone was extremely tense and stayed very quiet. You could clearly hear the sounds of the traffic around them. As soon as the car stopped in front of the house, she helped her mother out.

Marcia walked to the house very slowly with Lina still holding onto her. Lina brought her mother directly to her room. She helped her get ready for bed, settled her in, and then went down to the kitchen and asked a servant to make some tea for her mother. Lina sat at the table waiting for the tea, which was ready in a couple of minutes. She took the tray that the servant set up for her and went back up to her mother's room.

She settled the tray on the small table next to the couch, poured a cup for her mother, and added something to it. She went to the bed and helped her mother to sit up, then she went back and picked up the cup and brought it to her. Her mother took the cup and took a sip. Lina poured a cup for herself and sat on the bed next to her.

They sipped their tea slowly, savoring the wild berry taste——her mother's favorite. When Marcia stopped drinking her tea, Lina noticed that she still had some left in the cup.

"Two more sips, okay?" she coaxed her.

Her mother looked at her and gave her a smile. She drank the requested two sips before Lina took the cup from her. Lina went back to help her mother get comfortable. Marcia took the urn and pulled it closer to her chest.

"Good night honey, thanks," her mother said.

"Good night Mom," said Lina, giving her a kiss.

Lina shut the light off, walked out of the room, and closed the door. She went to her room, quickly changing into jeans and a sweatshirt. She picked up her phone and walked out of the room. When she made it to the foyer, she heard voices coming from the living room. She didn't want to face anyone right now so she went to the kitchen and out to the terrace. The garden lights were on, so she went out further. As soon as she was away from the house she made a call. Lina talked on the phone for a long time. After she hung up, she took a deep breath of relief. She knew right then that her plans had to change; she could no longer proceed to get the documents.

Her priority was her mother's health. Her revenge for her father's killer would have to wait. She walked back to the terrace and sat on one of the chairs. She heard someone coming out and looked up to see Daniel, Greg's older brother and the man she believed she was in love with. Daniel's face was serious, almost like he was angry.

"Daniel, hi," she said.

"Hi, that's all you have to say," he demanded of her.

"What do you want me to say?" she asked.

Daniel moved closer to her, he looked her up and down with what looked like disgust on his face. Lina took a step away from him.

"Look at you, the mighty Caroline. You don't belong in my house. All you're bringing is bad talk about my family. Your father was a criminal, and instead of facing his punishment, he took the easy way out. He was a coward."

Lina brought her hand up to slap him, but he was quicker than her and grabbed her hand. He lightly pushed her away.

"You're no good for my brother. You're nothing but a criminal's daughter now. Do me and my family a favor and take your mother and leave," he screamed at her, then he turned around and went back in the house.

Lina was shocked by his harsh words. He was the love of her life——the man she had dreamed she would marry since she was a little girl. Now his hatred for her was obvious. She brought her hands to her face and started to cry. She cried for the death of her father, and she cried for her mother's suffering, and now she cried for losing the man she thought she was in love with. Finally she cried for losing her best friend and her home.

"Enough," she said out loud.

She stopped crying and wiped her tears from her face. She needed to calm her nerves down and clear her head before she went back in the house. She took another long walk in the gardens. After she felt that she was in control, she went back inside the house.

She went upstairs and directly into Greg's room. She didn't knock; she just opened the door and walked in.

"I was waiting for you," he said sitting up on his bed. She went to him, sat next to him and gave him a hug.

"Shouldn't I be doing that?" he asked.

She smiled at him, "We're leaving tomorrow," she said with a shaky voice.

"You're going back home?" he asked.

"No, who knows how long the investigation will take. No, I mean we're leaving town; actually we're leaving the country," she said.

"What? Lina, things will get better, you'll see," said Greg.

"When? For how long? No, my mother needs closure. Having people staring at her because they believe my father is a criminal will tear her apart. I can't let that happen."

Greg didn't argue with her. They lived in a small town where everyone knew everyone else's business. He realized that it would be hell for them for a while.

"Where are you going?" he asked.

"Italy. My father has a second cousin from his mother's side there. I talked to him tonight about everything. He said his home is completely open to us," she answered.

"I'm going to miss you," he said with a soft voice.

"Me too," she said.

She gave him a kiss and slid off the bed. "Come in and see me in the morning before you leave for school, okay?"

"Okay."

Back in her room, she turned on her computer on and went to a travel website to buy the airline tickets for Italy. The sooner she got them, the better.

She finished making the arrangements and shut down the laptop. She changed into her pajamas and shut off the light and climbed into bed. She knew she would have enough time in the morning to go to see Len and Anna and go to the bank. She had to trust them with her secret. She closed her eyes but sleep didn't come. She turned so many times that after a while her body was exhausted and finally, she fell asleep.

Chapter 6

As Lina awoke, she felt someone touching her face. She opened her eyes to see Greg lying next to her.

"Good morning," he said, still caressing her face.

"Good morning," she said, leaning towards him.

"You know, I love you?"

"I know, I love you too," she said.

He brought her body close to his and held her for a few minutes in his arms. Lina inhaled his essence. She brought her face to his neck and kissed him.

"Promise me you'll call me every week and text me at least once a day," he said with a shaky voice.

"Yes I promise," she said with tears rolling down her face.

"You better go; you're going to be late for school."

"I love you," he said again giving her a quick kiss on the lips.

"I love you, too," she said.

He got off the bed," What will I tell Livy?" he asked.

"I already sent her a text message," she replied.

"Oh, you won't forget us."

"Never."

He walked to the door, opened it, and without looking back, walked out of the room. Lina touched her lips with her fingertips and stopped crying. She needed to get herself and her mother ready to travel. She got off the bed, took a shower, dressed, grabbed her bag and phone and left the room.

She knew that Len and Anna got up early. She made her way downstairs and out of the house, stopping at the coffee shop to get coffee and a bagel. On her way to Len's house, she sipped her coffee and ate her bagel while walking, ignoring everyone's stares. In about twenty minutes she arrived at Len's house.

She knocked at the door. She only waited a few seconds before Anna opened the door. Anna pulled her in the house and into her arms. "Caroline, honey," she said holding her. She called for her husband, "Len."

Len walked into the living room. Lina looked at him. He opened his arms and she ran into them. He hugged her tightly, not wanting to let her go. "Caroline, sweetie," he said, giving her a kiss on her forehead.

Lina missed them so much. They were like a second set of parents. Len let her go but still held her hand.

"I have to talk to you two," she said.

"Okay, come to the kitchen so Anna can make you breakfast."

"No, I'm okay. I just had coffee and a bagel on the way here," she showed them the empty coffee bag.

"That's not breakfast," said Anna.

Anna took her other hand and they pulled her to the kitchen. Len pulled out a stool for her to sit on and he sat next to her. Anna turned on the burners on the stove. She went to the refrigerator and pulled out all kinds of food to prepare. While Anna was cooking, Lina told her story to them. She told them about the documents her father had hidden and about the investigation at the house. When Anna brought her the breakfast, she stopped to take a few bites. She discredited the police report that said that her father had committed suicide.

While she was talking, she stopped between sentences to eat her breakfast. She went into detail about what she needed Anna and Len to do for her. She outlined the plans she had made for her mother and herself to leave the country.

"We understand sweetie. We'll do anything to help you and your mother and to bring justice to your father," said Len.

"Thank you. Here are our telephone numbers and also the number for my father's cousin," she said.

Lina finished her food and orange juice. Anna took the plates from the counter and brought them to the sink. Lina stood up from the stool. "I have to go. I need to get to the bank," she said.

Len and Anna hugged her and gave her kisses on her head.

"I'll call you when we get to Italy. Be very careful. Don't trust anyone except Greg and Livy, okay?"

"Caroline, you know we love you like a daughter," said Anna.

"I know. I love you, too," she said.

Lina gave them each one final hug and kiss and they walked her to the front door. Anna was already crying in her husband's arms. Lina turned, took one more look at them and walked out of the house. As she walked to the bank, she came to terms with the realization that she was leaving her home town——the place where she was born and the place her mother had lived her whole life.

When she got to the bank, she went straight to a customer service desk, signed her name in the log book and sat down to wait for help. She didn't have to wait long before a customer service representative called her name. She followed him to an office where she explained to him what she wanted for money from her account and what she wanted to go in her safety deposit box.

The customer rep took all the information down she gave him. He brought her to the safety deposit room and pulled the box for her, putting it on top of the table. He left her there while he went to fulfill all her requests.

Lina opened the box, took all the cash and put it in her bag. She also took her passport as well as her mother's. She left the rest of Marcia's legal documents and the savings bonds behind. She locked the box and left it on the table. When the customer service representative saw her coming out of the safety deposit room, he walked her back to his office where, after she signed several documents, he gave her all the money she had requested. "Thank you for your help," she said and left the bank.

Lina needed to get back to Greg's house and get her mother ready to go. She walked very fast and got back to the house in ten minutes. When she came in the front door, she could hear her mother's voice in the living room talking with someone. No time like the present to tell them all that they were leaving, including her mother.

She entered the living room, where her mother was sitting in a chair; Tim and Melissa were on the couch, while Daniel was standing.

"Well, it's about time. Your mother was ready to call the police," Daniel said in a biting tone.

She walked to her mother and kneeled in front of her, "I'm sorry. I had some things to do before we leave," she said.

"Leave?" said Tim.

"Yes, leave. We're going to Italy."

Marcia just stared at Lina, still holding her father's urn in her arms. She didn't say anything.

"Caroline, what are you talking about?" asked Melissa.

"Melissa, I made arrangements for us to go to live with my father's cousin in Italy," she said.

"Caroline, I know these are difficult times, but things will get better. Just wait a few more days," said Tim.

"No it won't get better. It may die down a bit, but everyone will always think of us as a family of criminals. No, it's time for us to go."

"Caroline," Tim started to argue again.

"Dad, let them go. It will be the best thing for everyone," said Daniel.

"Daniel, that's no way to talk about our close friends," said Melissa.

"Mom, let it be. Okay?"

"He's right. We'll call when we get to Italy. We'll stay in contact. It's just for a little while. In no time at all, we'll be back home," said Lina.

While they talked Marcia remained silent just listening to the conversation. She was gone already; Lina knew and Tim and Melissa knew it, too.

"Mom, let's go to your room. Melissa can I borrow a couple of travel bags?" she asked.

"Of course, I'll go with you upstairs."

"Caroline, are you going to need some money?" asked Tim.

"No, I'm all set," she answered.

Lina helped her mother to stand and got her upstairs. Melissa went with them, and helped Lina get the bags packed and ready. Lina assured her mother that the urn would be okay in the bag. She went back to her room and put her laptop in her bag.

She slung the bag over one her shoulders and took the other two bags, taking one more look at everything to make sure they didn't leave anything personal behind.

Back in the living room, she gave a hug to Tim, then Melissa. Marcia did the same. They still had some time, but she wanted her mother away from here, so she preferred to spend the time in the airport. "Thank you for everything," she said.

"I think I should go with you," said Tim.

"No. Tim, please. We'll be fine."

He sat back on the couch next to his wife. She was relieved to see that Daniel was not in the living room when they came back, so she didn't have to pretend to be nice to him. She grabbed the bags and her mother's hand and pulled her to the foyer. As Tim and Melissa waved goodbye, Lina helped her mother into the car and then joined her.

As the driver pulled away, Lina brought her mother closer to her. Marcia leaned her head on Lina's shoulder and closed her eyes. The drive to the airport was about forty-five minutes. She got her phone out and sent text messages to Greg and Livy. She shut off her phone and put it back in the bag, staying close to her mother and holding her tight.

After the car dropped them off at the airport, Lina checked them in at the airline desk and they went through security. She brought them to a small café and got them something to eat. After they ate, Lina went to one of the stands and bought a book for her mother and some magazines. Her mother loved to read; she hoped that this would keep her mind off her father.

After several hours of waiting, they finally boarded the plane. Once Lina had settled her mother in her seat. She pulled her phone out and sent one last message to Greg and Livy.

Chapter 7

Ten Years Later

Greg finished the document he was working on, saved it and closed his laptop. He checked his watch; he had ten minutes to make it down to the cafeteria to meet with Livy and Stacie. He had been busy all morning with the end of the month reports.

He left his office and took the elevator straight to the cafeteria. As soon as he walked in, he saw Livy and Stacie in line waiting to pay for lunch. He ordered a sandwich and got in line. After he paid for his lunch, he found Livy and Stacie at a table at the back of the cafeteria. He gave them each a hug and a kiss on the check and sat down. Greg smiled at them and started eating his sandwich. He stopped for a moment, "Did any of you hear from Jolene since the last text this morning?" he asked.

"Not me," answered Stacie.

"Me neither," answered Livy.

"I can't believe it's been a year since we've seen her and Gus," said Livy.

"It's going to be great to have her back."

"Yes, I missed her and Gus a lot," said Greg.

"It's hard to believe that it's been ten years since she left this town."

"I know, I'm so glad we were able to visit her in France for the past seven years," said Livy.

"It must been hard on you not to see your lovers for a whole year," said Stacie.

"Yes, our relationship is something that I never expected, but I'm so glad I have them both," he said.

They continued eating and talking for about an hour, reminiscing about their younger days together and the wonderful times they had together in Italy every summer, and the last four years in France.

Greg and Stacie had to go back to work. They all finished lunch and walked out of the cafeteria. Stacie brought Livy to the front lobby where they said goodbye, and Greg took the elevator back to his office.

The drive from the airport to the house was unbearable. Her heart was beating so fast, she was surprised she didn't collapse. The car stopped in front of the house——her childhood home where she had grown up with loving parents.

"No stay, let me go in alone," she said to Gus who was sitting next to her.

Jolene got out of the car and walked to the door. She took the key that she been holding onto so tightly that her knuckles had turned white and unlocked the front door. Slowly she opened the door and went inside.

She went down the two steps down to the foyer. Jolene couldn't believe she was standing in the foyer of the place she once called home. The house smelled the same as when she left it ten years ago. Len and Anna had done a good job with the upkeep.

She closed her eyes and a flash of memories came back of the awful ordeal she went through in the days before and after her father's unexpected and horrible death. She saw everything so vividly; it was like she was living those moments all over again.

Jolene opened her eyes. Her name was no longer Caroline, or Lina, as Greg and Livy used to call her. The fifteen-year-old girl who left her home and life behind to save her mother from imminent self-destruction no longer existed. That girl was long gone. She stood there for a long while.

Gus became impatient and decided to go in. Jolene didn't close the door, so he just walked in. He saw her standing there in a daze. "Tu vas bien, mon amour?" asked Gus with concerned in his voice.

"Oui," answered Jolene looking at the two people standing in front of her——Len and Anna.

"Gustave, anglais s'il vous plait," said Jolene.

"Yes, of course, sorry," he said.

He followed Jolene's gaze and saw the two people whom he recognized as Len and Anna by the pictures Jolene had showed to him. Jolene rushed to them and all three embraced in a group hug. They both gave Jolene a kiss on the cheek. Jolene went over to Gus, took his hand and brought him over to them.

"Len and Anna, this is my great friend Gustave Roux," she said.

Gus shook their hands, "Please call me Gus," he said.

Len and Anna smiled at him as each shook his hand.

Jolene was exhausted from the trip. "Len can you have someone bring in the luggage. I'm tired. I want to go to my room and take a quick shower and relax before dinner," she said.

"Okay," Len said as he made his way outside.

Gus stayed at her side. He put an arm around her waist and pulled her close to his body. Jolene didn't hesitate and leaned closer to him.

"We'll have dinner ready for you in about two hours. That should give you time to shower and rest for a bit," said Anna.

"Great. The house looks fantastic. You two did a great job with keeping it up."

When Len and the other servant came back in with the luggage, they went directly upstairs. "Let us know when dinner is ready, okay?"

"Okay."

Jolene and Gus went upstairs and walked towards her room. Len came towards them. "We set up the room next to you for Gus," he said.

"Great, thanks. Len, it's nice to see you," she said.

Gus followed Jolene as she turned and walked to her room, She hadn't set foot in this room since the night her father died. Her whole body shook with emotion. She could sense Gus behind her. He pulled her to him, so her back was tight against his body. He gently turned her head with his hand and met her lips in a kiss. She pulled herself tighter against him and kissed him back. They kissed for a while, not moving from that spot, just embracing and kissing each other. He pulled away and she looked at him and smiled. "Thank you," she said, "I need a shower. Meet me back here in ten minutes."

"Okay," he said as he took a couple of steps away from her and left the room.

Jolene only unpacked what she needed right now. She got under the shower and let the water run down her head, taking deep breaths to tried to slow down her heartbeat.

After her shower, she dried herself off and quickly got dressed. She was finishing brushing her hair when Gus walked into the room. He took the brush from her hand and took over brushing her hair. He was thinking about how beautiful her light brown hair was, and how much he loved the way it smelled as he leaned over and inhaled. He did a few more strokes before Jolene took the brush away and put it on the nightstand.

She took his hand, opened the sliding door to the porch and walked with him out of the room. From her porch, she had a great view of the garden and the small pond. He stood behind her with both arms wrapped around her waist and pulled her closer. She allowed her body to melt with his.

They stood there chatting as Gus continued to hold her close. She told him about the adventures she had had in the garden and the crazy but wonderful times she had with her parents. They heard a soft knock at the door. "Come in," she said from the porch.

Anna opened the door and walked through the room to the open sliding door. "Dinner is ready," she said.

"Thanks Anna. We'll be down in a minute."

Anna nodded her head to them and walked out of the room.

"She's a bit skittish with me around you," he said.

"She'll be fine," she said giving him a kiss.

He opened his lips and devoured her lips. They stopped and moved apart. "We better go down, mon amour," he said taking her hand and walking back into the room. She let him lead her and they walked down the stairs smiling at each other. When they got to the foyer she moved in front of him.

"This way," she said.

They went down the hallway and into the dining room where Anna and one of the servants were setting the last of the serving dishes on the table. Gus helped Jolene to her chair, then went around and sat across from her. They were both hungry, so they enthusiastically heaped food on their plates.

"Everything looks great," said Gus.

"Yes, Anna is a great cook. You're going to love her food."

"Um, I already do," he said taking a bite from his fork.

They chatted and laughed while eating. Dinner was perfect. She hoped she could get used to being back in the small town of Maidenville.

Will it ever feel like home again? she asked herself.

"What are you thinking?" he asked.

"Nothing," she answered.

"Something is making you frown. Tell me."

"I was wondering if it would ever feel like home again. I feel a distance, as if I don't belong here anymore."

He moved from his chair and went to her. He stood behind her, bent down and wrapped his arms around her shoulders. "You do belong," he whispered in her ear.

She patted his hands and looked up and smiled at him. "Thanks, I'm done eating. You want to go for a walk? I'll show you the pond."

"Maybe another time. I want you in my arms," he said.

"Gus, I'm exhausted," she said laughing.
"I just want to hold you, okay?"
"Okay but after the walk."

She got up from the table and he put an arm around her waist as they walked out of the dining room. They saw Anna coming down the hall, so Jolene went to her and gave her a hug. "Everything was delicious," she said.

"Yes dinner was fantastic," said Gus.

"Thank you."

"We're going for a walk. We won't need anything else for the rest of the night."

"Okay, goodnight," said Anna.

"Goodnight, see you tomorrow."

Anna took Gus's hand and walked towards the living room and then out to the terrace. They walked at a leisurely pace as Jolene pointed out various things she remembered. She brought him to a bench across from the pond. She sat down and pulled him down with her. He laughed and got closer to her. She pointed out the walkway that would take them to the tree house. She told him the story about when her father built it for her.

"Why don't we look for your father's papers now?" suggested Gus.

"No, I want everyone together. Besides, I promised Greg I would wait for him," she said.

"Okay, we'll wait," he said smiling at her.

He held her hand and brought his other arm over her shoulders. She leaned her head on his chest. She went back to telling stories about the pond until she yawned.

"Someone is really tired," he said lifting her face with the tips of his fingers and caressing her lips with his thumb. She opened her lips for him. He bent his head down and kissed her. She welcomed the kiss, but it didn't last as long as she expected. They stood and walked back to the house. He opened the sliding door for her and they went in. Quietly, they went upstairs. When they reached the second floor landing, Gus looked at her. "You want me to go to my room?" he asked.

"No. I want to be in your arms, too," she said pulling at his hand that she was still holding.

He smiled at her and went with her. When they reached her room, she opened the door and led him in. Someone had already gotten the bed ready for her. They both slept naked, so she started to take her clothes off. Gus did the same. She climbed in bed and Gus climbed in next to her. She wriggled her way backwards close to him. He held her waist and pulled her body close to his. He kissed her shoulder blade, then her neck.

"Gus."

"What? I'm helping you relax," he said.

"Sure," she said, closing her eyes and leaning her head back to his chest.

He knew she was tired so he stopped kissing her and closed his eyes, too. In a matter of seconds they were both fast asleep.

Chapter 8

It was Monday morning and Jolene was sitting at the dining table across from Gus. He was talking to her, but she wasn't really listening. She couldn't believe that it had been two weeks since she came back to her childhood home. She had done enough to make herself visible——she had been to the bank and opened an account; she had gone walking around downtown with Gus; she ate lunch with Gus at one of the cafés on Main Street where everyone, at one time or another, went to eat. She went shopping at the mall. She even bought a sport's car at the town's only dealership.

"Hey, you're not listening," Gus said.

"Sorry, I'm ready for the next step."

"Which is?" asked Gus.

"I will capture Daniel's attention. I know that there's a party at Greg's parents' house coming soon. He's going to get us an invitation," she said.

"Great, formal?"

"Yes."

He gave her a big smile and they went back to eating. This time she paid attention to what he was saying. They ate and talked for a while, in no rush to do anything. She loved his company; being around him made her happy, but she knew she would be happier if Greg were with them.

Jolene laughed at something funny he said. He was always making her laugh. "We have to go shopping," he said.

"Yes, let's go to the big mall in Aurora."

"Cool, shopping trip! I get to spoil you."

"Gus, I can buy my own things."

"I know," he said smiling at her, "but it gives me pleasure to buy you presents. Are you going to ruin that for me?"

"Fine."

They laughed out loud. They finished their breakfast and went back to their rooms to get ready for the drive to the mall. They met in the foyer; Gus took the keys from her and rushed out of the house with her fast behind him. He opened the passenger door for her and went to the driver's side and got in. He started the car and they drove off.

The shopping trip was a success. After several hours and many stores, they came home. Gus parked the car in front of the house and got out. He went around and opened the door for Jolene. He offered her a hand, which she took and he helped her out of the car. She grabbed a couple of the bags and left the rest behind.

As they entered the house, Anna greeted them in the foyer. Jolene went to her and kissed her on the cheek. "Anna, we have more things in the car. Can you please have someone get them and bring them to my room."

"Sure. Are you hungry? I just made some Danishes," said Anna.

"Oh my, yes. Let me go to my room and change into something more comfortable. I'll be right back."

"Okay,"

She and Gus went upstairs to their rooms. Gus quickly changed into jeans and a sweater and went to Jolene's room. She was about done, too; she was putting on her blouse. He went to her, moved her hands away and started to button the blouse. As he reached the top of the blouse and his hands were closer to her breasts, he caressed them with the back of his hand. He stroked them up and down. Jolene moaned in appreciation of his touch. "We better go down. Anna is waiting for us," she said with ecstasy in her voice.

Gus stopped, and finished buttoning her blouse. He coaxed her head up and they stared into one another's eyes. He could see the pleasure in her eyes. He stepped back from her, and she went to the closet and took out some flats. She put them on before they walked out of the room. They held hands while they went downstairs. She laughed at something he said.

They found Len and Anna in the kitchen. Jolene sat on the stool next to Len as he leaned over and gave her a kiss on the forehead. Gus sat next to her. "The kitchen smells fantastic! There's nothing like fresh-baked Danish," she said.

Anna brought them each a cup of coffee and put a plate full of Danishes in front of them.

"Wow, that really looks delicious," said Gus.

"Wait until you try them," Jolene said.

Gus smiled at her as he picked up the coffee and took a sip. Jolene reached over and picked out a Danish. She savored every bite. By the time she finished hers, Gus was already on his second. They made small talk with Len and Anna while drinking their coffee. When Jolene finished her coffee, Anna brought the pot over to give her some more, but Jolene waved her off. She offered coffee to Gus, too. He nodded yes.

They stayed almost an hour talking to Len and Anna. Jolene looked at her watch and saw that it was almost time for her to Skype her mother.

"I have to get ready to Skype Mom," she said as she stood up from the stool.

"Say hi to her for us," Len said.

"I will."

She gave Len and Anna kisses and walked out of the kitchen, leaving Gus with them. Gus continued to drink his second cup of coffee and finish his Danish. Anna stared at him. "She's very precious to us. If you hurt her, you will have to answer to us," said Len.

"She's precious to me, too. I love her very much. I would never do anything to hurt her," he said.

"Good," said Anna.

Gus finished his coffee and put the coffee cup on the counter. He got off the stool and walked out of the kitchen. He went to the study where he knew Jolene was talking to her mother. He walked into the room and sat on the couch next to Jolene.

"Hi Marcia," he said.

"Hi Gus," she said back.

Gus moved closer to Jolene. She leaned her head on his shoulder while talking to her mother.

"I heard you went shopping."

"Yes, you know how much I love buying pretty things for her."

"I know, you're spoiling her," said Marcia laughing.

"She deserves it," he said.

"Yes, she does."

"I'm going to do some work on my laptop, I'll see you later," he said kissing Jolene on her forehead, "Bye Marcia."

"Bye Gus, take care of her for me."

"Always."

He slid off the couch and walked out of the study. Jolene continued to talk to her mother, telling her about the changes she saw in the town. She mentioned the party at Greg's house on Saturday. "Honey, please be careful," Marcia said.

"I will Mom."

"Promise me."

"I promise."

They continued talking for a while longer. In his room, Gus was working on some documents on his computer. He went to his email inbox and checked for new mail, answering anything that was important and deleting the junk. He logged onto Facebook and looked at the new posts. He wrote a short post and signed out. He shut down the laptop and left it on the table.

He left his room and went to help Jolene with the things they bought today. As he started to take things out of the bags Jolene walked in. She grabbed him around the waist and rested her head on his back. Then she kissed his ear and nibbled on it. "I love your smell. You make my senses come alive," she said.

He turned around in her arms and brought his mouth to hers and kissed her deeply. She molded her body to his body while he caressed her back with his hand. Jolene's mind turned to mush with his kisses. She started to squirm in his arms. Gus pulled away. "We better stop. We have all this to put away," he said.

"Yes."

They moved to where the bags were and each took a few and brought them to the bed. Jolene went to the closet and got some hangers out. Gus took the clothes out and Jolene hung them. Together they managed to put away all her clothes. Jolene grabbed some of the hangers with his clothes and Gus grabbed the rest. She walked out of her room and Gus followed her. They went in his room to put the clothes in the closet. "Baby, I need a cold shower or I'll fuck you right now," he said with a grim look on his face.

"Gus, I want you to, but this isn't the right time. I'm sorry," she said.

"I know love. I'll meet you downstairs in an hour."

"Okay, Gus," she said.

"I'll be fine."

She turned away from him and walked out of the room. He closed the door and banged his forehead on it. He went to the bathroom quickly took of his clothes and got in the shower and put the water on. Next door, Jolene set out the clothes she was going to wear for dinner. She sat on the edge of the bed and closed her eyes. She smiled to herself remembering the moment she and Gustave met and how inseparable they became. She had never been close to anyone except Greg and Livy, but with Gustave, she immediately felt she had known him forever.

They had great times as they worked together modeling all over the world, except in the USA. Then she thought of the great time she had when she introduced Gus to Greg, and how wonderful the times were that they had spent together every summer. She cared for them both, but she couldn't get distracted from the tasks at hand. Nothing or no one could stop her from avenging her father's death and humiliating Daniel. She refused to let her mind go back to the bad years she spent with her mother after they left.

She got up from the bed, went to the bathroom and took a slow shower, trying to get her thoughts in order and calm her body. She dried off and went to her room to get dressed and do her hair. She looked in the mirror and felt satisfied with her choice of clothes and her hair, so she left her room.

She checked the living room but didn't see Gus, so she went to the kitchen to where Anna and her helper were working on dinner.

"Hi honey. Want something to drink?"

"Hi. I'm fine, just waiting for Gus to join me."

"Oh, you can stay with me in the kitchen."

"Okay," she said sliding onto one of the stools.

Gus walked into the kitchen after just a moment, smiling at her. He reached for her and leaned over to give her a soft, tender kiss on her lips.

"Hi," he said to Anna.

"Hi," she answered back.

"I'm taking her for a walk. How long before dinner is ready?" he asked.

"About forty-five minutes," Anna said.

"Great," he said taking Jolene's hand and pulling her off the stool.

She laughed out loud and brought her body close to him. They walked out of the kitchen and to the terrace, still laughing. He had his arm over her shoulder and she had hers around his waist. They walked out onto the terrace and to the garden, chatting and smiling at each other. They continued to the garden holding hands. He brought her to the pond and they sat on the bench across from it. He turned to face her and took her face on his hands.

"Je t'aime," he said to her as he took her lips in a passionate kiss.

She kissed him back with the same fervor. He took charge of the kiss; she opened her lips and he plunged his tongue in her mouth. They battled a delicious duel for a while; her body was on fire. He stopped the kiss and smiled at her. Jolene smiled back and laid her head on his chest.

"Gus, I...," she started to say, but he put a finger on her lips.

"I understand," he said, "we should go back," he grabbed her hand and stood up pulling her along with him.

They walked back to the house in silence. As Gus held her close with his arm over her shoulder, she lifted her face and smiled at him. In no time they were back at the house. Anna saw them and stopped them, "I was just coming to find you. The table is set up for dinner," she said to Jolene.

"Thanks," she said as they walked towards the dining room.

As they settled at the table, Anna and another servant brought the serving dishes with the food. Jolene and Gus ate quietly for a few minutes, then talked about what she planned to do at Saturday's party. They went over when to get together with Greg and Livy. She hadn't seen her best friends in almost a year, even though they talked or Skyped every week.

They finished dinner and Anna brought them dessert. Jolene smiled at Anna as she walked into the dining room with it. Anna had been making special desserts for her since Jolene was little. "Thank you," she said.

"You're welcome," said Anna giving her a kiss on the forehead and leaving them alone again. She and Gus ate the delicious dessert. They left the dining room, completely satiated, and went to the family room to watch some TV.

Anna brought them coffee, settling the tray on the coffee table. Gus found a movie on demand for them, while Jolene poured the coffee. He pushed the start button and went back to the couch and took his cup of coffee from her. She picked up her coffee and settled in next to him. They sipped their coffee and watched the movie.

Two hours later, the movie was over. Jolene felt so comfortable in Gus's arms that she didn't want to move. He shut the TV off and pulled her to his lap, stood up with her in his arms, and walked upstairs to her room. He opened the door without letting go of her. He stood her in front of him and slowly started to take off her clothes.

"Gus, Embrasse-moi," she pleaded to him.

Gus responded to her plea and kissed her. He pulled her closer and brought his hands to her bottom and pressed her tightly to him so she could feel his hard-on. She pushed her body into him, moaning and groaning into his mouth. They were both on fire, but he knew she wanted to wait, so he abruptly moved away from her.

"Gus," she said.

"Jolene, mon amour. I can't wait to be deep in your pussy. You're driving me crazy, baby."

"I want you, too," she said taking his hand and placing it on one of her breasts. That was all the invitation Gus needed. He swiftly helped her out of her clothes and proceeded to take off his own. He lifted her in his arms and gently laid her on the bed. He shut off the light and lay down next to her. Gus pulled Jolene to his body and brought his lips to hers. He kissed her for a while, then slowly began to caress her breasts, pinching one of her nipples with his fingers. He stopped kissing her and brought his mouth to the other nipple. He started to suck on the nipple hungrily.

Jolene moved her hands over every inch of his body she could reach while communicating her joy with soft moans. She dropped small, soft kisses on his shoulders and biceps and held tight to his arms as he moved to the other breast, taking a hold of the nipple between his teeth and biting it gently. She moaned her approval. He continued the delicious attack on her breasts for a bit longer, then moved slowly down her body, kissing her torso, her stomach, until he reached her mound.

Jolene moved her legs apart to give him better access. He caressed her pussy with his lips as he pushed one finger inside her. "Gus, s'il vous plaît," she whispered between moans.

"Please what my love?"

"More."

Gus took hold of her bottom and sucked harder as he pushed another finger inside her. Jolene started to ride his fingers and he began to pump in and out faster and faster. Her moans became louder and her body started to shake. He pulled his fingers out and gave her pussy one last hard suck.

He quickly moved on top of her, spreading her legs farther apart with his legs. He placed the tip of his cock in her pussy entrance and took his time pushing it inside her. She was in pure torment. The pace was driving her body wild. She tightened her hold on his arms, trying to pull him down for a kiss. Gus slid his cock completely inside and stopped and brought his body down. Jolene quickly devoured his lips with hers. Gus pushed his tongue into her mouth and started simultaneously to pump in and out of her pussy. Jolene lifted her legs and wrapped them around his waist to bring him deeper inside her. She gasped and moaned louder while kissing him. He stopped kissing her and brought his mouth to a breast and started to suck hard at her nipple. They continued moving at the same time. Jolene couldn't hold on any longer.

"Gus, hard. I need to come," she uttered between her moaning.

Gus pulled her tight to his body, lifting her by her bottom, and pumped faster and harder. He kept pumping her and taking little nibbles of her nipples. At that instant, Jolene broke into a wonderful climax that continued for several minutes. He pumped her for a while longer before he exploded inside her. Now both were shaking in each other's arms. He continued pumping until the last tremble came.

"That was fantastic," he said as they looked at each other with complete satisfaction.

"Yes, it was."

He gave her one last kiss, pulled from inside her and went to the bathroom. He took a washcloth and got clean, then took another one, dampened it with warm water and went back to the room to clean her as well.

"Thank you," she said.

He came back from the bathroom again and slid into the bed, taking her into his arms. They snuggled tight to each other and closed their eyes.

Chapter 9

Jolene was so nervous getting ready for this party. She couldn't believe it was already Saturday night. She kept going over and over in her head what to do when she got there. She had already done her makeup and was working on her hair, which took time because her curls were very wild. Gus walked in the room already completely dressed. He sat on the couch just watching her. "Wow, you look very handsome," she said.

"And you look stunning," he said smiling to her.

She put a few more pins on her up-do and used some hairspray. She looked at herself in the full-body mirror, then turned to face Gus. She did a twirl in front of him, "Beautiful, just exquisite," he said.

"Merci," she said.

He stood to take her hand and pulled her into his arms.

"Gus, don't," Jolene said smiling at him.

"Fine," he said taking two steps away from her.

They both laughed out loud. He started to walk out of the room still holding her hand. She stopped quickly and took her clutch from the nightstand. In the foyer, Len and Anna were waiting for her. They had expressed several times during the week their concern for her going to the party tonight. She could see the stress on their faces.

"Len, Anna, I'm going to be fine. Gus is not going to let anything happen to me. Besides, Greg will there, too," she said giving each kiss on the cheek.

"No one will hurt her, I promise," said Gus.

They said goodnight and walked out of the house. Gus helped her into the car and they drove off, arriving in only five minutes. They drove up to the front of Greg's parent's house and stopped the car where an attendant opened the door for Jolene. Gus got out and joined her at the steps. Jolene's nerves were in her throat; the last time she was in this house was ten years ago.

Gus noticed a bit of hesitation from her. He took her hand and proceeded to walk up the steps to the house. He gave her a big smile and a tender kiss on her cheek. Jolene smiled back at him as he knocked at the door. A few seconds later, a servant opened the door for them. Gus moved to the side, put his hand at her back and allowed her to go in first.

The servant walked them to the door of the ballroom. The room was already crowded with people, and when she and Gus appeared in the doorway, everyone turned to look at them. Gus gave her hand a quick squeeze and they moved into the room. They smiled to everyone they saw, saying hello as they continued to walk. They each took a glass of champagne from a tray as Jolene spotted Mr. Stutts, the bank executive who helped her with her account. They went over to greet him. "Good evening, Mr. Stutts" she said to him.

"Good evening Miss Moreau, Mr. Roux. This is my wife Stephanie," he said gesturing toward the woman standing next to him.

"Nice meeting you, please call me Jolene," she said shaking Stephanie's hand. Gus said hello and shook her hand as well. They chatted with the couple for a while until Jolene spotted Greg and Livy at the far side of the room. Her heart beat a bit faster. Gus moved closer to her and put his hand at her back as she gave him a very slight nod and continued the conversation with the bank executive's wife.

Greg and Livy saw Jolene and Gus talking to the banker, and slowly made their way over to them. As they approached, Greg said, "Good evening Mr. Stutts, Mrs. Stutts."

"Hello Gregory, Olivia," Mr. Stutts said.

"Hi," said Livy.

"This is Ms. Moreau and Mr. Roux. Ms. Moreau just moved to town from France. She's a model," he said.

"Oh yes, you bought the Jenkins place," he said shaking her hand, holding it for a bit before shaking Gus's hand.

"It's a beautiful place," said Livy.

"Yes, very beautiful," said Jolene.

As the group continued talking, Mr. Stutts and his wife made their excuses and moved to greet another couple. Greg moved close to Jolene; she tried to stay calm. He put one hand on her back, just where Gus had his hand. He gave a quick squeeze to Gus's hand and gently patted her back. Jolene took a deep breath. Greg smiled at her and quickly pulled his hand away.

They made the kind of small talk that strangers might make because there were several people around them. Daniel walked up to meet them. "Hi Brother, Olivia," said Daniel.

"Hi Daniel," said Livy. Greg didn't respond.

"Please, introduce me to this gorgeous lady."

Jolene didn't wait for an introduction. She stepped forward with an accentuated sway of her hips, keeping eye contact with him the whole time. She stood very close in front of him.

"Hi, I'm Jolene," she said, "Thanks for the compliment."

"You are beautiful," he said leaning closer to her.

Jolene laughed, turning her face and batting her eyes at him.

"Daniel, this is Mr. Roux," said Greg.

It took Daniel a few seconds to pull his eyes away from Jolene and look at Gus. "Hello," he said shaking his hand with very little interest.

His attention went quickly back to Jolene who gave him a seductive smile, which he took to heart and moved closer to her again. Gus knew about her plan, but it didn't mean he had to like it. He gave Greg a quick look and he could sense that Greg didn't like it either. The group continued talking while Daniel made small talk exclusively with Jolene. She laughed flirtatiously with him. For the moment, Daniel wasn't aware of anyone else in the room except for her, which was how she wanted it. "Look at me, hogging all your time. My apologies," Jolene said putting a hand on his forearm.

"Not at all. Would you like something to drink?" he asked her.

"Yes, please," she answered.

"What would you like?"

"I'll take a martini, please."

"I'll be right back," he said walking away from her.

Daniel walked directly to the bar and ordered her drink. Jolene stood between Gus and Greg. Both stayed close to her but didn't touch her. Livy noticed the tension between the lovers and tried to ease it. She said something funny and all three laughed.

"Thank you," Jolene said to Livy.

A few minutes later, Daniel came back with her drink, "Would you care to go for a walk in the gardens?" he asked.

"Sure," she said.

She moved towards him and they walked away from the other three. Daniel brought his hand to her back, but Jolene didn't feel any emotions from his touch. Daniel continued to talk to her as they walked out. She let him lead her to the gardens, even though she knew very well where they were. She smiled at him the whole time he talked and laughed in all the right places.

Jolene hoped she came off as calm and interested in him, but on the inside she wasn't either of those things. Her anxiety was giving her butterflies in her stomach. She took a sip of her martini and continued the talk with him. They continued to walk while he dominated most of the conversation. After a few minutes, she was completely bored with him. "We should go back. My companion will be worried about me," she said.

"Of course. Perhaps we can get together soon——maybe dinner?" he asked hopefully.

"Yes, that'll be nice. Let me give you my phone number," she said as he pulled out his cell phone and plugged the numbers in.

He walked her back to the house where she joined Gus who was still talking with Greg and Livy, except now Greg's father had joined them. Jolene smiled at them.

"Dad, let me introduce you to Jolene. She just moved to town a few weeks ago," Daniel said.

"Nice to meet you, Jolene," said Tim, shaking her hand.

"Nice to meet you, too," she said smiling at him.

The party was in full blast by now. She looked around checking out every one around her, recognizing the people that she grew up with. She felt disappointed that no one remembered her. Gus must have noticed the change in her expression because he moved closer to her.

She smiled at him, "I think it's time for us to go," she whispered to him in his ear.

"Okay," he whispered back.

They thanked Tim for inviting them to the party and said goodnight. She tried to see where Daniel was as they left and she spotted him on the dance floor with a beautiful blonde in his arms. She shook her head and left the house with Gus. They drove back to the house in silence. Jolene leaned her head back on the seat as Gus brought his hand to her face and caressed her.

Jolene closed her eyes, enjoying his touch. Gus parked the car in front of the house and Jolene opened her eyes and smiled at him. He got out of the car, went to her side and opened the door for her. They walked in the house holding hands. They stopped in the foyer where Jolene turned to face him and threw her arms around his neck. "Thank you," she said.

"For what?" he asked.

"For being so understanding," she said, bringing her lips to his.

Gus pulled her close against his body, putting one hand across her waist and the other at the back of her neck. He took over the kiss and plunged his tongue into her mouth as she opened her lips for him. They held each other kissing in the foyer until Gus lifted her in his arms and carried her upstairs. Jolene tucked her head on his chest and closed her eyes.

He brought her to her room and closed the door. He let go of her and pushed her gently against the door. He brought his lips back to hers and engulfed her mouth in a deep kiss. They kissed for several minutes. He pulled from her and slowly unzipped her dress, dropping kisses on every part of her body. At the same time, Jolene was pulling his tuxedo jacket off and unbuttoning his shirt. She caressed his bare chest, taking time to softly pinch each of his nipples. Gus finished taking her dress off.

Jolene wriggled her shoes off, leaving her only with a small thong on her body. Gus moved away from her and devoured her body with his eyes. He went back to her and started to pull the pins from her hair, dropping her beautiful hair onto her shoulders.

He took a handful of her hair in his hand and pulled her into another wild kiss. He took a step back; his kiss took her breath away. She swallowed quick short breaths and smiled at him. Gus took her hand and moved backwards towards the bed.

He stopped when he felt the bed at his back. Jolene let go of his hand and unbuckled his belt then pulled his pants zipper down. She pushed her hand under the waistband of his briefs and started to stroke his already hard shaft. She could feel him growing bigger in her hand.

He pulled her hand out as he kicked his shoes off and quickly pulled his socks off. He straightened up and pulled his briefs and pants off at once. He pulled her thong off then he lifted her up and settled her on the bed. He lay on top of her and rubbed his whole body on hers, slowly moving up and down. He propped himself up on his elbows and grabbed a nipple in his mouth as he rubbed the other between his fingers. He nipped her with his front teeth as Jolene gasped for air. "Gus, I want you inside me, please."

He spread her legs with a quick shove of his knees and positioned his shaft at her pussy entrance. Very slowly he thrust inside her, making her crazy with pleasure as he stretched her pussy walls completely. She loved the feel of his shaft inside her.

"Umm, Umm, Gus," she moaned out loud. Gus started to move faster in and out. Jolene couldn't stop from moaning and screaming from the pleasure he was giving at every thrust. Their love-making could be heard throughout the entire house. Two hours and several orgasms later, Gus kissed her one last time, moved to the side of the bed and cuddled her in his arms.

Chapter 10

Jolene's excitement was overwhelming. She gave everyone all kinds of orders to prepare the house for the weekend visitors. It had been a week since the party at Greg's parent's house. She had been on two dates with Daniel; both times he tried very hard to get into her pants, but she managed to give him the slip.

So far, the plan was working, but it was time for the second phase, and for that she needed Greg and Livy's help, which was why this weekend was very important to her. Greg, Livy and Stacie were all coming for the weekend.

She was so thrilled to be back with them. Gus came up to her and hugged her from the back. He pulled her closer to him and gave her a kiss on her neck. "Mon amour, you're glowing," he said.

"Yes, I can't wait to have them home with me," she said with a big smile on her face.

"I know," he said kissing her shoulders.

Anna walked in as they were kissing. "Ah-hem," she said.

Gus turned towards her with Jolene still in his arms.

"Anna," she said laughing.

"Everything is ready for dinner and the rooms are prepared for the guests," Anna said.

"Great, I'm going to take a shower and get ready."

"Me too," said Gus with a grin on his face.

Anna walked out of the living room and Jolene started to laugh out loud. "You need to stop inciting her," she said.

"I just want for once for her to smile back at me," he said.

"She will, just give her time. Let's get ready," she said.

He let go of her, grabbed her hand and they walked out of the room and upstairs. They went their separate ways into their rooms. After half an hour, Gus walked into her room while she was sitting on the bed putting her shoes on. He kneeled in front of her and helped her. She brought her hands to his face and with her thumb rubbed his lips.

He smiled at her. He stood up and brought her to her feet. She gave him another big smile then gave him a quick kiss on the lips and moved away from him. She checked herself in the mirror on the wall and took his hand, "Let's go down," she said.

They walked out of her room and downstairs. She checked with Anna again, who assured her that everything was ready. They went to the living room where she sat on the couch while Gus prepared drinks for them. He brought her drink to her and sat next to her. He grabbed the remote control and put soft music on, sitting back on the couch and pulling her with him. After ten minutes or so, she heard the doorbell. She moved to go but Gus held her. "That's why you have servants, to get the door. Relax, okay?" he said.

She smiled and nodded her head. She was holding her breath.

"Breathe, honey," he said rubbing her back softly.

She let her breath go as her childhood friend walked into the living room. Livy walked over to her and gave her a big hug and a kiss on the cheek. They held each other for several minutes.

"Hey, my turn," said Greg pulling Livy away from her.

Livy laughed and moved away, then walked to Gus and said hello to him and gave him a kiss. Greg embraced Jolene and brought his lips to hers. She instantly opened her mouth to him and they kissed deeply. He pulled her body against his and caressed her. Meanwhile, Stacie said hello to Gus.

"Hello, Greg," said Stacie poking him in his back. Greg stopped kissing Jolene and moved away from her. He went over to Gus. "Hi," he said and gave him a quick kiss on the lips.

Stacie approached Jolene and gave her a hug and a kiss on the cheek.

"Something to drink?" asked Gus as he moved to the bar.

"Yes," they all said.

Greg followed Gus to the bar and helped him with the drinks. They knew what the ladies liked for drinks because they had been friends for a long time.

When they all had their drinks, they sat down. Gus and Greg sat with Jolene on the couch, and Livy and Stacie sat in the large chair across from them. The conversation was lively and happy; they talked about old times. They reminisced about the good times they had together in Italy and France and caught up on how everyone's family was doing.

"Your mom really looks happy with Gus's uncle. You must be very pleased," said Livy.

"Yes, I didn't think she would ever smile again. Adrien brought her back to life. She's so happy," said Jolene.

After they talked for some time, Anna came in and announced that dinner was ready. They went to the dining room. Greg and Gus sat Jolene between them, and Livy and Stacie sat across from them.

The dinner was delicious as always, including the dessert. Jolene was happy everyone enjoyed dinner. When they finished, they congregated in the family room to watch a movie. Jolene, Greg and Gus got comfortable on the big couch and Livy and Stacie sat on the loveseat. Everyone was enjoying the movie, laughing and joking as they always did when they were together. Jolene smiled, feeling completely content now that Greg was with them.

"Honey, did you remember to give everyone the weekend off?" asked Gus.

"Yes, I reminded Anna this morning that after they were done with dinner, everyone was free to go home," she said.

"Great," he said giving her a kiss on her shoulder. Then they went back to watching the movie.

When the movie ended close to three hours later, Livy got up from the sofa and said, "Goodnight everyone," as she left the family room.

Everyone said goodnight back to her. Stacie gave her a look before she left the room. The other four stayed to watch the credits at the end the movie. Stacie waited a few minutes and then got up. "Goodnight," she said.

"Goodnight," said Jolene and the guys nodded their heads.

Livy went into her room, quickly changed into her pajamas and, after waiting a few minutes, left her room and went into Stacie's. Stacie was already in bed waiting for her. Stacie moved to the side of the bed and made space for her. She lifted the blanket and patted the bed for her to get in. Stacie leaned into Livy and gave her a kiss. Livy pulled her closer. They held each other kissing for long time.

Back in the family room, after another half an hour, Greg moved from his chair and started to leave the room. "Goodnight," he said to Gus and Jolene.

Jolene leaned over to Gus and stole a kiss from him. He pulled her on his lap and deepened the kiss. "We better go up. I'm sure Greg is anxious to be with you," said Gus.

"He's anxious to be with both of us," she said.

He stood up from the sofa with her in his arms. She laid her head on his shoulder as he left the room and he carried her upstairs. He got to the second floor and went directly to her room. Just as he let go of her and she stood in front of him, Greg walked into the room. Her back was to the door so she didn't see him, but she saw the change in Gus's expression. Greg moved behind her, wrapped one arm around her waist and pulled her close to his strong muscular body.

Greg was about 6'1" fair-skinned and built solid with beautiful dirty-blond hair and gorgeous hazel eyes, in contrast to Gus who had darker skin and was taller by an inch. He was fit, but not as muscular as Greg, and he had dark brown hair down to his shoulders and big green eyes. Each of them was gorgeous in his own way.

Gus moved in front of her while Greg turned her head to the side, devouring her lips in a kiss, and then he slid his tongue into her mouth. The kiss was fantastic; she loved the way he consumed her whole mouth with his kisses.

Gus unbuttoned her blouse and pulled her breasts out of the bra by tucking the bra under, quickly taking one in his mouth; he sucked hard and nibbled on her nipple. Jolene's body trembled in reaction. He took the other in his hand and pinched and rubbed it with his fingers.

Greg caressed her, slowly enjoying touching her soft skin. He let go of her head but continued kissing her. He undid her belt and pants then pushed her panties and pants over her hips.

Her pants dropped to the floor, and she moved to the side and kicked them out of the way. Gus never stopped playing with her nipples. Greg caressed the breast that Gus had let go, and with his other hand, he slowly traveled down her stomach to her mound. He loved when she shaved everything, enjoying the bare feeling in his hand. He slid two fingers between her pussy lips and slowly rubbed from front to back. He stopped kissing her, and Gus took over her lips.

After a few minutes, Greg pushed one finger inside her. Jolene squirmed in their arms, moaning into Gus's lips. Her body was ready to erupt. Greg pushed another finger inside her, pulling in and out faster; he could feel that she was ready to come because her pussy kept sucking his fingers in. He stopped and pulled his fingers out. "I want to taste your juices in my mouth. Gus switch with me," he said.

Gus moved to her back; she wanted to touch them but they wouldn't let her. Greg moved quickly in front of her then kneeled down. Gus started kissing and nibbling on her shoulder and back, as he did that he moved one hand to her breast and the other to her bottom. He brought his hand to her cheeks and slowly started to stroke them up and down, moving his hand between her cheeks and softly pressing a finger occasionally inside her.

Jolene's body was trembling in their hands. She was surprised that she was still standing with all the pleasure they were giving her. Meanwhile, Greg was having a feast sucking and biting on her clit while pushing three fingers in and out of her pussy.

As Greg pushed his fingers in, Gus slowly slid a finger completely inside her butt hole. Jolene's body was aching for release. Her head was resting on Gus's chest and if it weren't for Greg holding her up, she would haven fallen on the floor. Gus introduced one more finger into her butt as Greg quickened his movement and went deeper inside her, sucking harder on her clit. "Greg, please. Gus, don't stop."

They knew she was ready to come because she was squeezing the hell out of their fingers every time they went in. Greg and Gus continued with the fast pace. They were doing so well synchronizing their motions that Jolene had no cohesive thoughts anymore. Her body couldn't hold on any longer and when they simultaneously pushed their fingers inside her, she came all over Greg's mouth.

Greg continued in and out as well as Gus until they could feel her last tremor. Gus took a hold of her lips for one last kiss.

Jolene suddenly opened her eyes. Greg noticed the dazed look in her eyes that she always got after love-making. He lifted her in his arms and brought her to the bed. Gus moved the blanket to the side and Greg laid her on the bed. "I love the taste of your sweet juices in my mouth," Greg said.

As he was talking to her, he was taking his clothes off. Next to him was Gus doing the same. They looked at each other with their shirts off. Gus pulled Greg in an embrace and brought his mouth to his for a kiss. Their kissing was fierce; Greg brought his lower body right in top of Gus. He put his hands on Gus's hips and held tight to him while he rubbed his hard on. Jolene loved watching them make out. She got so hot just watching them together. Gus pulled away and started to take his pants off.

Gus kicked his shoes off and pushed his pants to the floor. Greg looked up to see Gus's massive erection in front of his face. Greg took Gus's dick in his hand started to stroke the whole length of it. Both were about the same size, but Gus was a bit thicker including the crown.

Greg stood up and looked at Gus, licking his lips. He moved closer to him and moved Gus's hand and took his dick in his hand. He proceeded to stroke it from the crown to the base. Gus closed his eye and enjoyed the touch of Greg on his cock. Greg kneeled in from of him and started to lick his dick from the base to the crown, taking the time to taste all of him. Jolene stood up from the bed and moved behind Gus and started to touch him all over his back giving him soft kisses.

Greg opened his mouth and slowly took Gus's dick in his mouth. He stayed a bit longer on the tip then opened wider and took all of him inside his mouth. Gus exhaled noisily. He didn't trust himself touching him so he kept his hands to his sides.

Greg's delicious mouth and Jolene's kisses were driving him out of his mind. He stopped Greg from sucking him. "I want to come in your ass, my love, but first let's do her together," he said to Greg as he pulled him up and kissed him, tasting himself in Greg's mouth.

Jolene pulled them closer to the bed. Greg kicked his shoes off and Jolene helped him take his pants off. Soon they were all naked together. She climbed in bed and pulled them with her.

The men lay on either side of her as she lay on her back. They kissed her all over. Greg brought his lips to her and gave her a kiss. He pushed his tongue in her mouth and they dueled with their tongues.

Gus moved slowly down her stomach, dropping kisses on her stomach on his way to her lower stomach. Greg put one of her breasts in his mouth while pinching and stroking the other one. Gus opened her legs wider and positioned himself between them.

He opened her pussy lips and started to lick her from front to back leaving no part of her pussy untasted. Then he pushed two fingers inside her. Jolene kept her hands at her side, scraping the sheet under her with her nails. "Stop Gus. I want one of your dicks inside me now," she said between groans.

Gus moved from between her legs and Greg took his place. Greg lay down on the bed and lifted Jolene on top of him. He placed his dick in her pussy entrance and pulled her down on top of him. He took both of her breasts on his hands and pinched them as he moved inside her. Gus moved behind her and with a soft push, he leaned her farther into Greg, making her butt lift up. Greg took one of her breasts in his mouth. Gus opened her butt cheeks and started to massage her butt hole then slowly pushed one finger inside her. After a few minutes he added another one and after another minute he inserted a third. He started to push in and out making sure she was ready for him. Through all this, Greg was pumping in and out of her. Jolene's moans were coming more frequently and louder now. Gus moved to the drawer and pulled the lubricant out. He put some on her butt and some on his cock, then he put the head of his dick to her hole and gradually started to push inside her.

"That's it baby, keep breathing, I'm almost there," said Gus. When he was completely inside, he stopped moving to give her the time to adjust to his size. After a few minutes, Jolene couldn't stand the waiting.

"Gus, please move."

Gus picked up Greg's motion and started to move in unison with him. After several minutes they started to move faster. Jolene was so full both ways; her body was trembling uncontrollably. They knew she was about to come, so they sped up and went deeper inside her. With them both pumping her together, in no time Jolene's body exploded into violent spasms. A moment later, both Greg and Gus came, too. The ripples of the aftermath orgasms continued for what seemed like forever. She couldn't hold herself up any longer and collapsed on top of Greg, bringing Gus with her.

Gus avoided going completely on top of Greg by slipping to his side and bringing both of them with him. Still together they rode the last of waves of trembling together. Gus massaged Jolene's back while Greg dropped tender kisses on her head.

"That was ecstatic. You two have drained me completely," she said with a big smile on her face.

Gus pulled himself from inside her and went to the bathroom. He came back with a wet cloth. Greg pulled out too and moved from her as Gus started to clean her. Greg got off the bed and went to the bathroom. He used the toilet, then started the water and got into the shower. "How is our girl doing?" asked Greg as Gus walked into the shower and stood behind him.

"She's knocked out," said Gus as he reached over and grabbed the washcloth from Greg and started to soap his back.

Greg closed his eyes and leaned into Gus's touch. Gus's hand trailed down his back and into his butt. He spread Greg's butt cheeks and with his free hand started to stroke his hole, then he pushed a finger into him. Greg groaned his approval.

Gus pulled him closer, then he dropped the cloth and wrapped his arm around him, and with his hand, slowly massaged his chest, down to his stomach and finally to his shaft. He took a firm hold of Greg's shaft while he pushed a second finger inside him.

"Gus," said Greg in a whisper.

"You like this, don't you mon amour," he whispered in Greg's ear.

"Yes," he barely got out when Gus pushed a third finger and stopped his massage on the crown of his dick and gave him a strong squeeze.

"I miss you so much."

"Me, too," said Gus. "I can't wait to feel my dick deep inside your ass."

"Gus I can't hold out any longer."

Gus let go of his dick turned him to face the shower wall.

"Spread them, baby."

Greg leaned his forearms and upper body to the wall and opened his legs wider to make room for Gus. Gus opened his cheeks and placed the head of his dick at his butt entrance. Slowly he started to thrust into him. Greg held his breath for a moment. "Oh God, I forgot how big your dick head is. I don't think I can open anymore," said Greg.

"Yes you can. You fit me like a glove."

Gus took it slow so Greg could get accustomed to him again. After a few seconds, he moved a bit faster. With another push he was all in. He turned Greg's face to the side with one hand, holding him still with the other while Greg wriggled on his arm.

Gus took his mouth in a voracious kiss. Then he started to move in and out of him with a steady thrusting motion, which gradually became harder and faster. Gus stopped kissing him and grabbed a hold of his hips. He held him tight while he continued to pump in and out frantically.

"Gus, now," said Greg holding his dick and stroking it hard and fast.

In a matter of seconds both men exploded in a simultaneous climax. Gus continued to thrust until both of their bodies stopped shaking. He leaned into Greg's back and kissed him on his shoulder. They stayed like this for a moment, enjoying their love-making. Gus pulled out and turned Greg to face him, he pushed him back into the wall and engulfed his mouth in a furious kiss. They stopped kissing to get some air. Greg savored Gus's lips with a stroke of his tongue.

"That was sensational," said Gus.

"Yes, I missed your kisses," said Greg.

"We better get out before we turn to prunes."

Quickly both took showers and dried off. They walked out of the bathroom naked and slid quietly in at each side of the bed, trying not to disturb Jolene. Greg wrapped an arm around her waist and pulled her to his body, while Gus moved in front of her and wrapped one arm around her hips. They both got comfortable around her and said goodnight to each other.

Chapter 11

Jolene's body was aching as she opened her eyes slowly with a smile on her face, but the aches were in the most wonderful places. She was so happy she had Greg and Gus together again. She could barely move surrounded as she was by two gorgeous bodies. Gus was plastered at her back with his arm over her thigh. She could feel his hard-on already, and Greg was in front with a handful of her breast. She turned and lay flat on her back.

"Good morning, honey," said Greg bringing his hand to her mound and softly rubbing it.

"Good morning, mon amour," said Gus stroking her nipple between his fingers.

"Good morning." she said softly grasping for air.

She closed her eyes and enjoyed them touching her body. Greg spread her legs a bit and used his fingers to open her pussy lips, while Gus moved and took the other nipple in his mouth.

Jolene couldn't stop the sounds from coming out of her mouth and she moaned loudly. Greg opened her more and slid a finger inside her. Slowly he pushed his finger in and out, spreading her juice all over her pussy.

Gus pinched one nipple with his fingers as he sucked hard on the other. Jolene's moans got even get louder. Greg inserted a second finger, pushing deep inside her. She lifted her hips off the bed trying to take his fingers in deeper.

Greg held her down by bringing a third finger inside her. Gus changed breasts and continued nibbling and nipping them. Jolene couldn't hold out any longer.

"Gus, Greg, please. I can't wait," she said between gasps.

"We know baby, soon. I want to taste your juices in my mouth," Greg said as he pulled his fingers out and spread her legs apart. He settled between them and quickly dropped his mouth on her mound.

Gus moved his mouth from her breast and consumed her lips with his. He pushed his tongue into her mouth and she immediately opened to accept his tongue. The kiss was dynamic. She brought her hand to his face then to his head and softly stroked his hair. At that moment, Greg sucked on her clit hard and pushed two fingers into her, pumping fast in and out. At the same time, Gus pinched and rubbed her nipple hard between his fingers.

Jolene's body burst into an immense climax as she groaned and moaned in Gus's mouth, they continued the assault on her body with their mouths and hands. At the other side of the hall in Livy's room, Stacie and Livy were also making love. The affection they had shared since high school had grown into a wonderful relationship that withstood the criticism and disapproval of their families. Livy kissed Stacie passionately and they held each other tight.

Back in Jolene's room, her body finally stopped trembling from the aftershock of her orgasm. Greg moved up her body, dropping soft kisses on the way. Gus moved to the side, giving himself the space to explore. He reached her face and brought his lips up to hers. Jolene could taste herself on his lips. She stroked his lips with her tongue. She opened her lips and they started to play with their tongues. He stopped the kiss and slid to her other side; both brought their hands to her stomach and held hands.

They moved closer to her, embracing her body like a cocoon. She brought her hands to their faces and caressed them then took hold of their hands. They stayed looking at each other for several minutes.

"We have to get up. There's a lot to do," she said.

Gus moved from her side and slid off the bed. "I'll take a shower," he said, walking naked into the bathroom.

Jolene rolled to her side facing Greg. He pulled her closer to his body. "I missed you so much," she said stroking his biceps.

"I missed you too, baby. I counted the days until you would come back to me," he said.

"We really have to get up," she said pulling away from him and sitting on the edge of the bed.

He sat behind her, "I love you," he said in her ear.

"Greg, I can't…" she started to say, when he stopped her.

"I know," he said sliding off the bed.

As he went into the bathroom, Gus came out of the shower.

"What's wrong?" asked Gus seeing the frown on his face.

"She can't admit she loves me," Greg said with a shaky voice.

"I know, me too. Give her time," said Gus wrapping the towel around his waist and pulling Greg into an embrace.

Greg rested his head on Gus's shoulder. "I'm scared. She's so full of revenge."

"Don't be. She'll come through, you'll see."

"Hey you two, I need to shower, too," she yelled from the room.

Gus let Greg go, placing a soft kiss on his lips and walked out of the bathroom. Greg took a fast one and went back to the room where Gus was still getting dressed. Jolene patted his butt on her way to the bathroom. Greg took the clothes out of his bag and got dressed. Both men were dressed quickly, then Gus craned his head through the open door of the bathroom. "Baby, we're going down. We'll start breakfast," he said loud enough for her to hear him over the running water.

"Okay, please knock at Livy's and wake them up," she said.

"Will do."

Gus wrapped an arm around Greg's shoulder and together they walked out of the room. They were walking down the hall when they encountered Livy and Stacie holding hands coming out of Livy's room.

"Good morning," Gus said.

"Good morning," they said together.

"Where's Jolene? It feels weird calling her that back here at home; in France it was okay," said Livy.

"I know. You think she'll ever go back to using her old name?" asked Stacie.

Gus looked at Greg who had an expression of grief on his face. Livy let go of Stacie and went to him and hugged him.

"I'm sorry. I didn't mean to upset you."

"I'm fine," he said smiling at her.

They went down to the kitchen. They were all dressed in comfortable clothes because they would be doing a lot of research today. In synchronized movement, they started to prepare breakfast. It was like when they were back in France together at Jolene's mother's villa.

They all moved comfortably around each other, joking and laughing. Jolene walked into the kitchen, stopping to watch them. She was so thrilled to have them all back together. "Good morning," she said walking over to Stacie and Livy to give them a kiss on the cheek.

"Good morning," they said back to her.

Jolene got in the flow of things and started to help, and in no time, breakfast was ready. They set up the food at the kitchen table and sat down to eat. They talk at the table was incredible——the atmosphere was full of love and caring. They laughed and talked the whole time they were eating. The best part was that they all enjoyed their time together so much. They all helped clean up the kitchen, and when they were done, Jolene brought them out to the terrace. They walked to the far side of the garden and stopped in front of a huge tree. "Look up," Jolene said, pointing up with her finger.

They all did what she said and saw her old tree house. The three of them knew about her tree house, but Gus didn't.

"Your old tree house," remarked Livy.

"Yes, I don't know if you remember when my father was building it. I asked him to build a secret compartment, remember," she said looking at Greg and Livy.

Livy slapped her hand over her mouth, looking completely stunned. "OMG, that's right. I remember you bugging him so much that he agreed to do it," said Livy.

"But you never told us anything about it," said Greg.

"That's right. He made me promise that it would be our secret. No one else was supposed to know, not even you two. He knew I would tell you otherwise," she said.

"Really?" said Greg in surprise.

"Yes."

They all looked up at the tree again and went around to the other side where the ladder was. Stacie and Livy moved away from the tree.

"I'm not going up there," said Stacie with a nervous voice.

Jolene moved to her side and patted her shoulder. "That's okay, you and Livy can be the lookouts. We'll go up," she said looking at Greg and Gus.

She moved in front of Greg and Gus and climbed up the ladder. Gus followed her then Greg went up. The tree house was solidly built so they had no worries. When they got to the top they crawled through the door. Jolene sat in the middle of the tree house on the floor. Greg and Gus looked at each other. They knew this was probably bringing back memories of her father. Gus moved next to her and tapped her shoulder. "Baby, where?" he asked.

She pointed to a wall that was covered with graffiti. She kneeled down in front of the wall and moved her hand to the bottom part of the wall. She pushed in several pieces of graffiti circles and suddenly a small door opened. They could see a box in the middle of the shelf. Gus reached for her hand as she reached in to grab the box. "Wait, let me. There are maybe all kinds of bugs and things in there."

Jolene moved aside and next to Greg. Gus reached his hand in and grabbed the box from the shelf. As he lifted the box, several bugs came out from the back and bottom of the box. She didn't scream but squirmed a bit. She was glad that it was not her holding the box that was for sure.

"How are you guys doing?" asked Livy from below.

"We got it. We're coming down," said Gus.

Jolene moved toward the steps, but Greg moved in front of her. "Let me go first, then you," he said.

"Really? You guys are a bit over-protective."

"Yes." was all he replied as he climbed down the rungs. Jolene followed behind him then Gus came, holding the box in one hand.

Greg took it slow going down. Once he made it down, he lifted her from the last step and stood her on the ground. Gus reached the ground a few seconds later. He handed the box to Jolene.

Everyone noticed how she hesitated to take it, but then she reached out and grabbed it. She turned around and walked back to the house. The rest of them followed her. She went directly to the study, putting the box on the coffee table. As she kneeled in front of it, Livy kneeled down next to her and Greg squatted at her other side.

With shaking hands, she slowly opened the box. There in front of them was the evidence she needed to find the person that framed her father for embezzlement. She pulled the envelope out and opened it, and as she turned it over to get the papers out, a flash drive dropped out on the table. Greg grabbed it.

"We need a laptop. Stacie, there's one on the desk," he said.

Stacie got up and grabbed the laptop, placing it on the table. Greg and Gus took the papers from the envelope and went to the couch. There were several pages of documents with reports. There was also a notebook filled with her father's handwriting.

Jolene took the notebook and sat on the small chair. Stacie and Livy took the flash drive and inserted it into the USB drive on the computer. They were all busy with their own tasks, not saying anything. After a long while, Greg put the documents down and stood up. "I need refreshment. Anyone interested?" he asked.

"Yes," answered Greg, Livy, and Stacie.

"Jolene, something to drink?" he asked.

"Oh, yes please," she answered.

He left the papers with Gus and walked out of the study. Gus continued reading while Livy and Stacie checked the information on the flash drive. Jolene was very quiet reading the notebook.

After ten minutes, Greg walked in with a tray full of drinks. He put the tray down on the table and everyone except Jolene stopped what they were doing and took a glass. Gus grabbed a glass and brought it to her. She looked up as he stood in front of her. He saw the anguish in her eyes. She put the notebook down and took the glass from him, absentmindedly sipping the juice. Greg went back to the table and took a glass for himself then went and sat next to her. "Are you okay?" he asked.

"Yes, I'm fine," she said firmly.

"Good."

They all finished their drinks and got back to the tasks at hand. They read and researched the information her father gathered and had left behind for several hours.

"Wow, look at the time," said Stacie. "It's almost time for dinner."

"What?" asked Jolene, looking at the desk clock.

"I'm sorry. I'll start dinner; you all worked on breakfast."

"No, we can all do it together," said Gus.

The others nodded their heads in agreement. Livy shut the laptop off and pulled the flash drive out and put it back in the box. Gus took the documents he was reading and put them back in the envelope and back into the box.

Jolene held the notebook tight against her chest. She looked at them. Gus reached for the notebook and she gave it to him. He put it inside the box. He closed the box and gave it to her.

Jolene opened a cabinet behind the desk against the wall and put the box in there. Greg and Gus each took one of her hands and walked with her out of the study. Livy and Stacie followed them. They got busy preparing dinner. Thanks to Anna, the meats were thawed out and already seasoned. Gus worked the grill with Greg, while the women prepared the salad and rice. In forty-five minutes, dinner was ready. Everything was put in serving dishes and set on the table.

Gus went to the wine rack and pulled a bottle of wine out, while Greg got five wine glasses and the women set the table. Dinner was going great——the conversation was very animated and there was plenty of laughter. Everyone was hungry so they ate everything.

After they were done with dinner, everyone helped clean up the kitchen. Livy prepared a carafe of coffee and set up a tray, which Greg carried to the study. Jolene got the box out and put it back on the table.

They all resumed what they were working on earlier. Each settled back in the same place as before and started to work. They was barely any conversation; the only activity was to get up for more coffee. They worked straight through for several hours.

"It looks like your father discovered the money discrepancy because the person got greedy and started to take too much at once. If he stayed with the small amounts, no one might have noticed," said Greg.

"We agree," said Livy, "the earlier amounts were small, then they became larger."

"In my father's notes, he wrote that he first noticed the problem with the larger amounts."

Everyone looked at each other perplexed. Jolene knew that they were getting close to finding the person who embezzled the funds and killed her father.

"Your father was close to discovering the person. He narrowed the search down to three executives," said Gus.

"One of them is the killer, too," said Greg.

"He must have found out about my father's investigation somehow and killed him."

They remained quiet for a few minutes, absorbing the information they were discovering.

"Is there anyone we know on the list?" asked Stacie.

Greg and Gus looked at Jolene. Jolene moved from the chair and sat next to Livy. She handed Livy the notebook and opened it to the page where her father wrote the names of the three executives he suspected. Livy nodded as Stacie read the page with her. Livy didn't say anything, not even trying to defend her father. "Livy, you're not surprised," said Jolene.

Livy turned to face her best friends," No, my father has no scruples," she said.

"And he's a mean son of a bitch, too. He was always mistreating Livy," said Stacie, holding her closer.

Jolene remembered the many times, late at night, when Livy would come to her room crying. "Livy, I'm sorry," she said giving her a hug.

"I'm not; he was and still is as cruel to my mother as he was to me. Embezzlement would be like him, but killing, that I can't believe."

"Livy we're not sure it's him. We need to finish the investigation my father started." They all looked at each other and nodded with approval.

"Stacie, our IT expert, will you find out for us where the money went or maybe, where it's still going?" requested Gus. "Greg, can you research this email and see if we can find out who it came from?"

He stopped and looked at Livy, "We need to get our hands on the police reports and any video from the days Jolene's father was in the police station. See what you can do."

Jolene waited for him to give her something to do, but he didn't. "What about me?"

"What about you?"

"What can I do to help?" she asked.

"Nothing, you need to stay far away from everything. We don't want anyone to connect you to your family," he said.

"Gus, I can't just sit here doing nothing."

"Don't you have the plan with Daniel? Work on that," said Greg in a sarcastic tone.

She knew that Greg was upset with her about Daniel, but she couldn't seem to leave it alone. There was something inside her that was demanding satisfaction for his betrayal. She stayed quiet for a moment. "Yes, of course," she said not making eye contact with them.

"Well, I think we've done enough for today. I'm ready for a quick shower and a movie. What do you think?" Gus asked in a cheerful tone.

"Yes," said Stacie.

The other two nodded their heads, but Jolene didn't say anything. They put everything back in the box and Jolene put it back in the cabinet. Livy and Stacie were the first to leave; the other three stayed behind. Greg moved closer to her, took her face in his hands and lifted it for her to look at him. He smiled at her and brought his lips to hers. She wrapped her arms around his neck and held to him for a fabulous kiss.

He stopped kissing her and took her hand. Gus took the other and they walked out of the room and straight up to her room. Greg walked into the bathroom, slowly taking her clothes off. He never took his eyes away from hers. At her back, Gus was helping, too.

After a few minutes she was completely naked in front of them. "Your turn," she said, "clothes off," as she put the water on.

Gus and Greg swiftly discarded their clothes. She laughed when Gus picked her up in his arms and walked into the shower with her. Greg followed behind them. Gus stood her in front of him and took the washcloth and soap. He started to wash her front. Greg grabbed the other washcloth and worked on her back.

Together they were setting her body on fire. She leaned back unto Greg, exposing her breasts to Gus. He took one breast in his mouth while washing the other. She gasped when he took her nipple between his teeth and bit it softly. Greg then turned her head to the side and placed his mouth to hers and pushed in his tongue. She sighed in complete surrender.

After a few minutes, Greg stopped kissing her and looked at Gus. Gus could see the passion in his eyes. Gus leaned over Jolene and while still holding Jolene's breast, he kissed Greg. Greg also had a hold of her by the waist. They stopped kissing, finished washing her and quickly washed themselves, too.

Gus stood her directly under the water to rinse off the soap. Greg brought his hand to her ass and spread her cheeks. He slid a finger inside her while kissing her neck, while at the same time, Gus brought his hand down to her mound and pushed two fingers inside her.

Jolene was in ecstasy. Her body was bursting with pleasure with all the pumping they were doing inside her with their fingers. They knew she was ready to come. They looked at each other, stopped and pulled their fingers out. Gus moved backwards against the wall and pulled her with him, lifting her right onto his shaft.

Jolene trembled as he took her, then Greg softly bent her forward and played with her butt hole before positioning his dick in her hole entrance and thrusting inside. Jolene gasped loudly with the sensation of how full she was. Not wasting anytime, the two men drove in and out of her. They picked up the pace of their thrusting. "I can't hold on any longer——she's so tight around my dick," gasped Greg.

"Me too, she's grasping my dick like a vise," Gus said.

"Come for us, baby," Greg said nibbling on her ear.

They thrust faster and deeper in and out. At the next thrust, she came to a full-blown orgasm. They continued pumping until they both came, too. Greg rested his head on her back and gave her a kiss, and Gus gave her a kiss on her head. She felt so lucky to have them, so what was keeping her from committing to them? They pulled out of her and quickly all three washed up. They dried off and went to the room and got dressed. Together they walked down to the family room.

The TV was already on but there was no one in the room. When they turned to go out, the girls walked in with a tray full of drinks and a bowl of popcorn. Stacie put the tray on the coffee table. Greg found a movie and started it. Everyone took a drink and got comfortable. Livy sat in the loveseat with Stacie and Greg and Gus sat with Jolene on the big couch.

Halfway thru the movie, the three girls were sound asleep, so Gus shut the TV off. Livy was completely stretched out on top of Stacie, and Jolene lay across both guys.

"You take Jolene. I'll take Livy and come back for Stacie," said Greg in a low voice.

Gus nodded to him. He lifted her into his arms and walked out. Greg went to the other chair and lifted Livy and walked behind him. They walked very slowly and quietly so as not to wake them up. Greg brought Livy to her room, laid her down on the bed and took off her shoes before going back down for Stacie.

Gus was already in the room with Jolene. He laid her on the bed, took her shoes off, and very patiently worked her clothes off. He covered her with the blanket and went back down to the family room.

He put all the glasses on the tray then picked up the tray from the table and brought it to the kitchen, going back to look for any mess that was left behind. He found a few napkins, which he picked up and shut the light off and went back to the kitchen where Greg was cleaning the glasses. He threw the napkins in the garbage can, found a dishtowel and started to dry what Greg had already washed. After they finished, Greg dried his hands. Gus turned him around to face him and pressed him against the sink, putting his arms on each side of Greg, trapping him with his body. Gus rubbed his hips against his then took his mouth in a wild kiss.

Greg brought his arms around Gus's waist and pulled him tighter to him. Hip against hip, they moved their bodies together as they continued kissing. Gus pulled his lips a few inches away from Greg's lips, "I want to be inside you," he said.

He moved him to the table. Frantically, they helped each other out of their shirts, touching and kissing every part of each other's upper body. Gus turned Greg around to face the table and pulled his zipper down. As usual, Greg wasn't wearing underwear.

Greg kicked his shoes and pants to the side. Right away, Gus moved a few inches back and took his off, too. He pressed Greg's upper body forward on the table and spread his legs apart. He took some of the oil he saw inside the cabinet and spread his cheeks apart and rubbed some of it all over his butt, pushing a finger inside him. Right away, he pushed another finger in and pushed in and out hard and fast.

Greg couldn't stop himself from moaning. Gus continued pumping inside him while with the other hand he rubbed oil on his shaft. He stopped fucking him with his fingers and slowly started to push his dick inside him. Greg slowed down his breathing, relaxing so he could take in all of Gus. Gus continued his slow thrust while touching him all over. As the crown went inside him, Greg felt the sweet pleasure of Gus's dick.

Gus pulled out a bit and thrust back in, this time going in farther. He kept thrusting in and out, eventually going all the way inside him.

Greg's body was trembling with pleasure, Gus could sense he would soon climax and went faster and harder in and out, clashing skin to skin. He was also rubbing Greg's dick up and down hard. He pushed one last time and erupted in a big orgasm. He gave Greg's dick a big squeeze. He continued pumping until he was spent.

He kissed Greg on his back and held him for a bit. He pulled out of him and turned him around. Greg already had a hold of his shaft and was stroking hard and fast. Gus went down to his knees and took Greg's dick in his mouth, licking and sucking him hard. Greg was so ready to come that on the next hard suck from Gus, he came in his mouth. Gus kept sucking until he swallowed the last drop of his cum. He moved his mouth to the tip and licked the last drop. Greg pulled him up and planted a kiss on his lips.

They kissed for a while, enjoying the touch of each other's tongues. They stopped kissing and held each other in a hug. They moved away from each other. They both grabbed dishtowels and cleaned up the mess they made. They picked up their shoes and clothes and walked hand-in-hand upstairs to Jolene's room.

They walked into the room in the dark, slowly sliding in the bed on each side of her. They moved closer to her and put an arm over her. Within minutes, they both closed their eyes and relaxed around her.

Chapter 12

Jolene sat on the bench across the pond. She was alone because Gus was on a conference call with his agent. She looked at the time; it was almost one o'clock in the afternoon on Friday. It had been five days since she saw Greg and the girls. Earlier, she was happy because she would be spending the weekend with them again, but then Daniel called and asked her out for a movie date. She had already seen him twice this week, but she didn't want him to lose interest in her so she said yes. She would have to way until late tonight to see them.

She stayed out in the garden for almost an hour until she saw Gus coming towards her. He sat next to her and held her in his arms. He knew she was disappointed that she would have to see Greg and Livy later than planned. She was looking forward to hearing the results of their research during the week. Jolene rested her head on Gus's shoulder and he smiled at her, holding her tighter. "I have to get ready for my date," she said pulling away from him.

He said nothing to her as they stood up and walked back to the house. As they walked through the kitchen, Anna gave them each a glass of lemonade. After they finished drinking their lemonade, she went up to her room while Gus went to the family room to catch up on the news.

He had been watching TV for an hour when he heard the doorbell ring. He saw Anna going for the door; she walked back with Daniel behind her. "Good evening," said Daniel stretching out his hand. Gus walked over to him and shook his hand.

"Good evening," replied Gus.

Gus showed him to a chair and they both sat down. Anna came back with two glasses of lemonade for them. "Anna please let Jolene know that Daniel is here," said Gus.

"Of course," she said leaving the family room. Anna knocked softly at Jolene's door.

"Come in," said Jolene.

Anna walked in the room where Jolene was putting the last touches on her makeup. Jolene looked at Anna and smiled. She spun around to show Anna her outfit. "What do you think?" she asked.

"You look beautiful," said Anna smiling back. "You were always beautiful, even from a young age. Daniel is here."

Jolene hugged her and gave her a kiss on the cheek. Anna hugged her back and held her for a few seconds. "I better go down," Jolene said.

She grabbed her small purse and walked out arm-in-arm with Anna. When they got to the foyer, Anna went to the kitchen and Jolene walked into the living room. "Daniel, hi," she said walking toward him.

Daniel stood up from the chair and met her halfway. He embraced her and went for a kiss on the lips, but Jolene turned her head and he ended up kissing her cheek. "Hi Jolene, you look beautiful," he stated.

"Thank you," she said.

"Ready?" he asked.

"Yes," she answered.

Gus was ignoring the whole encounter so she didn't want to make it any worse for him. She just waved goodbye to him instead of giving him a hug and kiss. He waved back without even looking at them. Daniel wrapped an arm around her waist and they walked out of the family room. Gus heard the door closing. He felt hurt; he didn't understand why it seemed so easy for her to switch off her emotions and go off with Daniel. Playing this all the way to the end was going to be painful, but he had promised to help her.

Gus brought his attention back to the news and tried to relax or Greg would sense that he was upset. After the news was over, he shut off the TV and went to the study. He turned on his computer and got himself busy working on some documents for his agent, trying to keep himself from thinking about Jolene.

He checked his watch; Greg and the girls would be here any minute. He went to the kitchen and checked with Anna on dinner.

"Everything is ready," Anna said.

"Great, thanks. You, Len, and the servants can go now. I'll take care of the rest. We'll eat out here," he said.

"You're sure?" she asked.

"Yes."

Anna showed him where everything was and then dismissed the servants. She said goodnight to Gus and left to find Len. A few minutes later, Gus saw them leaving the house. The servants were already gone. A few minutes later, he heard the front door opening; Jolene had given Greg and Livy a set of keys to the house. He walked to the foyer to greet Greg and the girls. Greg embraced and kissed him. After the kiss, they hugged for a while.

"Hey you two, we're starving. Dinner please," said Livy.

Gus and Greg laughed out loud and they all went out to the kitchen. Everyone helped setting the table and sat down to eat. They ate with no hurry, talking about everything that had happened during the week.

They laughed about a couple of stories that Stacie shared. After they were done with dinner, they stayed together at the table still talking and laughing. After an hour of conversation, they decided to watch a movie. Because Jolene wasn't there, they didn't feel that it was okay to talk about the research. They figured they should wait until the next day when they were all together.

Together they picked up the kitchen and washed the dishes. Stacie got a pitcher of lemonade from the refrigerator and glasses from the cabinet and put them on a tray. Greg took the tray and they all went to the family room. Gus turned on the TV, and went through the movie choices with them. Finally, they agreed on one. Gus settled on the big couch with Greg and again the girls got comfortable on the loveseat. They joked and laughed through the whole movie. Greg sensed the tension in Gus; he brought him closer and slowly rubbed his back.

Jolene got back to the house around one in the morning. After the movie, Daniel had insisted on going to a club. She didn't want to spoil the progress she had made with him so she agreed. She had a good time dancing, but she felt strange about being in his arms and kissing him. The kisses didn't do anything for her, but she kept up with the farce.

She grabbed a drink from the kitchen and went up to her room. Nobody was there. She felt sad while she went to the bathroom, cleaned her face, and put her pajamas on. She went back in the room, turned off the light and slid into bed. She turned and tossed for a bit before she fell asleep.

She was running fast, someone was chasing her. She kept running. The streets were empty. She couldn't get away. She started to scream and continued screaming.

Greg and Gus were startled by the screams. They looked at each other. "Jolene," said Greg moving quickly out of the bed and putting his briefs on. Gus was doing the same on the other side of the bed.

They heard Jolene scream again and quickly ran into her room. Livy and Stacie were behind them. Jolene was thrashing all over the bed, still screaming. They rushed to the bed and Gus kneeled next to her. He took her arm and started to shake her. Livy put the light on.

"Jolene, Jolene," he called her name.

She opened her eyes a little bit drowsy; she turned her face and looked at them. She covered her face with her hands and started to cry.

"What's wrong, mon amour," said Gus.

"It was awful," she said holding onto him. "Somebody was chasing me through the streets downtown; it was dark. I ran and ran and I couldn't get away."

"You're okay, baby," said Greg stroking her back. "We're here. No one is going to hurt you."

"Oh Greg, I was so scared."

Livy and Stacie sat on the other side of the bed, reached for her and comforted her. After some time, her trembling went away. Stacie slid from the bed. "I'll get you a nice cup of tea," she said rushing out of the room.

Gus lifted her from the bed and put her on his lap. She rested her head on his chest. Greg sat close to them and continued to stroke her back. Jolene felt at ease already by the time Stacie came back with her tea. She took the cup and slowly took a sip.

"Thank you, Stacie."

"You're welcome."

She sat up in Gus's lap and gave everyone a smile. She took Greg's face in her hands and brought it closer for a quick kiss, then did the same to Gus. "I'm sorry, I was being a baby. It's been a long time since I've had those nightmares," she said.

"Oh honey, why didn't you tell us about them?" asked Livy taking her hand.

"Because they stopped after awhile; they only lasted for about a year after we left."

Gus hugged her tighter and Greg held them both.

"Are you going to be okay?" asked Stacie seeing that they probably wanted to be alone.

"Yes, thanks. Sorry that I woke you up," she said.

"No problem, we're here for you any time, okay?" said Livy.

Jolene gave her hand a squeeze and smiled at them. Livy and Stacie said goodnight and left the room.

Jolene moved from Gus's lap and sat at the edge of the bed between them. She took a hand from each and brought them to her lips, kissing both hands. "I missed you in my bed," she said, "I know I've been selfish, but I feel so lost without you two."

Greg brought her lips to his; she opened her mouth for him. He kissed her for a few minutes, then stopped and Gus turned her to him and proceeded to kiss her, too.

"Please, for tonight I just want you two to hold me."

They smiled at her and they all crawled into bed with Jolene between them. Gus pulled her closer to him, pressing her back tight to his body. Greg moved with her. She relaxed her head on Greg's chest and closed her eyes.

"Je t'aime," said Gus softly in ear.

"I love you," said Greg too.

They could feel her body tense as they waited for her response, but it never came. Greg looked at Gus; they smiled at each other and closed their eyes. Jolene couldn't believe she didn't answer them. Deep in her heart, she knew she was in love with them both, but this was not the time to say it, not yet. She had to finish what she came to do, then she could think of a life with them. Jolene relaxed in their arms and quickly fell to sleep.

She woke up in a wonderful mood, her body already burning with the touch of the two men on either side of her. She had a big smile on her face when she opened her eyes and saw Gus pinching her breasts with his fingers, while Greg's hand was doing delicious twirls with his fingers on her mound.

"That feels wonderful," she said in a whisper.

She moaned with pleasure, her body engulfed in heat. Gus consumed her lips with his as she thrust her tongue in his mouth and they started a dance of tongues, tasting and savoring.

Greg inserted his fingers inside her, pumping in and out briskly. She squirmed under his fingers, pushing up to get him deeper. Gus softly kissed her from her face down to her breasts, then he put one nipple in his mouth while caressing the other breast. Greg positioned his body on top of her, spreading her thighs with his legs and thrust right into her.

Gus took his mouth off her nipple and positioned himself on top of her chest with his dick in his hand, stroking it up and down. Jolene opened her mouth in anticipation to taste him. He brought his dick up to her mouth and she slowly started to take it in. Jolene used her tongue to taste every inch of Gus's dick. She licked and sucked him while twisting her mouth all over it. She took a hand and started to massage his balls, squeezing softly and twirling them in her hand.

Greg picked up the pace and thrust harder and deeper. Gus kneeled closer to her mouth, took hold of the headboard and pumped in and out faster in her mouth. She continued to suck him harder, squeezing the balls tighter every time he got closer. All three were completely in tune with each other's needs and close to the point of orgasm. Jolene came first and seconds later Gus came, pumping all his cum in her mouth. She swallowed every drop. She continued to suck and lick him.

"Like that baby, suck me dry."

At that moment Greg exploded inside her, pumping in and out while she trembled all over. Gus took his dick out of her mouth and moved to the side, kissing her and tasting himself in her mouth. Greg stopped and lay on top of her, holding his weight on his forearms. Gus stopped kissing her and kissed Greg who was still semi-hard inside Jolene. She wriggled her body under him, feeling him grow hard again.

Gus's dick also was getting hard again. He stopped the kiss with Greg, moved to the nightstand and brought the lubricant out. He put lubricant on two fingers and went behind Greg, spread his butt cheeks and pushed two fingers inside him. Greg moaned out loud, lifting his butt higher for Gus to have better access.

"More, give me more," said Greg before bringing his lips to Jolene while, at the same time, he began to thrust in and out while Gus was pumping his butt with his fingers.

Gus pushed another finger in, pumping and spreading his butt hole. After a few minutes, he took his fingers out and pushed his shaft in, slowly working his dick head in. Once he was inside, he pushed harder and faster. He continued to move at the same time that Greg pushed inside Jolene. They worked together in such a delicious motion.

"God Greg, your butt is so tight around my dick," said Gus.

She couldn't hold out any longer. Greg could feel her heart speeding up as her pussy wall tightened around his dick, and he knew she was ready to come. He stopped the kiss, brought his arms up a bit for leverage and stared to push harder, going deeper inside her. Gus knew them both so well that he knew Jolene was about to come, so he followed Greg's lead and pumped hard to keep the tempo. In a matter of seconds, Jolene burst into climax.

"Greg, Gus," she screeched out their names thrashing her head all over the pillow, her body trembling.

Greg and Gus came together, and they kept moving until the last of their body tremors stopped. Gus pulled out from Greg, went to the bathroom, cleaned himself and brought washcloths for them. She smiled at them, "A girl could get used to waking up like this," she said.

Gus and Greg smiled back at her. They each cuddled one side of her.

"We better get up. We have work to do," said Jolene.

She climbed over Greg, "I'm first in the shower!" she said running into the bathroom. She started the water and quickly jumped in. The two men stayed behind and looked at each other.

"Will she ever admit she loves us?" asked Greg with sorrow in his tone.

"I don't know my love, I don't know," said Gus embracing him. They held each other for a while, and then Jolene came out of the bathroom with a towel wrapped around her body.

"Hey you two, time to get up," she said.

They moved apart. Greg went to the bathroom while Gus watched her dress. He knew every curve, every dimple on her body, yet he didn't know her heart. She smiled at him while she dressed, modeling to him the way he liked. Greg came out of the shower and Gus went in. She was almost done dressing when Greg had just started.

She sat on the couch and put her shoes on. Greg sat next to her and put his on, too. Gus came out of the bathroom and quickly dressed. He slid his shoes on and they walked out of the room. They went straight to the kitchen to get breakfast started. Jolene started the coffee while Greg and Gus worked on the eggs and bacon. A few minutes into breakfast, the girls walked into the kitchen. "Need help?" asked Livy.

"We got this. You want to get the table set up?" said Greg.

"Sure," they said.

They moved to the cabinets and got the dishes and glasses out, as well as the utensils. They were done setting the table by the time the food was ready. They put everything in serving dishes and brought it to the table. Gus grabbed the orange juice from the refrigerator.

Everyone sat down and ate; they kept the talk light and ate in no hurry, enjoying the food and each other's company. When they were done eating, the girls washed the dishes and the guys cleaned the table and stove. Jolene threw any garbage in the trashcan. When the kitchen was completely clean, they all went to the study to discuss the results of the week's research.

Everyone got comfortable in chairs while Jolene went to the cabinet and got the box out. She put it on the table then went and sat on the couch with Greg and Gus.

"Stacie you go first," said Gus, like always taking charge.

Stacie pulled some printed copies of documents from a manila envelope and she gave everyone a copy. "These are records of money that was transferred to the accounts. As you can see, the culprit moved money through several avenues. I checked all three executives and he's the only one that came up. I already told Livy my discovery," she said squeezing her loving partner's hand.

Daughter's Revenge

"Okay, Jolene. After Stacie told me about her research results, I decided to check my father's personal emails back at home," she said pulling some other printed papers from the same envelope Stacie had. She, too, gave everyone a copy.

"These are emails from my father's computer at home to two other people. As you can see, they're using code names. I tried to see if I could find their real names, but I had no luck." She found a specific email, "Listen to this," she said and started to read the email out loud. 'Let's meet. I have to move some money. We need to decide to what account and how much. The usual place at eleven tonight,'" she put the paper down.

They looked at each other, "I knew my father could do the embezzlement but not the killing. One of the other two is the killer," Livy said.

"How about the police reports?" Jolene asked.

"I was able to get copies of the reports. I made a copy for each of us," she said handing each one their copies, "I'm still working on getting the video."

They all read the reports quietly, "As you can see, the reports are very vague. I found nothing much related to the night he died," said Livy.

Everyone remained quiet. When they had all finished reading the reports, Gus turned his attention to Greg, "How about you?" he asked.

Greg handed them copies of the accounting reports. "Well I agree with Livy and Stacie that her father is guilty and also that he's not working alone. I found several discrepancies in the books too, and they all happen at the end of every quarter when the company moves money to the reserve, which is George's department," explained Greg.

He went thru all the transactions in all the documents he made copies of from the computer. They looked at the amounts transferred and the dates.

Jolene put her papers down. "We can bring all this documentation to the police. This will exonerate my father."

"Jolene, we need to find out who else is involved. Your father was killed in a police station. Who could get in so easily? Let's wait for the police station surveillance videos, okay?" said Livy.

"Livy is right, Jolene. This is circumstantial evidence. We need names and solid evidence," said Gus. The rest of them nodded in agreement. Gus pulled her closer and gave her a hug. Jolene rested her head on his shoulder.

They continued to discuss the matter until Gus put the papers down and looked at everyone. "Let's stop for now. Let's get dinner ready and watch some TV. There is a welterweight boxing match on demand tonight that I want to see.

"That's right. It's going to be a great match," said Stacie.

They put all the papers in the envelopes and in the box. Jolene put the box back in the cabinet and locked it. They left the room. Everyone took a quick bathroom break and met in the kitchen. They immediately divided the tasks and prepared the food. Greg and Gus again took the grill——this time they cooked fish——while Jolene steamed some vegetables, and the other two girls took care of dessert and drinks. Dinner was ready in no time, and everything was been put in serving dishes while Jolene set the table. Everyone sat down to eat.

They finished eating a very enjoyable dinner, and Stacie brought out the dessert. They all took some of the dessert and kept the talk going. As usual, everyone helped with the washing up before going to the entertainment room where the guys started a game of pool and Livy and Stacie played a video game.

Jolene sat in a chair and watched Greg and Gus play pool. After a couple of games, Gus went to put in the order for the boxing match on demand. Jolene took his place and played a game with Greg. Gus came to the doorway and called out, "Greg, how about a beer? Girls, drinks?"

"I'll take a beer," said Stacie.

"Me, too," said Livy.

Jolene took her shot, "Me too."

A few minutes later, Gus walked in with a tray full of beers. He gave everyone a bottle, put down the tray down and took his. Everyone took sips of their beers and went back to their games. Gus stood behind Jolene, who was watching Greg take his shot, and he started to caress her back.

She moved back into his touch and he moved closer to her. Greg got ready for his shot, and looked up to see Gus behind her. He smiled at them and brought his attention back to the game. He made his shot and continued with his turn. Jolene laughed at something Gus said in her ear. Greg heard her laugh and lost concentration on his shot and missed. "Man," he said snapping his hand to the side.

She moved next to him and took his face in her hand and gave him a quick kiss on the lips. "Sorry, babe," she said with a big smile on her face as she set up for her shot.

"Gus, you did that on purpose," he snapped.

Gus laughed out loud and went to him and gave him a kiss too. Jolene missed her shot, too.

"Aha, you deserve that, cheater," said Greg.

She laughed and moved away from the table, grabbed her beer and took a sip. With another couple of shots, Greg won the game. He went to her, grabbed the back her neck and gave her a deep, long kiss. "You owe me for that trick you pulled," he said.

"Me," she said laughing and putting on an innocent face. He laughed with her. They continued playing pool, joking and laughing for about another hour. Gus checked his watch and saw that it was close to nine o'clock——time for the boxing match.

"We have ten minutes before the boxing starts," he said.

Livy and Stacie finished the game they were playing and shut off the box. Gus and Greg played for a few minutes more before the game was over and Gus won the game.

"I'll get more beers," said Greg, picking up the empty bottles and bringing the tray with him to the bar.

Everyone cleaned up after themselves as Gus went to the family room and found the on-demand channel for the boxing match. He got comfortable on the big couch as Jolene settled in next to him. Livy and Stacie sat on the loveseat in each other's arms.

The boxing match started just as Greg walked in with more beers. He gave the girls theirs and went to sit on the couch with Gus and Jolene. They watched the first boxing match quietly and when it was over, Stacie stood up and said, "I'm making popcorn. Anyone wants anything?" she asked.

"I'll take potato chips," said Jolene.

"Okay."

She walked out of the room while the others stood up and stretched a bit. Gus sat back down and pulled her onto his lap. Jolene got comfortable and rested her head on his chest. Greg left the room for a few minutes to use the bathroom. When he came back, he saw Jolene sitting on Gus's lap. She lifted her head, smiled at him and patted the couch next to her.

He smiled back at her and went to sit next to Gus. She lifted her legs over his lap. Stacie came back with a full bowl of popcorn and another one of potato chips. She put the bowls on the table and went to sit with Livy who opened her arms for her. Everyone settled back and continued to watch the second match.

The rest of the evening was fun as they joked and laughed together. After the main match was over, about midnight, they picked up the mess in the room. Greg brought the empty beer bottles to the box at the bar, while the girls picked up the empty bowls and garbage and brought it to the kitchen. Livy washed the bowls and Stacie dried. When they were done, everyone went upstairs to their rooms.

Jolene, Gus and Greg each went to the bathroom and got ready for bed. Gus shut off the light and climbed into bed. Jolene got comfortable between them. Their love-making had been exceptional since they were back together. Jolene couldn't get enough of them and they felt the same way about her. Jolene started to caress Gus's chest with her hand and then licked it.

She put her mouth to one of his nipples and with the other hand caressed his lower stomach. Gus moaned in appreciation of her touch. Meanwhile, Greg had a hold of her breasts, caressing them and pinching gently. He held himself tight to her body, rubbing his erection on her buttocks.

She lowered her hand and started to caress the length of Gus's dick. He groaned louder now, tilting his head back as she squeezed him hard.

Greg continued to fondle her breasts while kissing her shoulders and back. Gus pulled her hand from his dick, rolled flat on his back, and pulled her on top of him. He lifted her up and positioned her directly onto his dick. Greg sat up and watched them. Jolene leaned her body forward on his and lifted her butt for Greg to take it

Greg grabbed the lubricant from the drawer and moved behind her. He put lubricant on his dick and then on her butt hole. Gently he started to push inside her while Gus was pumping in and out of her. Jolene's pussy was stretched completely. She loved the feel of both of their dicks inside her. She moaned and groaned frantically while the guys kept pumping in and out of her.

They moved continually in unison for some time until it was enough for her. She squeezed tight on their dicks and convulsed in orgasm. They pumped in and out and in minutes they both came inside her, keeping up the rhythm until her trembling stopped. After another hour or so of love-making, they all collapsed in bed, breathing hard. Jolene smiled at them. Gus pulled from her and went to the bathroom to get clean and brought washcloths back. He gave one to Greg, who had just pulled out of Jolene, and used the other one to clean Jolene. They cuddled closed to her, closed their eyes, and in seconds all three were fast asleep.

Chapter 13

Jolene checked her watch. In ten minutes, Daniel was coming to take her to lunch. It was Wednesday and she was still thinking about the great time she had with Gus and Greg on Saturday and Sunday. She wished for all this to be over soon so she could really make a life for herself——hopefully with both of them. Gus was out doing some shopping.

Jolene heard the doorbell ring. She left the study and went to open the door. When Daniel came in he gave her a hug and a kiss. Jolene tried to react as if she was glad to see him and enjoying the kiss. "Ready?" he asked.

"Yes, let me grab my purse," she answered moving toward the table by the wall and grabbing it.

She walked out of the house with Daniel behind her. He opened the car door for her and then got in. He drove off from the house and on toward the restaurant.

An hour or so after Jolene left the house, Gus walked in. He knew she was going to lunch with Daniel, and he didn't want to be here when he came to get her, so he made up the excuse that he needed to go to the mall. Now he was back home and upset that she insisted on going on with this farce with Daniel. He went into the kitchen.

"Hi," said Anna, who immediately noticed the strain in his face.

"Hi," he answered.

"How was shopping?" she asked.

"Ah," he said puzzled by her questions.

"Gus, shopping, you went out shopping, remember?"

"Oh, I didn't find anything that interested me," he said.

"Okay, coffee?"

"Please."

Anna got a cup from the cabinet and poured him fresh coffee. She brought the cream and sugar bowls and put them on the counter. Gus added a bit of cream and a teaspoon of sugar to his cup. He sat on the stool and quietly sipped his coffee. When he was finished, he left the cup on the counter and went back to his room where he sat in a chair and rested his head, closing his eyes for a moment.

The truth was that he was devastated that Jolene had not openly declared her love for him or even Greg. He was so sure she loved him, but why did she continue this false pretense with Daniel? He was afraid that the outcome could be disastrous. He shook his head. There was nothing he could do but be here for her. He promised to help her with both plans and he couldn't go back on his word. He brought his hand to his face and roared loudly in frustration.

At that moment, Jolene was in Daniel's car being driven back home. Lunch with him was pleasant, but it was such a one-way conversation. She was so tired of being with him. She was glad that it would be over soon. As they drove along, he received a phone call in the car. She was relieved that she didn't have to make small talk with him. When they got back home, Daniel was still on the phone, so Jolene opened her door and got out of the car. Daniel saw her walking away, so he quickly finished the phone call and followed her. She had reached the front door when he caught up with her. She opened the door and they walked into the house. "How about a drink?" he asked.

"Sure. This way," she said. He walked next to her and into the living room. He went behind the bar and prepared drinks for the two of them. Jolene went and sat on the couch. He picked up the full glasses and sat down next to her, handing one of the glasses to her. Jolene took a sip of her drink.

"Okay?" he asked.

"Yes very good."

Daniel put his arm over her shoulder and pulled her closer. Gus had heard the front door opening. He knew he should stay in his room, but it bothered him that Daniel was in the house with her. He walked downstairs and looked in the family room, the entertainment room, then to the living room where he saw them kissing. With difficulty, he kept control of his temper.

"Hello you two," he said loudly from the doorway.

Daniel stopped kissing her and turned to face him. Jolene moved away from him and sat up straight. "Gus, hi," said Daniel.

"Hi," said Gus walking into the room and sitting in a chair across from them. "How was lunch?" he asked.

"Great, we had a good time," said Daniel.

"Yes," said Jolene.

At that moment, Daniel got another phone call. "Sorry, I have to take this," he said." Hello, please give me a minute," he said to the person on the phone. He turned to Jolene and gave her a quick kiss on the cheek. "I'll call you tomorrow," he said.

"Okay," she said.

Gus didn't say anything to her; he just sat in the chair staring at her. Minutes later, he walked over to her, grabbed her hand and pulled her up from the couch. He pulled both her hands to her back and slammed his body against hers. "Why do you insist on doing this?" he asked.

"You know why," she said lifting her face to look at him.

"You like his kisses, don't you?"

"Gus, please."

"Don't you?" he yelled.

"No, I don't. I only like yours and Greg's," said Jolene firmly as she moved her lips over his. She softly nibbled on his lower lip and glided her tongue over his top one. Gus opened his mouth and let her invade his mouth, their tongues slowly and erotically wrapping around one another's. Their bodies writhed furiously, moving in each other's arms, trying to feel every inch of one another. He pulled her back to get access to her neck. He moved his lips with rough kisses down her neck to her cleavage.

He snapped her bra open and pulled her blouse to the side, spilling her breasts in front of him. Swiftly, he took a nipple in his mouth and the other in his free hand. He rhythmically caressed her nipples, then pinched hard and pulled. Jolene held his shoulders, pushing her head back to open more for him. He changed nipples, brought the hand slowly down her stomach then under her skirt.

He ran his hand under her thong and spread her legs with his knees. She couldn't think straight; her body was in agony from his touch. He opened her pussy lips and in an abrupt move, pushed two fingers inside her. Her pussy was already moist with her juices. Jolene moaned out loud, holding onto him so she wouldn't fall.

He pumped his fingers in and out her fast while he sucked and bit her nipple harder. He continued the delicious attack to her body, then in a swift move, he pinched her other nipple and squeezed her clit with two fingers, forcing her body to completely surrender to him. She erupted in an orgasm that he pumped until he felt the last shudder. He brought his lips to hers and gave her a quick kiss.

"Jolene..." he started to say something when she stopped him with a finger on his lips.

"That was amazing, I love the way you touch me," she said. He smiled at her and she relaxed in his arms.

"Gus, Jolene," Anna called out to them.

Jolene moved away from Gus. Her skirt was up around her hips her bra and blouse were all wrinkled under her breasts.

"Go. Over here Anna" he said pointing to the other door. Jolene walked quickly out of the room as Gus moved behind the bar and washed his hands in the sink. As he finished, Anna was standing in front of him. "I thought I heard Jolene."

"Yes, she's home. She went up to her room."

"Oh, I was wondering if it's going to be two or three for dinner, but I don't see Daniel."

"He left. It's going to be just the two of us."

"Oh, dinner will be ready at the usual time."

"Okay, I'll let Jolene know."

Anna walked out of the living room and back to the kitchen. Gus breathed a sigh of relief, as he walked out of the room and went up to Jolene's room. He could hear the shower going. He entered the bathroom and quietly took his clothes off. He stopped as he heard sobs coming from the shower and could see Jolene leaning against the wall with her head down.

"Oh Dad, what am I doing?" she asked herself out loud between sobs.

Gus got in the shower with her. Jolene turned and looked at him with tears running down her face. She put her arms around his neck and continued crying. "I'm so sorry, I didn't mean to hurt you," she said between sobs.

"Babe, look at me. I'm fine."

"You'll end up hating me."

"Never, mon amour. I could never hate you," he said kissing her.

He looked at her, "I'm exactly where I want to be," he said smiling.

"Thank you," she said burying her face in his chest.

He held her for a while as the sobs slowly stopped. Jolene could feel his hard-on on her stomach. She moved to kneel in front of him; he stopped her. "No baby, this isn't the time, let's just shower."

"But let me take care you," she said.

"I can handle a bit of a hard-on; it's not the first or the last," he said turning her to the water.

He turned off the water and grabbed a towel from the rack, opening it for Jolene. She walked into the towel. He dried her completely then sent her out to dress. He quickly dried himself off and went into the room and got dressed as well. "The movie you've been waiting for is on demand. We can see it before dinner."

"Okay."

They finished dressing and went straight into the family room. Gus turned on the TV and found the movie. Jolene got comfortable in his arms. The movie lasted two and a half hours. Gus changed the TV to the news while she relaxed in his arms, happy and content to be with him. Just when the local news was over, Anna walked in the room. "Dinner is ready."

"Thanks, Anna," Jolene said.

Anna walked out and left them alone. Jolene stood up and stretched her body. Gus put his arm around her waist, pulled her closer and gave her a kiss. They sat across from each other in the dining room while a servant finished setting the table. Gus smiled at her and they ate their dinner. They kept the talk light and nice. They both loved Anna's cooking. After dinner, Anna brought them dessert.

Jolene laughed a Gus as he devoured the dessert in seconds. He had a sweet tooth and Anna knew it. They sat for a while, just talking and enjoying each other's company. "You want to see your shows?"

"Yes."

He walked with her back into the family room and gave her a light kiss on the lips. "I have a couple of calls to make. I'll be right back."

"Okay," she said smiling at him.

He left the room and went to the study. He called his mother, talked to her for a bit then he called his agent and talked to him for some time. He looked at his watch; the call was longer than he expected. Finally he hung up with his agent.

When he got back to the family room, the TV was still on but Jolene was already asleep on the couch. He turned the TV off and lifted her from the couch and walked upstairs to her room. He turned the covers down slowly and laid her in the bed and carefully took her clothes off.

He covered her with the blanket. He took his clothes off and slid in beside her. She cuddled close to his body. He put his arm around her waist and brought her closer, gave her a kiss on the forehead. He would endure anything for her.

Chapter 14

Jolene was smiling as she joked with Anna who was preparing dinner for the night. It was early Friday evening and Jolene was happy because she would be seeing the girls and Greg. She took a sweep with her finger of the pudding Anna was preparing. Anna slapped her hand softly and laughed with her. Len and Gus walked into the kitchen. "What are you two up to?" Gus asked.

"Don't ask," said Len smiling, "They have trouble written all over them."

The two laughed harder and the men joined them. Jolene owed a lot to Len and Anna. They had maintained her home all those years and they were keeping her identity a secret. Their love for her was unconditional and she felt the same about them. She went to Len and gave him a hug; he smiled at her and kissed her on the forehead.

"Dinner is all set," said Anna putting the dessert bowl in the refrigerator.

"Okay, I'll send the others home. As soon as you're ready to leave, let me know honey," said Len to his wife, letting Jolene go and walking out of the kitchen.

"Okay."

Jolene went to Anna and gave her a hug and kiss. Anna kissed her back on the cheek. Anna checked everything on the stove one last time, then said goodbye to them and left the kitchen to meet her husband. Jolene and Gus moved to the living room. As Jolene sat down her cell phone rang. She looked to see that it was Livy. "Hey, girl. What's up?" she asked.

"I'm going to be late tonight; my father isn't leaving until after nine. I'll be there as soon as I get what we need, okay?"

"Be careful. Does Stacie know?"

"I will. Yes, she does."

"Livy, don't take any unnecessary risks. If anything happens to you, I won't forgive myself."

"Nothing is going to happen. See you soon, bye," said Livy and she hung up the phone.

Jolene hung up her phone, too. Gus sensed that she was worried. Jolene saw his the concern in his expression. "Everything is okay," she assured him, "Livy is going to be late," she said giving him a smile.

They heard the door opening. They went to the foyer to see Greg and Stacie just walking in. "Hi," said Stacie, giving Jolene and Gus each a kiss on the cheek.

Greg went to her and she wrapped her arms around his neck. They connected in a wild kiss. Their kisses were always explosive because they didn't see each other during the week. They kissed for a while. "Hi," he said holding her tight.

"Hi," she said back smiling at him.

Without letting her go, he walked to Gus and gave him a big kiss, too. "I missed you," he whispered in his ear.

"I missed you, too."

All three stayed together hugging each other for a few seconds. "Hey you three. How about me?" complained Stacie.

They laughed and pulled her into the hug with them. It was about six thirty, so they decided to go eat. They walked to the kitchen and like always everyone helped with dinner. A half hour later, they were sitting down and ready to eat. Dinner was pretty much perfect as always, thanks to Anna.

It was a little bit quieter than usual because Livy wasn't there. Jolene brought the dessert out and everyone served themselves. They finished eating and wrapped up the leftovers for Livy before cleaning the kitchen and washing the dishes.

Gus found a movie they all agreed on and Stacie lay across the loveseat with the other three taking their usual spot on the couch. They watched the movie more quietly than usual, probably because Livy still wasn't there. An hour into the movie, Livy walked into the house. No one turned to greet her because they all were engrossed in the movie. "Honey I'm home," she said laughing.

All four turned and laughed with her. Quickly, before Stacie could stand up to greet her, she sat at the edge of the couch and gave her a big kiss. Stacie shifted over a bit to give her some space. "I've been thinking about kissing you all day," said Livy smiling at Stacie.

"Me, too. Hungry?"

"Starving, Mom left early with her friends and Dad ate out, so no one prepared dinner," she said.

"I'll bring you dinner," said Stacie moving quickly from the couch.

"That's okay, I'll get it."

"No let me, please."

"Okay, but I'll eat in the kitchen."

Jolene looked at her, "No way, eat here with us."

"I'll be right back."

Greg lifted Jolene's legs and slid off the couch, "Beer anyone?"

"Oh my, yes. Get one for Stacie, too," said Livy taking her shoes off and leaning her head back on the seat.

"Jolene?"

"No thanks," she said.

Greg left the room and in two minutes he was back with four beers. He gave Livy hers and put Stacie's on the end table. He sat down next to Gus and handed the last one to him. They went back to watching the movie.

About ten minutes later, Stacie came back with Livy's dinner. She brought a tray table with her. She set the tray for her with the food. Livy started to eat right away. Everyone made small talk while she ate and they watched the movie. Livy stopped eating for a minute, "Hey honey, did you show them the DVDs?" she asked.

"DVDs, what DVDs?" asked Jolene, looking at her.

"The DVDs I copied of the surveillance and interrogation videos."

"No, I thought we should see them together," said Stacie.

"Oh okay. Why don't you get them? I'm about done here."

"Okay."

Stacie went and grabbed the bag she had left next to the stairs in the foyer and came back to the room. Livy finished eating and took her plate and tray back to the kitchen. As she came back to the family room, she went to Stacie who was holding the DVDs in her hands. She sat next to her and brought her closer in an embrace, giving her a quick kiss on her lips.

Jolene couldn't concentrate on the movie any longer. She was anxious to see the DVDs. Gus and Greg could sense that she was agitated. They exchanged an understanding look over her head. "Perhaps we should stop the movie and see the DVDs." Gus suggested.

"I agree," said Greg.

Gus stopped the movie and turned the Blu-ray player on. Livy went to the entertainment center, put one of the DVDs in the player, and grabbed the remote.

"Jolene, are you sure you want to watch this?" asked Livy.

"Yes," she answered firmly.

Livy started the DVD and settled back on the loveseat with Stacie. The first DVD was a recording of her father's interrogation. Her nerves started to get to her and she shook a bit. Gus tightened his hold on her and Greg reached out and held her hand. She smiled at them and went back to watching the DVD.

After two long hours the interrogation was over. She admired how her father kept so calm through the entire interrogation. Stacie went to the Blu-ray player and changed the DVD to the next one. The DVD was surveillance video of the two days before her father's death. Greg went to the bar and brought beers for everyone including Jolene. She took the beer he offered her and took a big sip.

Everyone was completely engrossed in the recording. They saw that her father was kept in the cell for two days and was only let out to go to the bathroom. They saw him eating and sleeping. Jolene's heart was deep with sadness to see her strong father incarcerated like a common criminal. She leaned her head on Gus's shoulders. The next DVD was the one of the night he got killed. They all watched carefully everything that happened. After several hours of watching the recording, Jolene was disappointed that it never showed the killer. "This is awful. How can this be? There is no recording of the killer."

Livy straightened up on the seat and looked at her.

"That's what we thought at first, too, but having an expert on videotaping as a lover has its advantages," she said smiling at Stacie, who smiled back at her.

"Jolene, to the normal eye, it seems that the video is good, but someone who has studied the video recording process can tell with certainty that this record was tampered with."

"How?" asked Gus.

"Some of the recording is deleted and the recording times have been changed. Someone was with your father for more than an hour."

"This proves that the last person who saw your father was the police captain——for only a few minutes according to the recording——but for much longer in reality. He was the one with your father the longest and probably was the one who killed him," said Livy.

Jolene's heart was rising and her hands were sweaty. Gus turned her to look at him. "Breathe, baby."

Jolene took short breaths. Greg rubbed her back softly in a circular motion. She brought her heart back to a steady and calm beat. "Better?" asked Greg.

"Yes, thanks," replied Jolene.

Livy looked at her; she went to her bag and pulled out copies of some documents. She gave everyone a copy. "I found plenty of information in my father's safe. The first document shows some of the transactions that Greg talked about. You can see the transaction from two months ago. The next one is several communications between my father and the police captain and——you won't believe this——the judge." She paused for a minute and took a sip of her beer.

"After several minutes of looking at everything, I remembered how close those three were. They had known each other since grammar school. I remember my father telling me stories about them when I was young."

Jolene couldn't believe it; now they had enough evidence to bring to the police. Gus and Greg gave her a hug.

"I have more; I remembered that he had his high school year book in his office so I found it. I want you to see this."

They opened the yearbook to the specific page on the book. Everyone was stunned by what they saw. The yearbook picture showed the three men together in football uniforms, and underneath their names were the nicknames they used at that time. These were the same names they used on the emails between them. Livy smiled at her. "We have them, Jolene."

Jolene leaped into her arms and held her tight, "Thank you." She moved back to Gus's lap, "We can bring this to the police."

"Not yet. We need to get all them together in an incriminating situation," said Greg.

"We have to make a plan," said Gus.

"Like what?" asked Jolene.

"Not tonight, baby. It's late; it's almost one in the morning," said Greg holding her face in his hands.

Jolene wanted to argue but she saw that everyone was tired. She nodded her head. Stacie took the DVD out of the Blu-ray and put it together with the others. She took the copies of the documents and put everything together and gave it all to Jolene who took everything into the study. The group followed her. She added everything to the pile of information they already had in the box.

Gus and Greg each took her hand and pulled her out of the room. The whole group went upstairs. Livy and Stacie said goodnight to them and went to their room. The guys brought her to her room. Greg went and got the bed ready while Gus helped her with her clothes. Greg took his clothes off too and climbed in bed. After Gus was done undressing Jolene, he took his clothes off, too.

Jolene slid into bed and got comfortable next to Greg. Gus lay down at her other side. Both cuddled her between them. They knew she was emotionally exhausted. She was asleep in their arms in a matter of seconds. Gus and Greg held her tight until they were sure she was calm and in a deep sleep. Gus reached to Greg and gave him a quick kiss on the lips.

Chapter 15

Jolene woke up a bit agitated. She was dreaming of her father. She moved very slowly, trying not to wake up Gus and Greg. She went under the blanket and slid down to the bottom of the bed, and with very stealthy moves, she got off the bed.

She went to the bathroom and grabbed her pajamas, still trying to be quiet, she walked out of her room. Her heart was beating fast as she took the stairs softly one at a time. She went directly to the study and pulled out the DVDs of the interrogation and surveillance videos.

She went into the family room and started the Blu-ray player. She put a DVD in the machine and saw her father being interrogated by the police. As always, he kept his cool. She listened very carefully to everything. Then she put in the first surveillance DVD. This one only showed the two nights before her father's death in the police cell. She stared at her father the last two days he was alive. By the end of this DVD, she was crying. She put in the third and last DVD, this time sitting directly in front of the TV.

She watched her father's every move from that last day——the way he ate his food; his body language as he sat on the cot. Now she was crying hard, her face completely wet. In Jolene's room, Stacie opened the door and walked in. She touched Gus on the shoulder. "What?" he said not completely awake.

Greg stirred beside him and both reached to the middle for Jolene. Quickly, they both opened their eyes. That was when they saw Stacie standing next to the bed at Gus's side.

"Stacie is something wrong?" asked Gus.

"Yes, Jolene," she said.

"What's wrong?" asked Greg brusquely sitting up.

"She's down in the family room watching the DVDs and balling her eyes out. She didn't even notice I was in the doorway watching her. She needs you two more than ever."

They moved fast and found their pajama pants and rushed out of the room. Stacie went to Livy's room. Greg and Gus ran downstairs. They hesitated at the threshold of the family room, watching her cry. "Jolene," said Gus rushing to her.

She turned to them, her face completely covered in tears. Gus kneeled next to her and opened his arms. She moved to him and buried her face in his chest. Greg moved to her back and hugged her. They surrounded her in a big embrace.

She couldn't stop crying. Gus stroked her head softly while Greg massaged her arm. They held her until only soft sobs were left. Gus stood up and pulled her with him. He lifted her in his arms and sat on the couch with her, settling her on his lap. Greg sat next to him. She lifted her face to them. "I'm sorry. I just wanted to see him one more time," she said still sobbing.

"That's okay, baby."

Gus moved her hair away from her face and caressed her chin with his fingers.

"Why didn't you wake us up? We would have watched it with you."

"Oh Gus, I miss him so much."

"I know, we know," Gus said.

Greg got the remote and stopped the DVD. He grabbed a box of tissues from the table and handed her a tissue. She wiped the tears off her face and blew her nose. "I should have done more——tried harder to get to the house," she said." "Maybe…" Greg stopped her.

"Jolene, you were just a teenager. There was nothing you could have done then, but now you are doing something, and you will bring justice for your father's death."

"People will know he was not a criminal, like they believed him to be," said Gus.

"Thank you. I don't know what I would do without you two."

"Now let's get you back upstairs and ready for breakfast," said Gus.

"Yes, we have plans to make and criminals to catch," said Greg.

"Let me take her," said Greg standing up.

"You know I can walk, right."

Greg took her from Gus and started to walk out of the room, "I know."

Gus walked along next to him. Jolene leaned her head on Greg's shoulder. When they got to the second floor, the girls came out of the room. "How are you doing sweetie?" asked Livy.

"I'm fine, thanks."

"We'll start breakfast. Meet us downstairs, okay?" she said patting her hand.

Livy and Stacie went down to the kitchen; meanwhile Greg brought Jolene to her room. He went directly into the bathroom. Everyone brushed their teeth. Gus turned on the water and took his pajama bottoms off, then helped Jolene off with hers. He got into the shower with her.

Greg waited a moment before taking off his pajamas, and then got in directly behind Jolene. He took the washcloth from Gus and started soaping her back while Gus grabbed her breasts and slowly circled her nipples between his fingers. Greg traveled with the washcloth down her back to her butt. He spread her cheeks and massaged her butt entrance, rubbing in a circle at the entrance, and poking a finger partially inside her then pulling it out. Gus moved one hand gently down to her stomach then lower. Jolene felt like her body would burst into flames; everywhere they touched left a trail of heat on her body.

Gus tapped her on the leg with his knee, signaling for her to spread her legs farther apart. Jolene didn't hesitate to open her legs for him. He brought his hand onto her mound and pressed hard down on her lips; he squeezed her clit hard between his fingers. Jolene screamed his name, "Gus, oh my, more."

Gus lowered his hand and pushed one finger inside her, while alternating between breasts and massaging them. Greg was pumping her butt with two fingers inside her. Both guys looked up and stared at each other. Gus reached over her and brushed a quick kiss over Greg's lips. They moved together to penetrate her with their fingers, pumping in and out faster and harder. Gus now had three fingers inside her. "Greg, Gus, I can't hold out anymore."

"Come for us baby," said Greg in her ear.

Gus pressed closer to her, keeping his fingers constantly moving. He brushed his tongue over her lips, and she opened her mouth for him to thrust his tongue in. The kiss continued as they pumped inside her, driving her to ecstasy. She moaned in his mouth when she came in a violent orgasm that continued in waves for several minutes. The guys kept pushing in and out until they felt her body had stopped trembling. Jolene settled her head on Gus's shoulder, breathing heavy and fast.

"That was amazing. You two are incredible," she said gasping for air.

All three finished showering and quickly got out. Greg brought a towel to her and proceeded to dry her. Gus moved behind him with a towel and dried him off. After they were done in the bathroom, they walked back in the room and got dressed. They went down to the kitchen where Livy and Stacie were pretty much done preparing breakfast.

"Need help?" asked Greg.

"You can set the table," answered Livy.

Greg pointed to Gus and Jolene to stay there while he got the plates and utensils. He brought everything back to the table and all three set it up in no time at all. Livy and Stacie brought the serving dishes with food and set them on the table.

"Everything looks great," said Gus.

Everyone sat down and started to eat. "I'm sorry if I got you all worried about me," Jolene said.

"Nothing to be sorry about, you're our friend," said Livy squeezing her hand.

"Thanks."

"Are you okay now?" asked Stacie.

"Yes, I'm fine. I just wanted to see him one more time."

"We understand, darling," said Gus.

Everyone was less tense after clearing the air. They joked around and laughed like usual. The atmosphere was much better now. Jolene loved all her friends so much; they had taken the time to help her, not asking anything of her. When they were done with breakfast they all chipped in to clean up.

They moved to the study room and Gus pulled Jolene to the couch where he sat down and settled her on his lap. Greg sat next to them and Livy and Stacie sat in a chair across from them; Stacie sat in Livy's lap. Gus took charge and started the conversation. "We have to plan this right to the smallest detail. Nothing can go wrong or we could lose the other two. Remember, one is the chief of police of the town now and the other has been a judge for many years in this community."

"Let's brainstorm ideas, then we can put the plan together," said Greg.

They all nodded their heads. Stacie went to the desk and grabbed a notepad and pen. Each of them took turns coming up with ideas on what to do. No one rejected any of the ideas yet. Jolene watched them with love, seeing their dedication for her and how determined they were to help her catch the awful people who had destroyed her life ten years ago——those terrible criminals.

They continued talking and came up with a few more ideas. After they completed this step, they revisited every idea once more, scratching out anything that wouldn't directly lead to the accomplishment of their goals. They spent several hours talking. Eventually, Stacie's stomach made a rumbling noise. "Sorry, who's ready for a break and a snack? I am, that's for sure."

Everybody looked at her and laughed, Stacie was the one from the group who was always hungry. She laughed with them, stole a quick kiss from Livy and left the room. The other four continued the discussion after she walked out. A few minutes later, she was back in the room with a handful of plates full of all kinds of vegetables, breads, and pastries.

They all stopped talking and helped set the plates on the table. Greg went and got beers for everyone. They took a few moments to snack and drink their beers.

The discussion resumed for another couple of hours, and at the end of that time, they had a complete plan with specific details for what each of them had to do to accomplish it. Jolene looked at everyone and smiled at them. They all had made a lot of sacrifices to be here with her—±she was very grateful to them. "What?" asked Livy.

"I owe you all so much. You have given up a lot to help me," she said.

"Speaking for myself, you don't owe me anything. I'll do anything for you. I love you," Greg said.

Tears rolled out of her eyes, "Oh Greg. I…" she hesitated for a moment.

"You don't have to say anything, baby."

"We all love you. You would do the same for us," said Livy.

Jolene couldn't stop crying. She got up from Gus's lap and walked away from the group. She turned and looked at them.

"I need some fresh air," she said walking out of the room. Greg stood up to go after her. Gus grabbed his arm and pulled him back.

"Let her be," said Gus, giving Greg a hug. He could see the concern for her in Greg's face.

"I don't know what I'll do if I lose her."

"She's scared to open up to you two," said Livy.

Greg and Gus stayed behind, holding each other. Outside in the garden, Jolene was still walking. She passed the garden and went to the tree house her father had made for her. Instead of going up, she slid herself down to the ground at the base of the tree. She brought her knees up close to her body and laid her head on them.

"Oh Dad, what I'm going to do?" she said out loud.

She closed her eyes and that brought memories of her and her father. She could vividly see the image of her father running after her in the garden, playing tag. He would catch her and tickle her until she gave in. The memories felt just like yesterday. She hated what they did to her father and the fact that they destroyed her life and her mother's. She lived these years with only revenge in her heart, and she didn't know what would happen after they caught the criminals. What would she do with her life?

She stayed there at the base of the tree until her tears stopped then walked back to the house. She was heading towards the study, but when she heard the voices in the entertainment room, she turned and walked that way. She stopped at the threshold and watched them. They were all playing the Mario Kart video game. She entered the room and stood next to Gus and Greg who moved apart so she could sit between them. She gave each of them a kiss on the cheek. After an hour of watching them play, she heard her phone ringing. She moved away from the group and answered her phone.

"Daniel," she said.

"Hi Jolene. Do you have any plans for tonight?" he asked.

"No, nothing."

"Good, I'll pick you up at seven. A friend invited me over to a small dinner party at his house."

"I don't know…" she started to say something else but he stopped her.

"Oh c'mon. I really don't want to go alone."

She didn't say anything right away. After a few seconds she gave in, "Okay," she said.

"Great," he said and hung up his cell phone.

She hung up too and stared at the cell phone. She had to bring closure to this situation with Daniel soon; she couldn't stand to be around him for any length of time. He had no sense of decency around her or any other woman. He treated them as objects who were only there to make him look good. His inability to carry on a decent conversation with her was frustrating. She wouldn't stop until she humiliated him just like he humiliated her ten years ago. Jolene walked back to the room.

"Who was that?" asked Livy.

She didn't answer her right away.

"Jolene, who was that?" she asked again.

"It was Daniel. He invited me to a friend's dinner party," she answered.

"And you said no," said Stacie.

"I…" she stopped, then continued, "I said yes. He's picking me up at seven."

"Jolene how far are you going to take this farce with Daniel?" Livy asked.

"I don't know."

With that answer, no one said anything else to her. Instead of going back to sit with Gus and Greg, she went to an empty chair. They didn't even look up from their game. She just sat and watched them. She checked her watch, "I should start dinner," she said moving from the chair.

"No need," said Gus.

"We can handle doing dinner," said Greg with a firm voice.

"I know. I just want to help before I get ready to go."

"We'll be fine. Go ahead and get ready," said Gus with a calm voice.

"Oh, okay," she said walking out of the room.

Greg slammed the control on the couch and stood up. The other three stopped playing and looked at him. "How could you be so calm?" he asked.

"Greg, please sit," Gus said tapping his hand on the couch. Greg didn't react right away to his request. "Please."

"Fine," he said swinging his arms in the air before he sat down again. The girls moved and sat in front of him. They each took a hand and held it while Gus wrapped an arm around his shoulders. Greg's body was literally shaking. "I don't want to lose her. I love her so much."

"Me, too."

The girls could hear the desperation in both of their voices. "You two have to be strong. She'll do the right thing. She does love you guys; it's just hard for her to say it," said Stacie.

"She'll come through, you'll see," said Livy.

Greg didn't go back to play but the other three continued with the game. Forty-five minutes later, Jolene came back into the room, everyone looked towards her. Her dress was a beautiful light blue summer dress tied over one shoulder. Trying hard to be casual, she sat next to Greg who was just watching the other three play. Greg inhaled her essence; she smiled at him. "Are you mad?" she asked.

"No, I'm fine," he answered.

She moved closer to him and took his hand in hers. Her touch sent chills up and down his spine. He turned to face her, lowering his head and taking her lips in a kiss. She opened her lips and he rushed in with his tongue. As they were kissing, the doorbell rang, which triggered a reaction in her; she stopped the kiss and moved away from him. She touched her lips, stood up and fixed her dress. "I'll get it. I'll see you sometime tonight," she said walking out of the room.

They all said goodbye to her. The three players went back to their game and Greg just pushed back on the couch. Jolene grabbed her shawl and clutch from the foyer table and walked to the door. They couldn't see Daniel, but they heard him as she opened the door. "Oh my God, you look stunning," Daniel said.

Quickly Jolene walked out of the house and closed the door.

"Thank you," she said.

Daniel bent and gave her a quick kiss on her lips. He moved back to look at her again. She took his arm and he walked her to his car. He opened the door for her and helped her in. He moved to the driver side, got in and drove off.

Back in the entertainment room, Greg's nerves were about to burst. He got up from the couch.

"I think I'll go for a run," he said walking out and going up to his room. Quickly he changed into running clothes and left the house. He went into a full run right away, leaving the house behind along with his worries about Jolene.

At the house, the girls were in no mood to play any longer. Gus felt the same way. They closed the game and shut off the box. "Let's get dinner ready," said Livy, moving to the kitchen.

Gus and Stacie followed her. They occupied themselves with dinner preparations, and half an hour later, they heard the front door opening and shutting. Greg walked into the kitchen, went to the refrigerator and pulled out a water bottle. He gulped the water in two swallows. "You need help?" he asked standing by the counter.

"No, I think we're all set. Why don't you go take a shower and get ready," said Gus.

"Yes, go. By the time you come down, everything will be all set, "said Livy.

He turned around without saying anything to them and went out of the kitchen. They continued cooking. Stacie got the plates and utensils from the cabinet and set the table. Just as Livy and Gus put the plates with the food on the table, Greg came back to the kitchen. "It's smells great," he said with a smile on his face.

They all took a seat and started to eat.

Jolene had been at the dinner party for only an hour and she already hated these people——they were so superficial it was pathetic. All they talked about was the business and their jobs while the ladies talked about shopping and more shopping. She kept her conversation to a minimum, making sure she was always eating something very slowly. She only spoke when directly spoken to.

The night was a disaster. Daniel only talked to her for two seconds, then he ignored her the rest of the dinner. After dinner, they moved to the living room where the host put on some soft jazz music. The talk got a little bit livelier as the ladies proceeded to trash every woman they knew.

The men kept talking about the economy and still more business. Jolene had never been so bored. She was glad she was good at hiding her feelings or they definitely would have discovered her dislike for them. After another two hours of more talking, Daniel decided it was time to go.

Jolene said thank you and goodbye to everyone. Daniel walked very close to her on the way to the car. Instead of opening the door for her, he encircled her with his arms against the car, bent his head and gave her a kiss. Jolene pressed her hands to his chest and kissed him back. "You're so beautiful," he said to her.

"Thanks."

He opened the door for her and got in the other side. The drive back was pleasant; as he drove he talked to her the entire time. Jolene made light conversation back. Sometimes when he was like this she felt guilty for what she was doing, but when she reminded herself of the night he humiliated her, the guilt quickly went away. She sat quietly for a few minutes. He turned to her and brought his hand to her face and softly caressed her.

He pulled into the driveway, parked in front of the house and shut off the car. He reached over to her again, pulled her closer and kissed her. His kiss lasted for a long time. When he stopped, he smiled at her. Jolene smiled back at him. He looked at his watch. "I have to go, I have a golf tournament tomorrow morning," he said as he gave her a quick kiss, "I'll call you, okay?"

"Okay."

He got out of the car and opened the door for her. He walked her to the door, gave her another quick kiss and said goodnight. Jolene opened the door and walked into the house. She walked into the kitchen, turned the light on and grabbed a bottle of water from the refrigerator. She sat on a stool and drank some of the water. Tears started to flow down her face as she brought her hands up and covered her face. She put her arms down, lay her head on her forearms over the counter and closed her eyes. She stayed like that for a long time. She hadn't heard anyone come in the room, but suddenly she felt arms encircling her and lifting her from the stool.

She knew who it was by his scent. She lifted her face, opened her eyes and smiled up at Greg, her best friend and lover. He smiled back at her as she rested her head on his chest and snuggled closer to him. He shut the light off and walked with her upstairs.

"Did I wake you up?" she asked him.

"No, I couldn't sleep," he answered.

"Because of me?" she said.

"Because of us," Greg emphasized.

He opened the room door where they saw Gus sitting on the couch. He moved over and made space for them. Greg walked to the couch and sat next to him with her in his lap. Gus smiled to them.

"Je t'aime," said Gus to her.

"I love you," Greg said.

Jolene tensed in Greg's arms when she heard these declarations of love. Greg brought a hand to her neck and caressed her softly with tender massages.

"Please don't. I just can't, not right now," she said.

"We know," said Gus slowly caressing her arm.

Jolene turned to him. Gus took her by her waist and lifted her to his lap. She straddled him, brought her hands to his bare chest and touched him. She leaned into him and kissed him. Gus held her tight to his body, taking over the kiss, devouring her lips, their tongues driving at each other. Greg brought his hand to the zipper of her dress, pulling it down. Gus stopped kissing her while Greg lifted the dress over her head, leaving her bare breasts for Gus to enjoy.

Gus moved sideways on the couch, giving Greg room behind her. He swiftly moved to take a breast in his mouth, rubbing the other between his fingers. Greg moved closer to her, dropping gentle kisses down her back and moving his hands all over her in a languorous motion. Her body was responsive, wriggling and moving every time one of them touched her.

Gus picked her up from his lap while Greg helped him pulled his pajama pants off. Greg ripped her panties from her. Jolene took Gus's dick in her hand and pointed it toward her entrance and gradually took him inside her. Greg moved fast and took his pajamas off, too. Gus lay down on his back on the couch, still holding her impaled on his dick. He brought her down closer to him, exposing her butt fully to Greg.

Greg could see Gus coming in and out of her. He used some of her juices and started to play with her butt, rubbing the entrance in circles and quickly poking in and out with a finger. He went to the nightstand and pulled out the lubricant tube from the drawer. He put some on his fingers, kneeling behind her with one leg on the couch and the other on the floor. He pressed his fingers into her hole. Gus held her down on top of him as Greg worked her butt. "Oh my, Greg please, I want to feel your dick in my ass, now," she said in a whisper.

Greg pulled his fingers out and positioned his shaft at her entrance and, bit by bit, thrust himself inside her. Jolene felt like she was stretched completely. She moaned and groaned, enjoying the feeling of both their dicks inside her. Greg pressed in and pulled out just up to his crown before quickly pushing back in, doing this several times until his whole dick was inside her. They stopped moving so she could adjust to them.

"Oh God, Jolene, you're so tight baby," said Greg.

"Yes, I can feel your juices soaking my balls, mon amour."

"Please less talking, more moving," she said gasping for air.

Both the men laughed out loud, and like a well-rehearsed movement, they thrust and parried at the same time. Jolene's body was burning with every thrust. She held tight to Gus's arms as they thrust harder and faster inside her. Jolene couldn't hold out any longer.

"Gus, Greg," was all she could whisper as she exploded in such a strong orgasm that her whole body shook in Gus's arms. They continued their motions, pressing deeper and harder.

"I'm coming baby," Greg said behind her at the moment he burst inside her.

"Me too," said Gus pushing deeper.

They continued moving until every drop of their cum was inside her. Jolene laid her head on Gus's chest, taking big gulps of air. Greg gave her a few kisses on her back.

"That was awesome, my love."

"Terrific, mon amour."

"You two spoil me," she said turning her head to see them both and smiling.

Greg pulled out of her and went to the bathroom to clean himself. He brought two washcloths back with him; one he used to clean Jolene's butt. Then Gus lifted her from him. Greg gave him the other washcloth and went back to clean her pussy as Gus cleaned himself.

Greg picked her up from the couch and settled her in the middle of the bed as he lay beside her. Then Gus lay down on the other side of her. Jolene snuggled closer to Greg and Gus got closer to both of them, putting an arm across his lovers. He pushed Jolene's hair to the side and kissed her on her shoulder. He held his body tightly against her. He could hear by her breathing that she was already fast asleep and noticed that Greg was asleep as well. He smiled and closed his eyes.

Chapter 16

She was standing on the porch outside her room enjoying the fantastic late spring weather. It was warmer than usual for this time of year. She couldn't believe it was already Monday morning. She smiled remembering the wonderful time she had over the weekend with her friends, and then she felt sad again that they had left. Livy left earlier than the other two; she wanted to go back to her father's house and see if she could discover the meeting place of her father and his criminal partners. A few hours later, Greg and Stacie left as well.

Jolene knew that in a matter of days her life would be turned upside down again, but this time it would be for the better. They would uncover the criminals and restore her father's good name. Jolene turned to see Gus admiring her from the porch doorway. "You're so beautiful. Let's go get some breakfast. I have a conference call with my agent this morning," he said stretching his hand out to her.

"Okay," she said taking his hand.

They went downstairs to the dining room. Anna walked in the room with food plates. She set them on the table and poured coffee for them then left them alone. Jolene took a sip of her coffee while Gus went to serve himself some food. She smiled to him as she drank her coffee.

She stopped drinking her coffee and served herself some food. They talked while they ate, Jolene expressing her concern about Livy going back to her father's house. "She knows what she's doing. We have to trust her decision," said Gus.

"I know, but that doesn't stop me from worrying."

"We all do."

They kept talking as they finished eating. Gus checked his watch and quickly stood up from his chair. "I have to go, mon amour."

"Okay, see you later."

Gus kissed her on the lips and walked out of the dining room. Jolene sat there for a bit longer. Her mind and her heart were in such a battle that she couldn't keep herself from crying anymore. She had to believe she was doing the right thing. Both Greg and Gus knew the plan from the beginning; she had never hid her intentions from them about Daniel. But now everything was changing as they continued to express their loves for her and she didn't know what to say or what to think anymore.

Jolene left the room and went straight out of the house through the living room sliding door. She hated facing anyone with tears in her eyes. She walked for a while around the garden, and then she went on to her tree house. She hesitated, but decided to climb up the ladder to the tree house. She crawled through the door and sat at the very spot where she used to sit when she had tea parties with her father.

Gus finished the conference call with his agent; the arrangements were made for him to go back to France for a small modeling job this weekend coming up. He checked his watch and realized that he had been on the phone for about an hour and a half. He shut down his laptop and left the study.

He walked to the living room where he thought he would find Jolene but she wasn't there. He checked the entertainment, family and dining rooms with no luck. He decided she was probably in her room, so he took the stairs two at a time, rushing to her room. The room was empty, too. He opened the sliding door and went out on the porch and looked down at the garden.

He knew if she was there or at the pond he would be able to see her from there. He searched as far as his eyes could see for her, but there was no sign of Jolene anywhere. He was getting a bit concerned; she would have told him if she had decided to go out.

At the other side of town, Greg was at the office. He started his laptop and checked his emails. He answered a few of them and proceeded with his workday. He was scheduled for a staff meeting in an hour. He looked over the reports he would be discussing at the meeting and put the reports together with his notepad and pen. He looked at his watch and wondered what Jolene and Gus were doing right now without him. He thought about the many great times they spent together in the summers when he and the girls went to visit Jolene in Italy and France.

Those memories were what gave him the encouragement that Jolene did love him, even if she still wouldn't admit it. He stopped thinking about the past; he needed to work things out with her so they could make a future together. He looked at his watch; ten minutes until the meeting. He took his notepad and reports and left his office.

Back at the house, Gus went downstairs and directly to the kitchen where he saw Anna cooking as always. Len was sitting on a stool talking to his wife. "Hi," said Len.

"Hi," replied Gus turning his attention to Anna, "Have you seen Jolene?" he asked.

"No, last I saw her she was with you in the dining room."

"Oh, I had a call to make. I left her in the dining room."

Anna saw he was worried about her. She moved next to him and put a hand on his arm. "She's probably somewhere in the house," said Len.

"I already checked all the rooms including her bedroom. She's nowhere to be found," said Gus, clenching his teeth.

Len and Anna looked at him. "Maybe the garden?"

"No, I looked out from her porch," Gus said starting to walk out of the kitchen.

"Gus, check the tree house," said Anna.

Gus turned to face her, "Shit, why didn't I think of that?" he said slapping his hands on his thighs, disgusted at himself.

He rushed out of the kitchen and ran towards the tree house. He didn't want to scare her, so he slowly climbed the ladder. He opened the trap door and saw Jolene lying on top of an old blanket. She opened her eyes, looked at him and smiled.

"Hi," she said.

"Hi," he replied.

He climbed through the door and sat next to her on the floor. He lifted her from the floor and onto his lap. She cuddled in his lap, resting her head on his chest and closed her eyes. "I love the way you hold me to your body," she whispered with her face on his chest.

He could feel the vibrations of her voice throughout his body. "Me too."

Downtown, Livy was at her office in the Realty Company. She looked over and over her father's yearbook. She shook her head and smiled; she couldn't believe her luck last night finding the secret meeting place of her father and his criminal friends.

It was right in front of her the whole time, but she never saw it until she read some of the emails again. The secret code for the location triggered a memory of her childhood——her father had taken her there once. She couldn't believe she forgot it because all three of the other suspects were there the time he took her.

Livy's smile got bigger. For the first time in her life, she felt completely free of her father's power. Now she could openly express her love for Stacie and there would be no more hiding it to anyone. She took out her cell phone and sent a text message to everyone. At the tree house, Jolene's phone vibrated; Gus's did, too. They both looked at the text message. Jolene read it out loud, "I found it. The plan is on."

Gus hugged her as she breathed a sigh a relief. Greg was at the meeting when his phone vibrated in his pocket. He discreetly pulled the phone out and looked at the text message. He read it and then he smiled. Daniel sneaked a look at his younger brother. They were never close during their childhood, but after the incident with Caroline's father his brother had distanced himself from him. And now they had drifted even further apart. They never even saw each other outside the office.

Daniel wondered who would be texting Greg and what they would be saying. Greg looked up at him and saw his brother watching him. He put the phone back in his pocket and turned his attention back to the staff meeting, ignoring his brother's stare.

Stacie was at her station working out some IT problems with one of the systems when her cell phone vibrated on top of her desk. She grabbed her phone and looked at her text message. She read the text, smiled, then felt a tear running down her face. She has been waiting a long time for the day she could openly show Livy how much she loved her.

In the tree house, Gus stood up and pulled Jolene up with him. He pulled her close, engulfing her with his body, and gave her a kiss that she frantically reciprocated. They stopped kissing and he pulled her towards the trap door. He opened the door and stepped down on the ladder with her behind him. He got to the ground and lifted her into his arms as soon as he could reach her. "Gus I'm capable of walking," she said laughing and wrapping her arms around his neck

"I know, but I love holding you in my arms," he said, laughing too as they walked towards the house.

It was already midday and he was hungry. She kissed him under his chin and started to tease him with her mouth and tongue. "Jolene, don't start something we can't finish right now," he said.

She ignored what he said and continued with her mouth, touching him with her hand on his chest. Jolene smiled when she felt Gus's body tense as he held her tighter. "Jolene, we have company on the terrace," he said with strain in his voice.

Jolene looked up to see Len and Anna on the terrace looking their way. She stopped touching him and waved at them, smiling.

"I'm going to get you for this," whispered Gus in her ear.

She laughed out loud. When Gus got to the terrace, he set her down. Anna and Len walked to her and both embraced her. Anna gave her a kiss on her cheek then Len kissed her on her forehead. "You okay?" asked Anna.

"Yes," she answered.

"Good, lunch is ready," she said with an arm wrapped over her shoulder, pulling her into the house. Len and Gus followed behind them.

"Anna, can we eat in the kitchen?" asked Jolene.

"Sure, honey. I'll set the table." Anna let go of her and walked to the stove to check the food. Jolene and Gus sat at the table. Anna put out the serving dishes and brought the plates to the table.

"Thanks," said Gus and Jolene together. They served themselves and began to eat. The talk was light; they continued enjoying Anna's delicious cooking as they always did.

"I have a short modeling job Saturday night. I'll be traveling Friday night and back Sunday night."

"Okay," said Jolene, smiling at him.

When they were done eating, Anna brought each of them a piece of pie. They both smiled at her and quickly devoured the pie. They laughed out loud like two kids. Anna looked at Len and smiled.

They stood up from the table, held hands and left the kitchen. They went to the family room, and while Gus found a movie, Jolene sat on the couch. Gus settled on the couch and Jolene sat between his legs, snuggling to his body. He wrapped his arms around her waist and she rested her head on his chest while they watched the movie.

They spent the rest of the day in front of the TV, watching one movie after another, just taking breaks to get snacks and go to the bathroom. Jolene was so comfortable in his arms. Anna walked into the room and announced, "Dinner is ready; I already set the dining room table."

"Thanks, Anna," said Jolene.

Gus stopped the movie they were watching and shut off the TV. He took her hand and walked into the dining room where a servant was pouring water into the glasses. They laughed and talked during dinner and she frequently looked at him and smiled. When they finished with dinner and the delicious dessert Anna had made for them, they left the dining room and went back to the family room for more movies.

After two more movies, Gus could tell that Jolene was asleep in his arms because her breathing was slow and shallow. He turned off the TV, settled her on his lap and stood up with her in his arms. She moved closer to him and he knew she was seeking out his body heat. He walked slowly upstairs and directly to her room.

He turned the covers down and settled her into bed. Carefully he took her shoes off and next her clothes. He covered her with the blanket and went to the bathroom. Her proximity to him all night drove him crazy; his body wanted relief. He didn't know how he was able to resist from making love to her the whole night. Every move she made brought a reaction from his body.

Gus took his clothes off and got in the shower. Just thinking about her gave him a hard on. He put some shower gel in his hand and brought it to his dick. Slowly at first he stroked the length of his dick up and down, eventually moving faster and squeezing harder every time. In a matter of minutes, he exploded and he kept pumping faster and harder until the last drop of cum was out. He got under the water and finished with his shower.

He came out, dried himself and went to the room where Jolene was peacefully sleeping. He softly climbed into bed and she immediately moved closer to his body. He wrapped an arm around her and closed his eyes.

For two days, Jolene was very anxious, waiting for news from Livy. Finally, Livy called with information for the meeting that was set up for Wednesday.

When Wednesday came Jolene called her mother like she did every Wednesday morning. After the call, Jolene and Gus went upstairs and got ready for their meeting with Livy's uncle. They needed someone in the police department to help them.

They didn't want anything to go wrong, which was why Livy suggested her uncle. She believed he would do the right thing. Gus and Jolene were ready. They walked downstairs then out of the house. Gus helped her into the car and he got in. He drove off towards the outskirts of town to a restaurant where Livy used to go with Stacie.

When they got there, Jolene saw that Livy's car was already in the parking lot. Gus parked the car and helped Jolene out. They walked into the restaurant and looked for Livy and her Uncle Phil. Livy saw them first and waved to them.

Gus indicated to the hostess that they were meeting Livy so she walked them over to their table. Gus could see that Jolene was nervous so he put a hand on her shoulders and gently squeezed. Jolene smiled at him and gave a quick squeeze back to his hand. He sat down next to her.

"Hi," said Livy, "Uncle Phil, this is Gus, a friend of mine." The two men shook hands. She hesitated for a moment before introducing Jolene. "Uncle…" she started to say but the waitress came with water for them.

"Ready to order?" the waitress asked.

"Yes," said Livy putting in her order. Her uncle ordered next while Gus and Jolene went over the menu. Gus ordered for both of them after Jolene approved his choices. Gus took her hand in his as the waitress left the table.

"Uncle Phil, please hear me out before you say anything, okay?"

Her uncle looked at all three with suspicion in his eyes, "Okay," he said hesitantly.

Livy told the story, starting when Jolene's father was killed. She paused when the waitress came back with their lunch. She continued after the waitress left the table, going back to when she and

Greg used to visit Jolene in France, and related how her best friend had become a famous model. She hesitated to tell him about Jolene, but there was no way to avoid it.

"Uncle Phil, Caroline changed her name," she said.

"Really?" her uncle said, mildly surprised.

"Yes," answered Jolene, "my new name now is Jolene Moreau," said Jolene looking him straight in the eyes.

Phil was stunned by the news. He stopped eating and looked around at all of them.

"Uncle, we have something to show you, but you have to promise that no one but you will see this documentation."

"Olivia what is this all about?" he asked.

"Promise me, or we will leave and you can forget you saw us."

"What's all this about?" he asked again but this time to Gus. Gus didn't answer.

"No, look at me," Livy said getting his attention, "Promise me, Uncle Phil."

"Fine, I promise," he said.

Livy pulled the file from her briefcase, and Jolene pulled the envelope and flash drive from her bag. "This information was compiled by Caroline's father——I mean Jolene's father——ten years ago," she said giving him the envelope and flash drive she had taken from Jolene. "This we compiled recently," she said giving him the envelope.

"What this?"

"This is all the information you're going to need to make the arrests for embezzlement and the murder of Jolene's father ten years ago."

Livy's uncle opened one of the envelopes and read some of the documents. He went through a few more papers before he put everything back in the envelope and closed it. He looked at Jolene with a grim face.

"Caroline," he started to say but Jolene stopped him.

"I no longer go by that name; please call me Jolene," she said. He looked at Livy and Gus and they both nodded their heads.

"Jolene, why didn't you bring this up before?" he asked.

"I had to leave town, my mother was on the brink of a breakdown, and I had no way to get back into my house," she said.

"What do you want from me?" he asked.

"Uncle, you're not surprised," observed Livy.

"Not at all. My brother has always been a greedy man."

"We need to have a solid case against them, which is why Livy will set a trap for them, and with all this evidence there's no question of their guilt," Jolene explained.

With no hesitation in his voice, Phil asked, "How and when are we going to do this?"

Livy smiled at Jolene and squeezed her hand. Jolene smiled back at her, then at Uncle Phil.

"I'll send a fake email to them for a meeting for tomorrow night. Then we'll set up the cameras and microphones."

"I see you have everything planned. Who's helping you with the cameras?"

"Stacie," answered Livy.

"Well, let's get things rolling then," he said.

They finished their lunch while they went over more of the details. When it was time for Livy to say goodbye to her uncle, she hugged him and kissed him on the cheek. Phil smiled at her. Livy sat back down and they continued talking for a while longer. Gus paid the bill and all three left the restaurant. They walked to Livy's car. She hugged and kissed them both and drove off.

Gus and Jolene drove back to the house. The drive was mostly quiet with Gus doing most of the talking. Jolene rested her head back on the seat and closed her eyes. Gus reached over and caressed her face. She turned her head and kissed his hand.

Jolene knew that now it was up to Livy and Stacie to set up everything. They reached the house in an hour and walked into the house.

Jolene needed some time alone she turned to Gus, "I'm going for a walk in the garden," she said.

"You want company?" he asked.

She shook her head, "Not this time."

He gave her a quick kiss on the lips and let her go. He walked to the study and Jolene went out to the garden. She walked slowly, deep in thought. Most of her teenage years and all of her adult life had been spent planning revenge for her father's death and humiliation for Daniel for his betrayal.

She always thought that the killer and the person who framed her father for embezzlement was the same man, but now she knew that there were more people involved. She would have revenge on them all and justice would be served for her father. Jolene continued her slow pace, and sat down on the bench across the pond.

Back in the house, Gus called Greg and expressed his concern for Jolene. He hung up the phone and went to check on her discreetly. He went to her room where he could see the garden from the porch. He saw her sitting on the bench across the pond holding her head in her hands.

He knew that she had a lot on her mind, which was why he tried to give her space on the situation with Daniel and tried to keep Greg calm, too. He saw her stand and walk back to the house; she looked up and saw him. He waved to her; she waved back with a smile on her face. He went downstairs and out to the terrace to meet her. The weather was very nice, so he took her hand and pulled her over to the swing at the far side of the garden. She dropped her shoes and curled up on his lap. He wrapped his arms around her and held her tightly to his body. She put one hand on his chest as she rested her head under his chin. She loved being this close to him. He swung with her as they talked and laughed, enjoying the sun on their faces.

"Embrasse-moi," she said looking up at him.

"Mon amour," he said bending down and capturing her lips on his. He kissed her with such passion——she could feel the emotion he put into his kisses. They kissed for a while until they heard the sliding door open and footsteps. "I'm sorry, I didn't mean to interrupt," said Len.

"It's okay," said Jolene.

"Anna sent me to tell you that dinner is ready,"

"Thanks," said Gus and Jolene at the same time.

They both laughed. Len turned around and went back into the house. They walked back to the house, hand-in-hand, and into the dining room. Anna already had the table set so they sat down and served themselves. They continued talking while they ate. When they were done with lunch, they ate the delicious dessert Anna gave them. Afterwards, they went to the family room where Gus turned on the TV and found the basketball game.

Jolene and Gus were big sports fans. They cuddled next to each other on the big couch and watched the game. They both enjoyed the game, laughing and yelling at the referees as if they could be heard through the television. They were happy because their team was winning. Jolene stretched out on to of him; Gus could feel her whole body on him. She gave him a big smile and he laughed at her teasing. After the game was over, he started a movie and she continued to snuggle with him.

He pulled her onto his lap and she made herself comfortable as the movie began. The movie was a good action movie, but within an hour, she fell asleep——he could tell by her breathing and relaxed body. He kept her close to him as he continued to watch the movie. When the movie was over, he turned the TV off, and carried her quietly and slowly up the stairs and into her room. Like the night before, he undressed her and settled her into the bed. He brushed his teeth in the bathroom, took his clothes off and slid into bed next to her. Like always, she responded to the warmth of his body and snuggled next to him.

Chapter 17

Jolene woke up disturbed——something had scared her. She looked around in the dark but didn't see anything. She moved closer to Gus. She couldn't completely go back into a deep sleep, but she was able to rest for a bit longer. She opened her eyes and looked at the clock on her nightstand. It was still early but she couldn't sleep any longer. She slowly moved away from Gus and slid out of the bed. She went to the bathroom, brushed her teeth and put her robe on.

She dressed herself in a jogging suit, being so quiet that Gus didn't wake up. She left the house and went directly to the gym. Jolene got on a treadmill and ran for about forty minutes, then cooled down. After that, she did some free weights then some pushups and sit-ups. She exercised for about two hours.

She went into the locker room and took a quick shower and put on one of the robes hanging on the wall. By the time she finished it was about nine o'clock. When she got back home, she went upstairs, but instead of going back to her room, she went to the room at the far side of the house where she had extra clothes in the closet. She quickly dressed and found a pair of sandals she had left in the closet. She sat on a chair, reclined her head back and stared at the ceiling. Her emotions were in overdrive——the meeting to set the trap for Livy's father and his partners was today at noon.

Her mind was going in circles; she worried about Livy and what would happen with Daniel. On top of all that, she was still trying to figure out her feelings for Gus and Greg.

She was so scared to love anyone, to get close. She closed her eyes for a moment. She could here Gus coming out of the room. She stood up right away went to the door and opened it.

"Gus," she called him. He walked towards her as she came out of the room; they met in the hallway. "Good morning, Mon amour," he said bending down and kissing her.

She opened her lips giving him access to her tongue. He responded and they were quickly involved in a full passionate kiss that lasted for a few minutes. They stopped kissing to come up for air. She held onto him and took short shallow breaths. They both got control of their bodies. "I'm starving," he said.

Jolene laughed out loud, "You're always hungry."

He took her hand and they went to the dining room where Anna was just starting to set up their breakfast. "Good morning," Jolene said, giving Anna a kiss on the cheek. Anna turned and kissed her back on the cheek and said, "Good morning Gus."

"Good morning Anna," he replied.

Anna went back to finish setting the table as Gus and Jolene sat at the table talking. A few minutes later, Anna came back with a servant and the food. They set all the serving dishes down and left. Anna came back with a pitcher of orange juice and coffee for them. They ate slowly to prolong their time together. Jolene chatted about anything and everything. After they were done eating, they stayed there and continued talking, Gus resting his hand on hers.

"Let's go for a walk," she said.

"Okay," he said.

They walked out to the terrace. He took her to the garden, slowly walking and enjoying the sun. Jolene loved flowers, so she stopped several times to admire them. They continued walking for an hour or so. He checked his watch. "We should get ready to go. Remember, Livy suggested that we dress with warm clothes and hiking boots."

"Okay," she said.

He moved his hand to her waist and brought her closer. They walked that way back to the house. As they went into the house, Gus's cell phone rang. He got his phone from his pocket and checked who was calling. "It's Greg, you go up. I'll catch up with you."

"Okay," she said as she moved away from him.

"Hello," he answered his phone.

"Hi, how's she doing?" asked Greg.

"Nervous, she won't say anything but I can tell," answered Gus.

"Are you worried about today?"

"No, she'll be fine. She'll come through, you'll see."

"Good, I'll see you soon."

"See you."

Gus hung up the phone and went to his room. He found his hiking clothes and boots. He dressed quickly and went to her room. She was sitting in a chair tying up her boots. He kneeled in front of her and helped her with the boots. She smiled at him and caressed his cheek with the back of her hand. "Everything okay?" she asked.

He looked up, "Yes, we're all set for today."

"Good." He finished with her boots, she stood up and they went downstairs.

"I need something to drink," said Jolene.

They walked to the kitchen. Jolene saw Anna and Len sitting on the stools drinking coffee. "Hi, can I get you something?" asked Anna, starting to stand up.

"No, No, sit. I can get it myself."

Jolene went to the cabinet, pulled out a glass and pulled out a pitcher of lemonade from the refrigerator. She poured some in the glass and put the pitcher back. She drank her lemonade and put the glass in the sink. She said goodbye to Anna and Len and she and Gus walked out of the house. They got in the car and drove off to meet with Greg and the girls. The drive was to the outskirts of town. She settled back on the seat and put the radio on.

Stacie picked up Livy at the real estate office downtown and drove directly to the meeting spot. They drove for a while on a winding road on the outskirts of town then passed some clearings surrounded by woods where teenagers met on the weekends to drink. It had been the place to gather for many years. The meeting place was deep in the woods. When Livy's father had taken her here, years ago, Livy remembered that they had hiked for a while.

When they got to the spot where the path headed deeper into the woods, they got off the road and hid the car from view. Livy checked her watch while they went to the back of the car and got the equipment she needed out of the trunk. When they heard a car coming, they turned around to see Greg's car. He parked next to them just as Gus and Jolene pulled up.

Jolene went to the girls and gave a kiss on the cheek to each. Greg and Gus did the same as they took the equipment from their hands.

"This way," said Livy as she moved in front of them and led the way. The group followed her into the woods. They walked for about fifteen minutes going deeper in the woods. Suddenly, the woods began to thin out, and they could see a clearing ahead of them. Livy quickened the page until they were all out in the clearing. In front of them was a shed with a big sign that read "KEEP OUT."

"This is it," said Livy.

"Okay, let's get working. We don't want to get caught out here," said Gus.

"Right, I'll put the microphones inside the shed along with the small camera," said Stacie relieving them of the equipment she needed. "You four work on the cameras outside. Make sure to use good hiding places, but with good views of the shed, okay?"

"Okay. Greg, you and Livy take the left side. Jolene and I will take the right," said Gus.

Quickly everyone grabbed the equipment they needed and moved to their assigned side. Gus and Greg climbed the trees, while Jolene and Livy connected the equipment together and gave it to them. They all worked very quietly and speedily. Gus switched the power button on and moved on to the next tree.

At the other side, Greg was doing the same. It took them about an hour. When they were done, Stacie came out of the shed and pulled the wireless receiver out and turned it on, checking that all cameras and microphones were transmitting properly.

After a second check on the sound, they picked up the rest of the equipment and walked back to their cars where they finalized the plans for what time and where to meet that night. Everyone was anxious to get this done and over, especially Jolene. She smiled at them, "Thank you, I couldn't ever have done this without you all," she said as she gave the girls a hug and kisses to the guys.

"This will all be over soon and you can live free of revenge," said Stacie.

They got in their cars and drove off. Greg followed Gus to Jolene's house while Stacie drove Livy back to the office. Livy gave her a quick kiss on the lips and got out of the car. Stacie went back to the office where she parked the car in the employee's garage and trying to look calm as she walked back to the building.

At that very moment, on the other side of town, Jolene, Greg and Gus had just arrived at Jolene's place. Greg stopped in front of the house behind Gus's car. "You have time to come in?" asked Jolene.

"No, sorry baby. I have to go," he answered.

"Oh, okay," she said.

He turned to look at her in the front seat. "Come here," he said as he pushed his body through the window.

Jolene moved to the edge of the seat to get closer to him. He brought his hand behind her neck and pulled her toward him for a kiss. His kiss was ravishing and wild. Jolene put her hands around his neck and opened her mouth to welcome his tongue. The kiss lasted for a moment. "I'll see you tonight, my love."

Jolene moved back on the seat, trying to catch her breath. Greg went around to the other side of the car to give Gus a kiss, too. He hopped back in his car and waved goodbye to them as he drove off. Jolene just sat there for a moment, staring at the empty driveway. Gus tapped her on the shoulder and grabbed her hand. "C'mon baby," he said pulling her towards the door.

Jolene smiled and went with him. As they walked into the foyer, Anna came over. "Good, you're here. I was getting worried. Everything okay?"

"Yes, everything went according to plan," said Jolene.

"Great," she said, giving her a quick kiss on the cheek.

Jolene smiled at her and wrapped her arms around her waist for a hug. They held each other for a few minutes. Anna brushed Jolene's hair back from her forehead, "I have lunch warming, and I will serve it in five minutes."

"Okay, thanks," said Gus.

Anna let go of Jolene and walked back to the kitchen. Gus brought his arms around her waist and pulled her to his body. He brought his lips to her and she immediately opened her mouth for him. He tightened his hold on her as she moved her hands from his chest and wrapped them around his neck. Her nipples were hard and the touch of the bra was making them very sensitive. She rubbed her breasts to his chest. Gus took small grasps of air and continued kissing her. They were still kissing when they heard someone coughing behind them. Jolene hid her face on his chest and laughed.

Gus laughed too as he turned to see who it was behind them.

Anna was standing with her arms crossed with a serious look on her face. Gus gave Anna a big smile. "Lunch is already set in the dining room," she said.

"Thanks, Anna," mumbled Jolene still with her face burrowed in Gus's chest.

Anna turned around and left them alone. Jolene and Gus both burst into laughter, as they walked to the dining room holding, each other by the waist.

Back at his office, Greg tried hard to stay calm and be civilized to George and not jump him and beat the hell out of him. Sitting across from him, he watched George talking as if nothing was wrong. He couldn't believe for how many years he had stolen from the company without anyone noticing it.

They were going over the quarterly numbers like always, but now Greg knew that George was a thief and an accomplice to murder. Greg couldn't smile at him without feeling as if he were betraying Jolene's father. They finished the meeting and Greg managed to say goodbye to George and went back to work on his laptop.

Gus and Jolene were done eating. Gus took her hand and walked her to the entertainment room where they started a video game. Jolene knew that he was trying to keep her occupied. She appreciated his efforts and played along.

Jolene was startled when Gus's phone rang. He paused the game and answered his phone. Jolene checked her watch. She couldn't believe how long they had been playing. She heard Gus agreeing with whomever was on the phone with. When he hung up, he smiled at her and brought her closer to him and kissed her on the forehead. "That was Greg, he's getting ready. He says it's cool outside and to wear warm clothes."

"Oh, okay. We should go up and change then."

"Yes," he said as he stopped the game and shut off the video box.

He extended his hand for her; she took it and stood up from the couch. They went upstairs where she went to her room and Gus to his.

After ten minutes or so Gus walked into her room. She was already dressed and sitting on the couch tightening her hiking boots. Gus sat next to her and lifted her leg to his lap where he finished tightening the boot and then did the other one.

Jolene gave him a sweet smile. She leaned over to him and gave him a kiss. Gus put her leg down and lifted her onto his lap. She wrapped her arms around his neck and they continued kissing. He devoured her lips and when she opened her mouth for him, his tongue engaged in a wild dance with hers. The kiss was hot; he pulled his lips from her mouth and started to run a trail of kisses to her chin, then her neck.

He kissed and tasted her neck with his tongue, then moved to her ears where he nibbled her earlobe and took gentle bites of it. She squirmed on his lap, rubbing her butt on his shaft, which immediately reacted to her rubbing and got hard. He stopped the trail of kisses and looked at her; both of their bodies were on fire. He took her face with his hands, "Je t'aime," he said to her.

Jolene's eyes widened with his declaration of love. She didn't answer him. "We should go," she said in a shaky voice.

"Yes," he said standing up with her in his arms.

He let her go and she stood up. He grabbed the backpack next to her and then grabbed his own. Together they left the house and got into his car. The ride was quiet and she kept her attention on the road. He concentrated on the driving, giving her some space. This time, they parked farther away at a small string of local stores located at the front entrance to the woods.

He parked the car far away from the stores, close to the small trail going into the woods. The stores were already closed; the parking lot was empty. He shut the car off. They stayed in the car for a few minutes in the dark. There were no light poles around them to light up that corner. He made sure to have the inside lights off so when they opened the doors, they didn't light up. He reached into the back seat, grabbed both backpacks and opened the door. Jolene opened her door and got out. She walked to the front of the car and stopped to wait for him.

He grasped her hand, "I know you know your way in the woods, but I want you to let me lead," he whispered to her.

"Gus, I…" she started to whisper back to him, but he stopped her from saying anything.

"Just tell me where to go okay? I will lead," he said softly but firmly.

"Fine," she said agitated by his tone.

"Just point, let's stay quiet," he said pulling flashlights from his backpack and special night vision goggles. He gave her one of each.

They walked quietly for a while until Gus was sure they couldn't see the lights from the parking lot. "I'm sorry. I didn't mean to be pushy," he said slowing down the pace and looking back at her.

"I know," she said.

There was not much to see on their way to the location, mostly trees. He kept a firm grip on her hand as they continued walking. They walked for about forty-five minutes before finally reaching the destination. He shut his flashlight off and she did the same. He crouched down to the ground and pulled her with him.

They stayed behind a tree near where Stacie had put the equipment. They needed to connect the equipment to the receiver that Stacie had. They only had to wait a few minutes before they could hear Livy calling them. They moved from behind the tree and joined the rest of the group who each pulled the required electronics from their backpacks.

"Greg, Gus, please check the cameras for me one more time while I set up the receiver and DVD player," said Stacie.

Gus pulled the other sets of goggles out and distributed them. Quickly Greg and Gus moved to the trees that they had set up earlier to check the cameras. Stacie and Livy worked on the electronics while Jolene held the flashlight for them. After a few minutes, Greg and Gus came back.

"Everything is okay," said Greg.

"Good, we're almost done with the set up here," said Livy.

"Did you cover your tracks?" asked Jolene.

"Yes," answered Gus.

Livy and Stacie connected the last cable from the DVD to the receiver. Stacie turned the receiver on and checked the reception on all the cameras. She tweaked the controls until she was happy with the clarity of the images. "We're ready," said Stacie.

Jolene turned off the flashlight and put it inside her backpack. They all helped cover the equipment with the camouflage material Stacie had left there earlier. Then they moved to cover the area under several trees and shrubs.

Stacie and Livy found a cozy spot under a tree and sat down together. Gus and Greg found a spot a few feet from the girls where Gus sat down on the ground pulling Jolene next to him. Greg sat at her other side and pulled a blanket out of his backpack and covered all of them.

They still had an hour until the meeting time, so they got comfortable and kept quiet. The night was getting cool. Jolene shivered a bit when she felt a breeze of cool air go through the woods. Gus and Greg moved closer to her to protect her from the wind. Jolene was getting edgy; it felt as if they had been waiting forever. She tucked her head into Gus's chest. He caressed her face while Greg rubbed her back.

At last, Gus signaled to them to stay still; he heard movement from the other side of the clearing. After hearing footsteps, they saw three men come out of the woods and into the clearing.

Jolene's nerves were on the brink of betraying her. She concentrated very hard to keep still. The men were too far away and they were speaking in very low voices so they couldn't hear their conversation. After several minutes of standing in front of the shed the three men went inside.

Livy texted her uncle telling him that her father and the other two were together at the meeting place. A few seconds later, her uncle texted her back saying that he was on his way. The time slowed down——seconds seemed like hours to Jolene. The waiting was killing her.

After what seemed like an eternity, she heard Livy's uncle calling out to his brother. It was several minutes before the three men came out of the shed. The lights from the shed illuminated the whole area.

"Phil, what are you doing here?" asked George.

"George you're under arrest," said Phil walking towards him.

"Ha, ha, ha, funny," said his brother. The other two joined in.

"No joke," said Phil with a firm voice.

George stopped laughing and the other two looked at him. In that instant, Cliff, the police chief, reached under his jacket for his gun. Phil pulled the gun from the holster located at his belt and fired on the chief, shooting him in the shoulder.

The chief's gun dropped to the ground, and a police officer quickly picked it up and put it in his waistband. George and Steve were in shock and didn't move from where they were standing.

Jolene heard the gun firing and screamed. Gus and Greg ran towards the clearing. The girls ran behind them. When they got there, they saw one of the police officers picking up the gun from the ground. They stopped running and slowly came out of the woods. Greg and Gus kept the girls behind them. Livy's uncle was standing across from her father.

"Phil what's going? What are you doing?" asked George.

"I'm doing my job. You are all are under arrest for embezzlement, and you chief, you're under arrest for murder, too," Phil said.

He pulled handcuff from his belt and handcuffed his brother while the other police officers handcuffed the other two men.

"Livy, what are you doing here? I demand an explanation," her father yelled.

"An explanation, ha. The fact that you framed Jolene's father for embezzlement and then allowed him to be killed," she said pointing to Cliff.

"Who the hell is Jolene?" he asked.

Jolene moved from behind the girls and stood in front of him. "Perhaps you remember me better as Caroline Jenkins, daughter of Joshua Jenkins," said Jolene almost inaudibly because she was shaking all over.

Greg and Gus moved next to her and embraced her. All three of the handcuffed men turned pale. George was furious. He turned to his brother. Phil was already calling it in to the police station and requesting an ambulance.

"You believe the memories of a fifteen-year-old girl over your own brother?" he yelled.

"You're done, brother; all of you are. The compiled evidence against you three is solid. And with the recording of tonight's little meeting, there will be no doubt of your guilt."

It was several minutes before the rest of the police arrived at the scene. All the police were stunned at what they saw. Livy and Stacie went back into the woods and collected the DVD that recorded the information in the clearing as well as in the shed. They walked back to the clearing.

Livy hesitated a bit and looked at her father who was being taken away by one of the police. Another police officer helped Cliff with his injury. They wrapped the injured shoulder and started to walk him away. Phil could see the indecision on Livy's face as she stood there holding the DVD. "I promise to take care of it," he said as he took it from her.

Livy gave him a hug as he gave her a kiss on the forehead. He let her go and gave an order to his officers to search for any additional evidence. Livy and Stacie went to where Greg and Gus were holding very tightly to Jolene. They all walked back to the woods and collected their equipment on the ground.

"We'll collect the rest another time," said Stacie.

They walked back to where Phil was standing. "Uncle Phil, please take care of the video and audio equipment you find in the shed, okay?"

"Okay honey. I'll give you all a ride to your cars."

"Mine is the closest," said Greg.

Phil went back to the shed and left orders on what to do with the electronic equipment. He came out and walked into the woods via the trail towards his police car. The group followed him and they all got in his car and he drove off. Greg gave him directions to his car. When they got back to Greg's car, Livy, Stacie and Greg got out. Phil lowered his car window and spoke to them, "I'll meet you three at the police station. Okay?"

They all nodded their heads and got into Greg's car. The drive to Gus's car was very tense; Jolene was barely holding it together. She looked terribly pale and fragile. Gus moved her closer to him on the seat, and she clung to him. Phil pulled over next to their car and Gus and Jolene got out. Phil got out and stood next to Jolene. "How are you doing?" he asked her.

Jolene didn't reply immediately. She looked up at him, "I'm holding my own. I'm fine," she said.

"Can you meet me at the police station?" he asked a bit hesitantly.

Jolene hadn't been in the police station since the last time she saw her father———the night a horrible crime was committed that destroyed her family. She closed her eyes for a moment, took a deep breath looked at him again.

"Yes," she answered.

"Good, I'll see you there."

They all got into their cars and drove away from the parking lot and headed downtown to the police station. Gus reached for her hand and held to it. Jolene smiled at him and he brought her hand to his mouth and gave her a kiss on her palm. The drive to the police station was short; they were there in no time at all. As they parked, they saw the girls and Greg waiting for them at the walkway of the main entrance of the station.

Gus quickly got out of the car and went to the other side and opened the door for Jolene who was very still in the seat, not making a move to come out. Greg, Livy and Stacie sensed something was the matter so they walked over to the car. Greg bent down to her and took her hands, "Are you okay, honey? We're here for you," he said.

"I know," she said giving him shaky smile then looking up to the other three.

I can finish this, she thought to herself as she closed her eyes and let go of the breath she had been holding.

She moved closer to the door and let Greg pull her out of the car. He and Gus wrapped their arms around her waist and slowly started to walk towards the police station. Livy and Stacie followed them. Gus opened the door and led her into the main hall of the station. When they got inside, they looked around and saw that everything was in chaos.

Police officers were passing them, moving fast and the atmosphere was hectic. They went to the front desk where a policeman was on the phone. The moment they approached the desk, Livy's uncle came from one of the side doors towards them. "This way," he said leading them through the door he just came out of.

The girls knew where they were going because they been to this side of the station the night Jolene's father died. Phil brought them to a large room and asked them to sit down around a large table. "I'll take statements from all of you, one at a time, I'll start with you," he said pointing to Gus.

Gus stood up, "Sure."

Phil opened a door at the end of the room. Jolene looked up to Gus and he smiled at her and winked as he left the room. It was already past midnight. She knew it was going to be a long night. They stayed quiet for a bit, then Greg started to make small talk with them. After half an hour, Gus came back in the room and pointed to Greg to go next. Greg stood and walked out the door.

Gus sat next to Jolene and wrapped his arms around her shoulders. She leaned her head on his side. Gus said something funny to the girls and they all laughed. Greg came back in after a few minutes. The next one to go in was Stacie. She smiled to Livy and walked out. Livy's face looked concerned. "She's going to be fine," said Greg softly tapping her arm and smiling at her.

Livy smiled back to him. Jolene was so nervous she couldn't sit still any longer. She stood up and started to pace a bit. Gus went over and stood in front of her. He wrapped his arms around her waist and pulled her to his body. He put a hand behind her head as she hid her head on his chest. She wrapped her arms around his neck and held tight to him. She started to shake.

Gus rubbed his hands on her back. Greg moved behind her and also wrapped his arms around her. Jolene's body slowly stopped shaking. She relaxed a bit in their arms and leaned back into Greg. They kept holding her as Stacie came in and Livy went out. Stacie sat down and said nothing to anyone.

The room was quiet, Stacie was worried about Livy, and Greg and Gus were comforting Jolene. The time had basically stopped for Jolene. Her mind kept going over everything that had happened. She and her friends had done it: Her father's killer and the men guilty of embezzlement had been caught. So why wasn't she relieved? After what seemed like hours, Livy came in. Jolene looked up to see Phil coming out behind her. He walked over to Jolene. "Can you do this?" he asked.

She nodded her head and said, "Yes."

Phil wrapped his arm over her shoulder and they both walked out of the room. The other four sat down and kept themselves occupied talking. Phil brought her to a smaller room where there was a small table and two chairs. He got her seated then went across from her and sat down.

"How are you doing?" he asked.

"Okay," she answered.

"I'll be recording your statement."

"Okay."

Jolene's nerves tightened her throat. She put her hands on the table to keep them from shaking. Phil turned the recorder on. "Please, for the record, state your name and then proceed with your statement."

Jolene took a big breath and started talking. She started by explaining her new name, then went into what happened ten years before with her father. She repeated everything he told her the night before he died. She continued by describing the documents her father left behind and the research the group had done to gather the information they needed to prove the criminals' guilt. She talked for a long time, going over every detail of the plan she put together for the last ten years. After saying what she felt was all she needed to say, she stopped.

"Why not come to us ten years ago?" he asked.

"Would you have believed a fifteen year old?"

Phil didn't say anything. "No, you wouldn't," she said.

Phil put one hand over hers and gave them a soft squeeze.

"Caroline, I'm so sorry," he said.

Jolene's eyes opened wide. Calling her by her childhood name opened the gates for all her childhood memories. The wonderful memories with her father and mother flashed in her mind: the great times they spent together, the happy times she had with her father. She was so overwhelmed that she started to cry. Phil moved from his chair and rushed to her. "I'm so sorry, please don't cry," he said.

In a matter of seconds Greg and Gus walked in the room and went to her. Jolene stood up from her chair and rushed to Gus who had his arms opened for her. He engulfed her in a big embrace. Greg moved behind her and embraced her, too. They both surrounded her body. Phil stood there just looking at the three of them. "We're done here," he said walking out of the room.

Greg and Gus followed him, still holding tight to Jolene who was still crying. As they walked into the other room, the girls reached out to her to comfort her, too.

Phil opened the door to the corridor, then he stood in the doorway and he spoke to them, "Stay here, I'll be back as soon as I can. Livy come with me."

Livy followed him out of the room. A few minutes later, she walked back in with her hands full of drinks and snacks. Gus and Greg were still standing, holding onto Jolene, while Stacie was sitting in a chair.

Livy put everything on top of the table and brought a drink to Stacie, leaning over to give her a quick kiss on the lips. Greg and Gus settled Jolene in a chair, and Greg grabbed a couple drinks for her and Gus. He handed Gus his and opened the drink for Jolene.

Jolene took the soda can and took a few sips then put it down. She looked around the room, then at her friends and she gave them a weak smile. Everyone stayed quiet while they drink the beverages.

Jolene checked her watch; it was past one in the morning now. She took another sip from her drink. After fifteen minutes, Phil came back into the room. He pointed for everyone to sit down and then he sat down, too.

"I have great news," he said looking at Jolene. "The judge confessed to everything including the decision about your father. He confessed to the embezzlement and to conspiring to get rid of your father, but the decision to kill him was entirely the captain's."

Jolene concentrated on staying calm. She took the can from the table and took small sips as Phil continued talking. "The confession will ensure that all three will spend a long time in jail," he finished.

"That's great," said Greg.

"On the other hand, my brother and the chief have lawyered up already, so they're not saying anything, but with all the evidence you collected and the judge's confession we have a very strong case. It's been a long night so I'm letting you go home. Don't speak to anyone about this matter, okay?"

They all nodded their heads and quickly stood up. Greg and Gus stuck to Jolene and Livy and Stacie walked together. Phil brought them back to the main floor. The front room was in less chaos than before, but there were still police officers everywhere. Phil walked them out of the station.

"Go home and rest. I'll call you if I need anything else."

"Thanks," said Gus as Phil shook his hand, then Greg's, Jolene's and Stacie's.

Livy walked to him and gave him a big hug. "Thank you, Uncle Phil, for everything."

"You're welcome, honey." he said lifting her face to his. "You know I'm here if you need me."

"I know," she said giving him a quick kiss on the cheek.

They walked to their cars. Greg moved next to the girls. "I'm going with Gus and Jolene. Livy you take my car, okay?" he said handing the car keys to her.

"Okay," she said as she gave him a kiss on the cheek, then Stacie did the same. Jolene went over and gave them kisses, too. They said goodbye and walked to Greg's car. Greg helped Jolene into the car while Gus went to the driver's side and goy in. Greg climbed in the back. The drive was very quiet. Jolene turned her head to the side and closed her eyes; after a few seconds she was fast asleep.

Gus parked the car in front of the house and Greg quickly got out from the back seat and quietly opened Jolene's door. Gus undid the seat belt and Greg lifted her in his arms.

Gus got out and walked to the front door with Greg walking behind him. He opened the door and let Greg go in first with Jolene in his arms. They walked upstairs and straight to her room.

Gus pulled the blankets back and Greg settled her in the bed. Greg started to take her shoes off while Greg worked with the jacket. Slowly he pulled the zipper down and next took her arms out. Jolene was so exhausted that she didn't even move. Finally they got her clothes off and left her underwear on. Greg moved her to the center of the bed and Gus covered her with the blanket. Greg moved next to Gus, "I should be going; I have to go to work for at least a few hours. I'll take the car, okay?" he said.

"No stay," Gus said pulling him closer and consuming Greg's mouth with his. The kiss was needy and desperate. Greg wrapped his arms around his waist and tightened the hold. They kissed for a long while. Gus stopped kissing him and leaned his forehead to his. They stayed like for a few minutes.

"Okay," said Greg.

Greg went to the bathroom while Gus started to take his clothes off and put his pajamas on. After Greg came out, Gus went in. Greg found a pair of Gus's pajama pants and put them on. Then he very slowly slid in bed next to Jolene. When Gus came out, he shut the light off and slid in the other side.

Instantly, Jolene felt his body heat and moved closer to him. Gus settled her tight against him then reached for Greg to move closer. Together they made a cocoon around her body. They could feel Jolene's body relax. Finally, Gus tenderly caressed Greg's face for a moment then closed his eyes. Greg watched over them for a few minutes.

Chapter 18

Caroline walked out to the garden——there standing at the terrace was her father.

"Daddy," she said rushing to him and giving him a big hug.

"Hi Caroline, my princess," he said hugging her back and giving her a kiss on the forehead. They stayed holding each other for awhile; she didn't want to let go.

"Walk with me, sweetie," he said taking her hand and starting to walk.

"Where are we going, Daddy?" she asked.

"Let's go to the tree house," Joshua said.

They walked slowly, just talking about anything and everything. Joshua reached over and moved strands of hairs that the wind had blown onto her face. He held the strand for a bit, then brought it to his nose. "I've always loved the way your hair smells, my sweet," he said. "You smell of sunshine and flowers."

Caroline laughed out loud, "Daddy, you say the funniest things."

They continued walking towards the tree house, still laughing and talking. He let her take the ladder first then followed her. She opened the door and went in with her father behind her. She sat at her usual corner; her father sat across from her like he always did. He took her hands in his.

"You did well, my princess. You brought the guilty to justice and cleared my name. I'm so proud of you and what you have become."

"Oh, daddy. I miss you so much!"

"I miss you and your mother very much," he said. "It's time for me to go, you know?"

Caroline moved next to him and leaned her head on his shoulder. "No, daddy. Don't go. Stay with me" she pleaded with him.

"My love, you're a grown woman now. It's your turn to live. Be at peace, my love."

Caroline held tight to him, "No daddy, I'm lost without you."

"No you're not. Do the right thing my love, okay? And know that I love you with all my heart," he said as he started to fade away.

Caroline called for him, *"Daddy no. Come back. I need you."*

She started to cry uncontrollably; she covered her face with her hands and continued to cry.

Greg woke up to the desperate cries coming from Jolene. Greg looked up at her with her hands on her face.

"Daddy no. Come back. I need you," he heard, as she started screaming, thrashing her head and crying.

"Daddy, Daddy," she continued screaming.

A few seconds later, Gus woke up, too. He looked over and saw Greg already awake. He saw Jolene crying. He pulled her closer as Greg moved closer to them and surrounded them both in a hug. "Jolene," he said softly in her ear.

She didn't respond but just kept crying. "Daddy no. Don't go," she said again in the middle of her cries.

"Jolene," he said in a firm tone this time.

"Jolene," said Greg from the front, touching her face.

He sensed that the touch surprised her. He continued touching her face as Gus called her name again, "Jolene, my love wake up."

"Jolene," said Greg with his lips on her forehead.

Jolene opened her eyes. She looked straight at Greg and it was as if she didn't know where she was. She closed her eyes again quickly and one more time yelled for her father, "Daddy, I love you," she said one last time and quickly opened her eyes again.

She looked at Greg, then turned flat on her back and looked at Gus. She didn't say anything; tears were still flowing down her face. She took her hands and wiped her tears away.

"Hi, mon amour," said Gus smiling at her.

"Hi," she said in soft voice, almost a whisper.

"Hi, my love," said Greg at her other side.

"Hi," she said, again in a whisper.

They held her close, saying nothing. Jolene closed her eyes for a second time, trying to hold onto her father's image in her mind.

"Jolene, are you okay?" asked Greg.

"Yes," she answered with her eyes still closed.

She moved up, opened her eyes and checked the time from the clock on the nightstand. She saw that it was past ten o'clock in the morning. She threw the covers off her and crawled down to the bottom of the bed. Gus and Greg left her alone; they could sense the tension in her.

She slid off the bed and went directly into the bathroom. Greg and Gus looked at each other. Gus turned and sat up at the edge of the bed. Greg got close to him and wrapped his arms around his shoulders. Gus brought his hands to Greg's arms and held tightly to him.

They heard the faucet going, then after few seconds, they could hear the shower running. Gus got up and put his pajama bottoms on, noticing that the bathroom door was open a bit. He went over closer to the door and heard Jolene crying. His heart broke hearing her cry. He signaled with his finger for Greg to come over. Greg slid off the bed and stood next to him.

Jolene's cries were louder and could be heard in the room now. They looked at each, opened the door and walked into the bathroom. Quietly, Greg reached for the shower door and pushed it open and walked in. Gus took his pajamas off and walked in behind him. Jolene was crying so hard now that she didn't even notice them in the shower stall.

"Jolene, baby," said Gus pulling her in an embrace. He surrounded her with his arms. Jolene didn't pull away. Greg moved behind her and they both captured her in a big circle. Jolene wrapped her arms around Gus's waist and continued to cry.

"Mon amour, please stop crying," he said.

"Baby, we're here for you. Please tell us what's wrong," said Greg.

After a few more minutes of crying, Jolene's sobbing slowed down enough for her to be able to talk. "I can't. I'm fine," she said moving her arms from Gus and trying to move away.

"Honey, let us take care of you," said Gus.

"I can't, not now," she said.

"Honey, we're not asking for anything. We're just helping you bathe, okay?" said Greg.

Jolene nodded her head. Gus and Greg each took a washcloth and started to wash her. It was not like her to not react to their touch, but she was so distraught that she didn't even flinch when Greg touched her on her pussy. They quickly finished washing her.

"Now your hair," said Gus.

He poured shampoo in his hand and gently started to wash her hair. Jolene closed her eyes and enjoyed the gentle massage Gus gave to her head. She saw herself back in the tree house, but this time it was empty and old, the way they found it when she came back from France. "Daddy," was all that escaped from her mouth in a whisper.

"Jolene," whispered Gus in her ear. It took a few seconds for her to react then she opened her eyes to see Greg and Gus looking at her with concern on their faces.

"Thanks," she said as she dipped under the water and rinsed her hair.

They both quickly soaped up. She moved to the door as Gus moved behind her and went under the water. She pulled the door open and got out of the stall. Gus went out behind her. She took a towel and dried herself. Gus did the same. A few seconds later, Greg shut the water off and came out. Gus handed him a towel.

Jolene kept her distance from them as she finished drying. She wrapped the towel around her body and left the bathroom. She dressed quickly and was putting her shoes on when they came out of the bathroom. Jolene tried not to look up at them. They were both totally naked. They found their clothes and started to dress.

Jolene grabbed her cell phone and walked out of the room leaving Gus and Greg behind. Gus saw that Greg was getting angry with her. He moved next to Greg and lifted his face with his finger. He brought his lips to his and gave him a kiss. They kissed for a few minutes then Gus stopped and said, "Give her time, okay?"

Greg's anger was gone already. Gus always knew how to take his mind off things. He smiled at Gus, "Okay."

They walked slowly downstairs and to the dining room. Jolene was already there eating her breakfast. They sat next to her at the table. She kept to herself as they sat down. Anna walked in with their coffee. Gus and Greg started to serve themselves food. They quietly ate, trying not to upset her any more. She finished eating and slowly drank her coffee. She stood up from her chair and moved behind Gus, bringing her arms around his neck. "I'm so sorry. I'm just a bit distressed," she said.

"It's understandable, honey."

She looked over to Greg and smiled at him, "I had a dream about Dad, and I just can't stop thinking about it," she said.

"Anything we can help with?" asked Greg smiling back at her.

"No, I just have to face this alone, but thank you for offering," she said.

Gus finished his breakfast and stood up from the chair with her arms still around him. He stood next to her and Greg moved to her other side; she wrapped one of her arms around his neck. She was sandwiched between both men. "Okay, but only this once. We don't want you to keep anything from us," said Greg.

"I know. I'll tell you. It's just too painful right now."

"Okay, mon amour," said Gus.

Greg moved away from her. "Let's go for a walk. Get some fresh air."

"Good idea," said Gus.

They each took one of Jolene's hands and walked out of the dining room to the terrace. Gus and Greg just walked, not forcing any kind of talk. She was thankful that they weren't trying to get her to talk. They walked through the garden and towards the pond. As they were walking, Greg's phone started to ring. He pulled it from his pants pocket and looked at it. He made a troubled face then slapped his hand to the side of his leg. "Damn, shit," he said reading the text message from his mother.

"What's wrong?" asked Jolene.

"I forgot I have my cousin's wedding Saturday plus the dinner party tomorrow night, damn it."

"That's right, you mentioned that the other day," said Gus.

"Yea, well I forgot," said Greg pissed off. "I don't want to leave you alone."

"I'll be fine. You two needn't worry. Besides, the girls will be around."

"I'll cancel my modeling gig," said Gus.

Jolene turned to him and let go of his hand and touched his face, "No, I'll be fine. I'm a grown woman. I've been on my own for a while now. There's no need to babysit me."

Gus and Greg smiled to her and then laughed out loud. "Believe me, we know you're a grown woman. I'll be back early Sunday. It's just for two days," said Gus.

She smiled back at them and they started walking again. They made it to the pond and sat down on the bench. The guys wrapped their arms around her shoulders. She lay her head on Gus's shoulder. They stayed close to each other for some time. The rest of the day went slow. They watched TV for most of the afternoon then, in the early evening, they switched on the local station. The scandal about the police chief, judge, and Livy's father was all over the news.

Jolene sat quietly just listening. Gus and Greg didn't say much either. Jolene was sitting comfortably between them, wrapped in Gus's arms. Greg hung out with them right up to dinnertime.

Anna walked into the family room and let them know that dinner was ready. Greg stood up from the couch and pulled Jolene up.

He took one hand and Gus, who was standing beside her, took the other one. They held each other as they entered to the dining room. Greg pulled out the chair for her and the guys sat on either side of her.

They ate quietly until Greg brought them into a conversation. The rest of the dinner was pleasant. After they finished with dinner, Anna brought them one of her fabulous desserts, which they ate in no time. Instead of going back to the family room afterwards, Gus brought her to the entertainment room. He settled on the couch to start a game. Greg held her hand and pulled her closer to him. "Baby, I have to go," he said kissing her softly on the lips.

"Okay," she said.

"I have things to finish at work before I leave for the wedding tomorrow."

"I know. I'll be fine."

"Are you sure?" he asked holding her against him.

"Yes," she said bringing her arms around his neck and her lips to his for another kiss.

This time she launched her tongue into his mouth as soon as he opened it. They stopped kissing. She was left breathless and shaky. Her body demanded more of him. Greg pulled away from her. The proof of how much he wanted her was apparent by the bulge in the front of his pants.

She looked up at him, "I'm sorry. I didn't mean to…" she started to say, but he stopped her with a finger on her lips.

He smiled at her and she smiled back. "I'm fine," He said.

He let go of her and walked over to Gus who had been watching their loving exchange. Greg bent over and gave him a quick kiss that Gus accepted willingly. Greg stopped the kiss and moved back from him; he smiled to Gus as he caressed his face with his hand. He walked back to Jolene and kissed her quickly on the lips. "Goodbye, my love," he said.

He walked away from her and out of the room. Jolene watched him leave and continued to stand there for a few seconds after he was gone.

"Jolene, mon amour," said Gus.

She turned to him; he tapped the couch for her to sit next to him. Jolene laughed, went to the couch and sat down. The rest of the night was quiet as she sat watching Gus play his video game. After a few hours, she fell asleep curled up in a ball at the end of the couch.

He stopped the game, shut off the box and put the control away. He went to her and lifted her into his arms, holding her close to his chest. Slowly, he walked up the stairs and to her room. The blanket was already pulled down so he settled her on the bed. He took her shoes off then continued with her clothes. He covered her with the blanket, tucked it tight around her body and left the room.

Gus went to his room where he quickly took his clothes off and got into the shower. He turned the water on cold; he needed to take the edge off of wanting to fuck her. After a few minutes of letting the cold water run down his body, he shut off the water and came out. He dried himself off and put his pajama pants on. He left his room and went back into hers. Very patiently, he slid under the blanket and lay next to her. Instantly she found his body heat and curled against him.

Chapter 19

Jolene's body was on fire as his hands caressed her breasts. She turned towards him and slowly opened her eyes.

"Hi, embrasse-moi," he said.

Jolene quickly complied with his desire and kissed him on the lips. Gus took over the kiss and immediately thrust his tongue into her mouth and they went into a passionate duel of tongues. He let go of her breasts and pressed his body into hers.

She rubbed against him as he continued the attack on her mouth. With a swift movement, he brought her flat on her back and climbed on top of her. He spread her legs with his thigh and settled between them, keeping most of his body weight on his forearms. He stopped kissing her and brought his lips on a slow path of soft kisses from her neck to her breasts where he took one of nipples into his mouth, making Jolene gasp for air. She wrapped her arms around his waist and pulled him closer to her breasts. Gus took the nipple between his teeth and softly took little bites of the tip. Jolene couldn't hold out any longer and started to rub her pussy on the hard flesh of his shaft. With one hand, he positioned his dick in her entrance and, with a sudden move, thrust inside her. Jolene was now completely immersed in an uncontrollable heat throughout her whole body.

Gus moved in and out of her in rhythmically, touching her all the way to her core, but then slowing down and pulling partially out. He kept her near climax without allowing her to come. He thrust in and out faster. Jolene's head was thrashing on the pillow. Her eyes were open; she did not take them away from his face for a second. He brought one hand to the other nipple and started to rub it between his fingers and gave it a quick, hard pinch. Jolene moaned, driving him to move faster. "Oh, yes Gus," she said pulling him away from her nipple and kissing him.

Gus devoured her mouth with his while continuing to thrust harder and faster in and out of her pussy. Jolene was ready, he could tell by the way she tightened her pussy around his dick, but he didn't want her to come yet. He thrust deep inside her and stayed still there as they continued the delicious battle of tongues.

He stopped kissing her, "I love your mouth, mon amour."

"Gus, please. I need to come," she said trying to make him move. Gus took hold of her hips and stopped them from grinding on his dick and lifted her legs higher on his chest and pulled out partially and then thrust hard back in. He moved fast and hard getting her into a frenzy that lasted only a few minutes before she exploded into a climax. He continued thrusting in and out after he came, too. He pushed in and out of her until the last drop of his cum and her tremors stopped.

She pulled him down to her and kissed him tenderly and softly with just her lips. He deepened the kiss as she welcomed his tongue into her mouth. He kept balance with one arm as he caressed her face with his hand. When they stopped kissing, he stopped and collapsed next to her. He smiled at her and brought her fingers to his mouth and kissed them. "I love making love to you."

"Me too," she said.

"I have to get up and get ready to go," he said sliding out of the bed.

"Okay."

He walked into the bathroom. Jolene heard the faucet running, then the shower. She stayed in bed for a bit longer. In a matter of minutes, he was out of the bathroom and getting dressed.

She got up and went to the bathroom, took a quick shower and came out with a towel wrapped around her body. She went to the drawers and closet to pick out what to wear and started dressing. Gus grabbed some of his personal things from the bathroom. "I'll be right back," he said leaving the room.

"Okay."

She finished dressing and got her shoes out of the closet. As she finished putting them on, he walked back into the room with a travel bag in hand. He stretched a hand out to her and she took it. "Let's get breakfast," he said leading her out of the room.

They walked downstairs and into the dining room where Anna was setting the table for them. Gus set his suitcase to the side and walked to the table. They sat down and Anna brought them breakfast.

"I'll be back early Sunday evening," he said between bites.

"Okay."

They continued eating mostly making small talk. Anna brought more coffee to them, which Jolene welcomed right away. "Thanks," she said as Anna poured coffee in her cup, then she went and poured more into Gus's cup.

"Anna, please have the driver bring the car over," he said to her as she filled his cup. They finished their second cup of coffee.

"Baby, I have to go, so I can make it to the airport on time."

"Okay," she said with a sad tone in her voice.

He moved to her chair, pulled her up and embraced her. She wrapped her arms around his waist. "Je t'aime," he said to her and kissed her.

Jolene held tight to him as they continued kissing. He stopped kissing her and loosened his hold on her. He wrapped an arm around her waist and walked to where he left his bag. He grabbed the bag and walked out the door. He put the bag down and hugged her again and gave her a quick kiss. He caressed her face with the back of his hand, "See you soon, mon amour," he said.

"See you soon," she said back.

He walked out of the house as she stood there staring at the door. She stood for a while until she saw movement at her side. Anna looked at her and smiled, so she smiled back. "I'll be in my room," she said and walked upstairs.

She went in and sat on the couch and turned on the TV. She found the news channel and left it there. The news about the firm scandal was still being reported heavily. She was relieved that Phil kept his promise to keep her name out of the press. She didn't know how long she was staring at the TV without listening when she heard a knock at the door. "Come in," she said.

Anna opened the door and walked in the room, "Dinner is ready," she said.

"Thanks. Anna I'll eat in the kitchen, okay?"

"Okay." Anna left the room and closed the door. Jolene went to the bathroom and freshened up. She went down to the kitchen where Anna had already set a place for her at the table. She sat down and Anna brought her dinner. "Thanks," she said in a soft voice.

Anna went to the refrigerator to get Jolene something to drink and went back to check the food on the stove. She stayed quiet as she saw Jolene eating very slowly, just moving the food around on her plate and taking small bites.

Jolene finished eating as much as her stomach would allow. She hasn't been feeling well for the past few days and figured it was nerves with everything that was going on.

She was about to get up from the table when Anna brought her a plate of chocolate cake. Jolene smiled at her and started to eat the cake. She just took a few bites then stopped. "Thanks, Anna. Everything was delicious," she said as she got up and walked out of the kitchen.

Jolene decided to take a walk in the garden. She found a secluded bench away from anyone's view and sat, contemplating everything that had happened to her over the past weeks and her relationship with Greg and Gus. On top of all that, she still had to handle the situation with Daniel. Jolene was heading back to the house when her cell phone rang. "Hi, Livy," she answered.

"Hi. Listen, we won't be going to your place tonight. Mom called me and she wants me to come over the house; she wants to talk to me."

"I understand, honey. We'll see each other tomorrow."

"Okay sweetie. See you tomorrow."

She hung up the phone and walked upstairs to her room. She grabbed a book from the shelf and read for an hour or so when her cell phone rang again. "Hi," she answered the phone.

"Hi, mon amour. How are you doing?" asked Gus.

"I'm doing well. How was the trip?" she asked.

"Lousy and boring without you. I missed you," he said.

"Missed you, too," she said with a shaky voice.

"I have to go. I just wanted to hear your voice, mon amour."

"Gus…" she said hesitating for a moment, "see you soon."

"Oui. Goodnight."

"Goodnight." Jolene hung up the phone and quickly it rang again. It was Greg this time. "Hi."

"Hi, my love. Miss me?"

"Yes. How was the flight?" she asked.

"Ah, okay. I guess. Hanging with your father and mother at my age is not cool," he said.

She laughed out loud, "Greg stop it. You love your parents."

"Yes I do. How are you doing?"

"I'm fine. It's a bit quiet here for my taste, but I'm okay."

"I have to go. I just wanted to take a minute from the dinner party to call you. I'll call you tomorrow. I love you," he said.

"Okay, I'll wait anxiously for your call," she said.

She hung up the phone and went into the bathroom. She got ready for bed, but instead of going to the bed, she lay on the couch and put the TV on. She woke up there, not knowing how long she'd been asleep. She shut off the TV and light and got into bed. She closed her eyes and quickly fell to sleep.

Jolene woke alarmed and disturbed about her surroundings. She wasn't accustomed to waking up alone. She checked the time;

it was 9:00 am. She went to the bathroom and took a quick shower. She came back to the room and got dressed and went down to the kitchen where Len and Anna were talking.

"Good morning," she said.

"Good morning," said Len going to her and giving her a kiss on the forehead, Jolene smiled at him.

Anna came over and gave her a kiss on the cheek, "Good morning. Ready for breakfast?"

"Yes, something simple, please. I'm not very hungry," she said.

Len brought her over to the stool and they both sat down. Anna quickly prepared breakfast for her. She brought Jolene a plate with eggs, sausage and toast, then a cup of coffee. Jolene ate slowly, making small talk with Len. Anna brought a cup of coffee to Len and one for herself. She sat at Jolene's other side and they all talked while Jolene picked at her food. Her cell phone rang and she saw that it was Daniel. She hesitated before she answered, "Hi."

"Hi, Jolene."

"Daniel. Where are you?"

"I'm on my way to your place. I thought we could spend a couple of days together," he said.

"Together, us? I don't know."

"C'mon, give me chance, okay?"

Jolene stayed quiet for a few minutes, her mind racing. This might be the perfect time for her to get her revenge on him. "Jolene, are you there?" he asked.

"Yes, I'm here. Okay."

"Great, I'll be there in an hour. Just bring a small overnight bag." "Okay, an hour. See you."

"Bye."

She hung up the phone. Her mind was going through different scenarios. She sat there for a while, just staring at nothing.

"Jolene," called Anna.

"Ah. Sorry, what?" she asked.

"I asked you. What was that about?"

"Oh, Daniel is coming to get me," she said as she got off the stool.

"Oh," was all Anna said.

"I'll have to get ready," she said walking out of the kitchen.

Anna and Len looked at each other and shook their heads. They knew nothing good would come out of this. Quickly, she went to her room and got her travel bag ready. She changed her clothes and went downstairs. She made a call to Livy, which went to voicemail. She left her a voice message and hung up the phone.

Jolene went to the living room and turned on the TV. She sat on the couch watching the midday news. The news was still reporting the embezzlement scandal of Barnes and Jenkins Investments, LLC. She was still listening to the news when she heard a knock at the door. She got up and went to the foyer, "I'll get it, Anna," she said as Anna was walking to open the door.

Anna turned around and went back to what she was doing. Jolene opened the door to see Daniel with a big smile in his face. He took her in an embrace and gave her a quick kiss on the lips. He let go of her and walked into the house. "Ready to go?" he asked.

"Yes, let me tell Anna that I'm leaving," she said walking towards the kitchen.

"Okay, I'll wait for you in the car. I'll take your bag."

"Okay, thanks."

Jolene walked into the kitchen and gave Anna a kiss on the cheek. "I'm leaving. See you Sunday," she said.

"Okay. Jolene, be careful."

"I will."

Jolene got into Daniel's car. Right away, Daniel put the car in drive and took off. He talked the whole time he was driving. Jolene talked back to him, making very idle conversation. He drove for close to two hours before they arrived at a very pretty cottage. Daniel got out and went to help her out of the car. He took the bags out of the trunk and took her hand and walked her to the front door. He opened the door for her and led her into the house.

"This is beautiful, Daniel," she said with sincerity in her voice.

Daniel saw the smile on her face and was very happy. He embraced her and gave her a kiss. "Get comfortable, I'll bring your bag to the room," he said walking to the back of the house and down the hall. Jolene sat on the couch. He came back and sat next to her. "I'm so happy you're here with me," he said taking her hands into his.

Jolene smiled at him, saying nothing. Daniel stood up from the couch, "I'm glad you wore comfortable clothes and boots. Let's go for a walk. There's a beautiful trail at the back of the house."

"Sure," she said.

She stood up beside him and he took her hand and walked out the side sliding door. They started to walk the trail, slowly and in no rush, just walking and talking. The afternoon was very pleasant and sunny. She loved the smell of the trees and the singing of the birds. After walking for a while they went back to the cottage. "I made a reservation at a nice restaurant by the highway. Why don't you go and get ready while I check my emails."

Jolene hated his condescending tone, but didn't say anything. Instead she just turned and went down the hall to find the room. She took a quick shower and got dressed. As she finished putting on her shoes, Daniel walked in. He hugged and kissed her, deepening the kiss by thrusting his tongue in her mouth. Jolene let him set the pace of the kiss. She hesitated a bit, but then kissed him back.

"I love your lips," he said, "My turn to get ready."

She walked out of the room and left him alone to do his thing. She went back to the living room and sat down and turned the TV on. Turning on the news, she found that the story about her father's firm had spread. When she heard Daniel coming out of the room, she shut off the TV and stood up.

"You're so beautiful," he said caressing her face.

"Thanks," she said smiling at him.

"Let's get going or we're going to be late."

They walked out of the cottage and got into his car. The drive to the restaurant was about half an hour. He pulled up in front of the restaurant and an attendant opened the car for her and another one for him. He went to her and took her hand and walked her into the restaurant.

"Good evening, Mr. Barnes," said the hostess.

"Good evening," he said.

"Your table is ready," she said as she led them through the restaurant. Daniel pulled out Jolene's chair for her and then he sat down. The hostess left them alone and a few seconds later, the waitress came over. "Good evening, I'm Kelly. I'll be your waitress this evening."

"Kelly, please bring a bottle of your best wine," said Daniel

"Yes, sir," said the waitress and left the table.

"This is a very nice place," said Jolene, opening her menu and looking it over. She was so nervous she didn't know what to order.

"They have fantastic dinner choices. Let me order for you."

"Sure, thank you," she said breathing a sigh of relief.

The waitress came back with a bottle of wine and she served a sample for him. Daniel tried the wine and gave the waitress a smile of approval. Kelly poured the wine for them and took their food order from Daniel. Daniel made a toast to them and they sipped their wine. He made some conversation with her in between answering his phone, which was constantly ringing.

Jolene took small sips of her wine while smiling and shaking her head to him as he continued to talk. She took a deep breath and relaxed, happy when dinner finally came. Right away, she started to eat. For the most part, he ate quietly only making small comments about the food.

Her face hurt from all the smiling she was doing to pretend she was interested in his conversation. Jolene did like her dinner even if she didn't choose it herself. "That was delicious," she said.

"Yes, it was. How about dessert? They have a delicious cheese cake," he said.

"Sure."

The waitress cleared the dinner plates and took the dessert order. Daniel took her hand in his and gave her a quick kiss on the palm. "You're so beautiful," he repeated to her caressing her face.

"Thanks," was all she could say.

He put his hand down when the waitress came back with dessert. Jolene loved cheese cake so this was perfect for her. They stayed quiet as they ate the dessert. After more than two hours of dinner together, Daniel was ready to leave. She was glad of it. He paid the bill, took her hand and left the restaurant. His car was already in front when they came out. He tipped the attendant and helped Jolene into the car.

During the drive he received several more calls. She stayed quiet, listening to his boring conversation with whomever he was talking. The drive back seemed shorter and in no time they were back at the cottage. He turned off the car and went to her side and helped her get out. He took her hand and walked her into the house.

Suddenly, he pinned her against the wall with his body and proceeded to give her a kiss. Jolene opened her mouth for him and he thrust his tongue into her mouth. He kissed her for a while, then stopped and started a trail of small kisses down her neck to her shoulder. He pulled her blouse down and kept trailing kisses down her arm, then going back again to her neck.

"You have a gorgeous neck," he said and slowly started to caress one of her breasts over her blouse.

Jolene's body reacted to his touch. She felt her body heat up right to her core. She wrapped her arms around his back and held onto him because her legs were becoming wobbly. Daniel pulled away from her and she could see his eyes were glassy with desire. He took her hand and walked towards the bedroom. She kept pace with him, but wasn't completely certain that this was what she wanted.

He opened the bedroom door and walked in, pulling her behind him. Jolene stood beside him. He took his time to approach her, but when he did he started to very patiently take her clothes off. Jolene's body was burning as he softly touched every part of her body as he took off her clothes. Jolene needed to do something, so she began to take his shirt off then went to his pants. He kicked his shoes off, then moved her hands from his belt and started to take his pants off.

Jolene was standing in front of him in just her bra and panties. He took a handful of her breasts and caressed them over the bra. Then he snapped the front of the bra and pulled it off her. He took one in his hands and lowered his mouth to the other one. He sucked the nipple hard and pinched the other between his fingers and pulled it. Jolene's body was on fire. Her reaction to his touch was more intense that she had expected.

He settled her on the bed and lay down next to her. He leaned over her and started kissing her, bringing a hand to her stomach and slowly stroking her. He moved his hand under her underwear where he started to push his finger through her pussy lips. He slowly massaged her pussy with his finger, touching her up and down. Jolene's body responded to his touch and she wriggled her hips for more. Daniel stopped kissing her and quickly moved to her breast, keeping the motion of his finger on her pussy. "Open up for me, sweetie," he said softly in her ear.

Jolene spread her legs apart and he moved his fingers down, and with a swift move, pushed two of his fingers inside her while taking a nibble of her nipple. She moaned out loud in response. He kept pumping his fingers in and out, faster now as he devoured her entire nipple in his mouth, nibbling and rubbing it with his teeth.

Jolene's mind felt detached from her body, as if her body was betraying her. It was like she was watching from the outside as someone fucked her body and she had no emotions.

He stopped and pulled a condom from the nightstand drawer. He put it on and rapidly moved on top of her and quickly positioned his dick at her entrance. "I love the feel of your body against mine."

With a sudden move he entered her. Right away he set the speed on fast. He moved in and out in a hurried pace. Her body complicated everything by responding to every move he made. She always thought she would hate his touch, but he was proving to be an excellent lover.

"C'mon, come for me," he said pushing faster and harder in and out of her.

Jolene held to his lean body. Daniel rode her faster, going deeper. After several thrusts deep inside her, Jolene exploded in an orgasm. Daniel brought his lips to her and kissed her, continuing to ride her for a few minutes longer until he exploded in his own orgasm.

He pushed in and out until he stopped coming. He stopped kissing her while he pulled out of her. He went to the bathroom, pulled the condom off and flushed it down the toilet. He cleaned himself and went back to the room. He brought a towel and gave it to her. Jolene took the towel and cleaned herself while he lay next to her and started to stroke her arm softly. "That was fantastic, you're so beautiful," he said kissing her shoulder.

They lay next to each other for a while. Jolene felt the need to move away from him. She needed to wash up. She started to slide out of the bed. He put a hand on her arm, "Where you going?" he asked.

"I want to take a quick shower," she answered.

"Oh, okay," he said smiling at her.

She got off the bed and went to the bathroom. She turned the water on and got into the stall. She quickly washed her body, rubbing hard everywhere she could. All of a sudden she started to cry. She felt so guilty; she knew she had betrayed the trust Greg and Gus had given her. She couldn't stop crying and the tears were running in streams down her face.

She stayed in the shower until she calmed herself down and managed to stop the tears, and got out of the stall. She dried, wrapped her body with the towel, and went back into the room.

When she got closer to the bed she could see that Daniel was already asleep. She couldn't get close to him; she felt so sickened about what she had done. Quickly she got the jogging suit out of her bag and put it on.

She went to the living and sat on the couch. Resting her head on the armrest, she immediately began to cry again. She didn't know how long she had been crying, but when she looked at the clock on the wall, she realized it was past two o'clock in the morning. She lay down and grabbed the quilt from the back of the couch and closed her eyes. After another half an hour she fell asleep.

She woke up a bit lost, not aware of where she was. She opened her eyes and saw the sun shining through the window. She looked up at the clock and saw that it was just a little past seven o'clock. She pulled the quilt off and stood up, folding the quilt and putting it back on the couch. Then she went to the bathroom down the hall.

She felt worn out emotionally and physically. She went in the room and pulled her toothbrush from her bag and went back to the bathroom to brush her teeth. After she was done, she went back to the living room. Quietly, she opened the sliding door to the backyard. She went out and stood on the deck enjoying the sun on her face.

The sun was warm but it was a bit nippy in the shade. Still, she preferred to be outside than inside the cottage with him. She felt the need to work out her body so she went back in the house and, still being very quiet, went in the room. She pulled her sneakers out of the bag and put them on and wrote a note to Daniel.

She walked to the beginning of the trail and started her run. She ran for several miles until she noticed she was getting too far away from the cottage. She turned around and ran back the way she had come. As she walked into the cottage, Daniel wrapped her in a hug. "Good morning, gorgeous," he said kissing her.

"Good morning," she replied.

"How about getting breakfast ready for us," he said to her.

Jolene looked at him a bit disturbed, but quickly she switched her expression to a smile. "Okay," she said.

She went to the kitchen, washed her hands and prepared breakfast while Daniel sat down and talked on his phone as usual. Daniel ate his breakfast in between phone calls. Jolene felt so detached from the whole situation, like it was happening to someone else. He finished eating and received one more call; he took the phone and got up from the stool.

Jolene picked up the dishes and brought them to the sink where she washed them. After she was done, she cleaned the counter and stove. She put everything back in the cabinets and went to the room get all her things back in the bag. She went back to the living and sat on the couch to wait for him. Daniel walked in the room and sat next to Jolene. It was already past one o'clock; he had been on the phone for over an hour.

"I have a special place I want to show you," he said smiling at her and wrapping his arm around her waist.

"Sure," she said, "I'm ready to go."

"Good. Give me a couple of minutes to get my bag ready and we'll go, okay?"

"Okay."

Several minutes later, he came out with his bag in his hand. He took her bag and walked out of the house. Jolene followed him. He opened the door for her and then went to the trunk and put the bags in. She got in the car and a couple of minutes later, Daniel got in, too. He started the car and drove off. The ride in the car was the usual thing, with him on the phone alternating with him making small talk with her. She answered him in one-syllable words and shook her head a lot. After driving for a bit, she noticed they were not going the same way they had come.

"Where are we going?" she asked him.

"It's a surprise. You'll see. Just sit back and relax," he said. She wanted to insist on an answer but refrained from saying anything. He drove for another half an hour then took a turn on a long gravel road. He drove ten more minutes and stopped at what it looked like a rest area. He pulled closer to the railing and shut off the car.

"C'mon, I want to show you something." He got out of the car; she hesitated for a moment but then got out, too. Taking her hand, he walked her close to a railing. Jolene looked out onto the beautiful panorama in front of her. Her face said it all; the view was so fantastic that she just gazed at it, amazed.

"It's beautiful, isn't it?" he asked standing behind her wrapping his arms around her waist and pulling her close to him. Jolene was so overtaken by the view that she ignored his hold. "I can't tell you enough how beautiful you are," he whispered in her ear.

He turned her around to face him and moved a few steps away from her. He pulled something from his pants pocket.

He took her hands, then opened his hand, "Jolene, marry me?" he asked.

"What? Daniel!"

"Jolene, I find you extremely beautiful and I want to marry you. What do you say?"

"Daniel, I don't know what to think. I need time to give you an answer."

He looked at her for a few seconds then pulled her in a hug, "Of course, sweetie." he said, handing her the ring. She took it and put in her sweater pocket.

"Let's go have a bite. I know of a really nice place just a couple of miles from here," he said taking her hand and walking back to the car.

Jolene was still in shock from his proposal; this just didn't feel right at all. They drove for about ten minutes, and arrived at a small, cozy restaurant——not the kind of place she expected him to go.

Jolene passed the rest of the afternoon in a daze. She was sat back in the car seat looking out the window on their way to her house. The drive was longer because they had to double back to get there. It was early evening and they were just minutes from the house. The whole drive there she kept playing with the ring in her pocket.

Back at the house, Greg and Gus were desperately pacing the living room rug up and down, worried sick about her. Both had been calling her for the past two days with no answer. When they got to the house, Anna told them that she left with Daniel early Saturday. "I can't believe she's with my brother," said Greg furious.

"Greg, please don't jump to conclusions. You know she always planned to get revenge on your brother. That's probably what she's doing right now," said Gus.

"How could you be so calm? The woman we love is with another man," screamed Greg.

Gus moved behind him and embraced. Greg kissed his forearm. "I don't feel good about this," said Greg with a sad tone in his voice.

"You knew she was serious about getting your brother back."

"I know, but this? I was hoping she would change her mind after everything with her father was resolved," he said. They turned when they heard a car coming down the driveway. Greg moved to go to the door but Gus stopped him. "No, let her come in," Gus said in his ear.

"Fine," snapped Greg back at him.

Jolene looked at Daniel when he stopped the car. He pulled her to him and gave her a kiss. "I'll wait anxiously for your call," he said with a smile on his face.

"Okay," was all she could manage.

Greg and Gus heard the car stop in front of the house. A few seconds later, they heard a car door closing. Jolene waved to Daniel as he drove off. She walked to the front door and went in the house. She started to walk towards the stairs when she heard someone behind her.

She turned to see Greg and Gus staring at her from the threshold of the family room. Greg was furious, she could see it on his face, while Gus was serious but looked calm. Quickly Greg approached her. Jolene looked away from him and moved back, ending up against the door. Greg moved closer to her. "You slept with him, didn't you?" he demanded.

Jolene looked up at him with tears already running down her face, but she didn't say anything. Gus moved closer to them, but stayed behind Greg. "You slept with him," he repeated but now he was yelling as he slammed his hands against the door on each side of her.

Jolene saw Anna and Len rushing towards the foyer. "Everything is fine," she told them with a shaky voice, "Please, leave us alone."

Anna hesitated for a moment, but Len pulled her away from the foyer. "If you hurt her…" she started to say, but Gus interrupted her.

"He's not going to hurt her," Gus assured Anna.

Anna and Len left the foyer. Jolene brought her eyes back to Greg. This time he was right on top of her. His anger showed in the tension of his jaw. "You slept with him," he stated with a firm voice next to her face.

Again, Jolene didn't say anything but put her hand in her sweater pocket and pulled out the ring. She opened her hand and showed it to him. "He asked me to marry him," she said tears continuing to run down her cheeks.

Greg turned brusquely taking two steps away from her. "So, you whore yourself to my brother for revenge?" he screamed.

"Greg," said Gus.

"How dare you?" she said as she went to slap him, but he grabbed her hand before she got the chance and let it go.

"How dare me? All we have ever given you is love and this is how you pay us in return," he said looking at Gus with so much pain. He started to move away from her.

"Greg, please," she pleaded with him as she grabbed his arm. He pulled the arm away from her and went towards the door.

"I'm out of here," he said not looking back as he opened the door, "Goodbye, Jolene," he said as he walked out of the house.

Jolene's face was covered in tears. She moved towards Gus who was standing just staring at the door. "No," he said moving away, "I may not yell like Greg, but I'm as hurt as he is. I need to rest. I had a long flight and I've been sitting here for hours waiting for you," he said walking towards the stairs.

Jolene stood there, her body barely functioning. She was shaking now and more tears were coming down her face. She stood there for a while then turned and walked to the study. She went in and sat down on the couch, resting her head on the armrest. She completely lost control and broke into sobs, no longer holding back anything. She didn't know how long she had been crying, but by the time she looked up, it was almost three o'clock in the morning.

She went up to her room and got her pajamas on and lay down in the bed for almost an hour until her eyes could no longer produce tears. She was so tired that she finally fell to sleep.

Gus could not sleep at all until he heard her go into her room. Now that he knew where she was, he could settle down and get some sleep, too.

Chapter 20

Gus was still exhausted when the morning came. He got out of bed and went to the bathroom to take a quick shower. He got dressed then put the last of his clothes in one the bags he had gotten ready the night before. He made sure he had all his personal documents in his blazer pocket. He sat on the couch and wrote a letter to Jolene. He finished the letter, put it in an envelope and sealed it, putting it in his other pocket. He grabbed his bags and walked out of the room. He left the bags in the foyer and went to the kitchen. Len and Anna were sitting down drinking coffee. "Hi," he said standing next to them.

"Hi," both said back.

"I'm leaving for a while. I need time to think," he said.

"We understand," said Len.

Gus pulled the letter from his pocket and gave it to Anna, "Please give Jolene this letter," he said. "Len, can you drive me to the airport?" he asked.

"Of course," Len said as he stood up and left the kitchen.

"She loves you two. She's confused. Please just be patient with her," said Anna now standing next to him.

Gus nodded his head and smiled at her; she gave him a hug and a kiss on the cheek. Gus hugged her back. He said goodbye to her and left the kitchen. He grabbed his bags and left the house. Len helped Gus with the bags and Gus got into the car. The drive to the airport was awful, the farther he went from her, the more his heart felt like it was breaking. He closed his eyes and a few tears ran down his face.

Downtown at the office, Greg was trying very hard to do some work. He completed some paperwork before his eleven o'clock meeting. He checked his watch and saw that he had five minutes before the meeting. He sent the email he was working on and closed his laptop. He picked up his notepad and left his office.

Jolene woke up exhausted. It was like she didn't rest at all. She couldn't believe how late it was——almost eleven o'clock. She got out of bed and went in the bathroom to take a shower and then got dressed. She went to Gus's room but he wasn't there, so she went down to the kitchen where she saw Anna making lemonade. "Good morning," Jolene said.

"Good morning, sweetie. Did you get any sleep?" asked Anna.

"Very little. Any coffee?"

"Yes, sit. I'll get it for you."

Jolene sat down on the stool. Anna poured a cup for her and brought it to her. "Anna, have you seen Gus? He's not in his room," said Jolene.

Anna didn't answer right away; she took the envelope from her pocket and gave it to her. "He left. He gave me this envelope for you," said Anna.

Across town at Barnes and Jenkins Investments, LLC building, Greg was getting ready to enter the conference room. Behind him was his father. As he walked into the room, he saw Daniel talking to a group of executives. As he passed by them, he heard Daniel talking about Jolene. "She's the sweetest piece of ass I've ever had. She's gorgeous!" said Daniel.

Greg turned and pushed Daniel against the wall. "What the fuck is wrong with you?" Daniel gasped.

"You are a mother-fucking bastard." Greg spat at him.

Daniel looked at him and smiled, "What brother? It bothers you that I got to her first," he said laughing.

"Wrong, all you got are my leftovers. She was mine a long time before she was yours. Not only mine she was with Gus, too," said Greg giving him another shove and walking away.

"Son of a bitch," said Daniel as he rushed Greg. Greg turned around and threw a punch that hit Daniel right on his jaw, Daniel stumbled back.

"Enough," screamed Tim, "Greg sit down. Everyone sit down. You too Daniel" he said.

Daniel found a chair far away from his brother and sat down, rubbing his sore jaw. Everyone was stupefied with what happened but no one said anything. Tim looked around the room and, after a few minutes, he started the meeting.

He spoke to them about the situation with George and the other two accomplices. Then he went into detail about what the company was ready to do with Joshua's part of the business, which legally belonged to his family. After he talked for a while everyone agreed on what to do. "Now, Greg is going to bring us up to speed regarding Josh's daughter. Greg."

"Ten years ago, an injustice was done to Caroline's father, and she swore she would get revenge against the people responsible. Caroline grew up into a beautiful woman and on her eighteenth birthday, she legally changed her name to Jolene Moreau."

"What? No way. You're lying," said Daniel, livid.

"Daniel, stop talking," said his father.

"I'm not lying. Jolene is Caroline. She came back to her hometown and after several weeks of research, she did exactly what she promised she would do ten years ago," said Greg.

"All this time you knew who she was and didn't say anything to us?" screamed Daniel.

"Yes. Furthermore, I was part of the team that helped her do it."

"So, was I part of this game?" he asked.

"You most definitely were," said Greg with great pleasure in his voice.

Daniel stood and tried to rush him, "No more. Daniel leave. This meeting is finished. I'll contact the legal department and start the process for the division of Joshua's part of the company," said Tim.

Daniel moved away from his father and furiously walked out of the room. The rest of the executives left, too.

Tim walked over to Greg, "What now?" he asked him.

"I need time to think. I'm taking a couple of weeks off."

"Okay. Greg, do you care for her?"

"Yes, I love her and I love Gus, too."

"I don't presume to know your life but this is definitely a surprise. Take all the time you need."

"Thanks, Dad."

Tim left the room leaving Greg behind. Greg sat back down and just stared out of the window. He got up and left the conference room and went straight to his office where he continued to do more paperwork. Daniel was infuriated with his brother and Jolene. He left the building, got in his car and drove like a maniac all the way to Jolene's house.

Jolene drank her coffee quietly and took a few bites of the breakfast Anna had made for her. She stopped eating and stared at the envelope Anna had given her. She heard the doorbell ring. "I'll get it," she said standing up, folding the envelope and putting it in her pants pocket.

Jolene walked out of the kitchen and towards the front door. The doorbell rang again. Jolene opened the door and saw Daniel standing in front of her. He pushed past her and into the foyer. He turned around and gave her an awful look. "Jolene, or should I call you Caroline?" he snapped at her.

Jolene didn't know what to say; she just stared at him.

"You're wondering how I know. My brother, your lover——let me correct that statement——ONE of your lovers told me."

"He did," she said, "Daniel…"

"You bitch. You played me for a fool," he yelled at her.

"Daniel, I don't know what to say."

"There is nothing TO say. I want my ring back."

Jolene pulled the ring from her pants pocket. She opened her hand. Daniel quickly snatched the ring from her. He moved closer to her, "Stay away from me," he snapped at her.

He shoved her out of the way and walked out of the house. Jolene couldn't believe how badly she managed to mess up the situation with Daniel. And how high the price was for her mistake. But there was nothing she could do now; it was probably too late to mend it. Jolene touched the outside of her pocket where she had put the envelope.

She went out to the terrace and walked straight to the tree house. She climbed the ladder, undid the latch on the door and went in. She sat in her favorite corner and took the letter out.

Back at the office, Greg was talking on his cell phone with Gus. "I told Dad about us and Jolene."

"What did he say?"

"He didn't judge us or anything. I told him I was taking some time off."

"And?"

"He said okay."

"Great. When will I see you?"

"Wednesday night. I have to go. I need to do a lot of work before tomorrow."

"Okay, my love. See you soon."

"Yes. Gus, I love you."

"I love you, too. Bye."

Greg hung up the phone. His mind wandered to the last words he said to Jolene, but it was too late to take them back. He shook his head and got back to his paperwork.

Jolene couldn't stop crying. She put the letter back in the envelope and held it to her chest. She had lost the two men that meant so much to her and now she was alone.

"Oh God, Dad. What have I done?" she said out loud, tears pouring down her face. She leaned her head against the wall and closed her eyes, just letting her tears roll down. She heard the sound of her name; someone was calling her, it sounded like it was coming from far away. She opened her eyes and shook her head; she realized she was still sitting in the tree house. She heard someone calling her name again, this time it sounded louder. Jolene went to the door and opened it. There below her, next to the ladder was Len calling her name. "Jolene, you have a guest," was all he said, and he turned around and left her alone.

Who can it possibly be now, she thought.

She was not ready to see anyone. She climbed down the ladder and walked into the house but before she saw anyone, she went to the bathroom and freshened up her face. She looked at herself in the mirror; her eyes were totally red and there was sadness in them. Her face was all drained and strained. She dried her face and went to the living room.

Anna was standing talking to someone standing in front of her. Jolene couldn't see who it was because of the angle. She moved farther inside the living and recognized her visitor. "Melissa," she said moving towards her.

Melissa stood up and rushed to her, giving her a big hug. Jolene wrapped her arms around the woman she always saw as her second mother. Anna left them alone in the living room.

"Oh, Caroline," she said pulling back a bit so she could look at her. Jolene looked up to see Melissa's face full of tears.

"Please don't cry. I'm fine. Look at me."

Melissa pulled her to the couch and sat down, still holding onto to her. Jolene had no choice but to sit down next to her.

"Why. Why not tell us?" she asked.

"I couldn't."

"You didn't believe we had anything to do with your father's…" Melissa started to say, but Jolene stopped her before she could finish the sentence.

"Oh God, no. But we knew that Tim would want to do his own investigation within the company and that would have attracted too much attention, maybe even alert the guilty person. He killed once and we weren't sure he wouldn't kill again."

"So you did it to protect us," said Melissa still crying.

"Yes, next to my parents, you're my family and I couldn't take the chance you would get hurt.

"Oh, Caroline."

"Please Melissa, call me Jolene. That's my legal name now. Caroline died ten years ago when someone snatched her father out of her life. I'm now Jolene."

"I'm sorry, I'll try."

Jolene smiled to her. Melissa hugged her again and kissed her on the forehead. "How's Marcia doing?"

"She's doing great. She missed you a lot. She didn't just lose her husband, she also lost her best friend."

"Why not call me?"

"I asked her not to. I needed to disappear out of your life for the plan to work. Mom would never be able to keep a secret from you."

"True," Melissa said.

"She wants you to call her; I'll give you her phone number."

"Great. What now?"

Jolene stood up straight and looked out the window. Her face was very serious and full of vengeance.

"Now we wait for justice to be done for my father," said Jolene in a harsh voice.

"Yes."

Anna brought them some refreshment and they continued talking. Jolene handed Melissa a piece of paper with her mother's phone number and her own number as well. Melissa put it in her purse. "Thank you, I have to go," said Melissa getting up from the couch.

"Okay."

"I'll call you so we can get together."

"Yes."

Melissa gave her a hug and kiss on the cheek and Jolene walked her to the front door. "Bye," she said giving her another quick kiss on the cheek.

"Bye," said Jolene with a big smile.

Jolene watched Melissa drive away, then closed the door and went to the study. She got her phone out and dialed Greg's number. The phone rang several times then went to voicemail. She didn't know what to say so she hung up.

Jolene stayed in the study for some time, just sitting with her eyes closed. Her mind was going over and over Greg's words to her. How hateful they were, how angry he was at her.

He's right, I'm a whore. How could I betray them like that? **she thought.**

There was a knock at the door so she opened her eyes. "Come in," she said. Anna came in the study and walked over to her on the couch. Anna saw the strain on her face.

"Dinner is ready. I set the kitchen table instead of the dining room; I hope that's okay with you."

"Yes, that's fine. Thanks. I'll be there in a minute."

"Okay," said Anna, walking out of the study.

Jolene went to the bathroom to check on her face. She looked as bad as before; nothing she could do would erase the strain on her face. She went to the kitchen and sat at the table. Anna brought her a plate with dinner. Jolene wasn't very hungry, but Anna would get on her case if she didn't eat something. She took a few bites but couldn't eat anymore because her stomach was getting upset. She pushed the plate away and stood up from her chair. Anna came to the table, "I made you dessert," she said.

"Anna, I can't eat one more bite. I'll eat the dessert later, okay?"

"Are you okay?" she asked.

"I'm fine, my stomach just feels funny, that' all," answered Jolene.

Jolene walked out of the kitchen. Anna stood there watching her go, tears rolling down her face. Len came up behind her and gave her a hug. "She's going to be fine, you'll see."

"I hope so," Anna said.

Jolene went straight to her room. Her stomach was more upset now. A few seconds later, she was in the bathroom vomiting up everything she had eaten. She blamed it on nerves. She got comfortable on a corner of the couch, turned on the TV and settled back to watch a movie. She rested her head back and looked at the TV. She must have closed her eyes sometime during the movie because when she looked up the late news was on.

Jolene shut off the TV and made her way to the bathroom. She took a quick shower, dressed in her pajamas and lay down on the bed. Hours passed and she was still not able to fall asleep. Her throat felt dry so she got up and went down to the kitchen to get some juice. She finished drinking the juice, rinsed the cup and went back to her room. She settled back in bed, but a few minutes later, her stomach rejected the juice and she ended up in the toilet puking it all up. She rinsed her mouth and went back to bed. She was so exhausted that she quickly fell to sleep.

Chapter 21

Jolene woke up as exhausted as she was when she went to bed. She had spent a restless night filled with awful nightmares beginning with her father and ending with Gus and Greg. She got up and went to the bathroom, brushed her teeth and dressed in casual clothes. She walked slowly down to the kitchen, her upper body hunched over. Anna was just pouring another cup of coffee for her husband, Len. "Please pour one for me," said Jolene as she sat on the stool next to Len.

"Are you okay? You look tired," said Len.

"I'm fine, just a restless night, that's all."

Anna brought her a cup of coffee and went back to the stove to prepare her breakfast. The smell in the kitchen was making Jolene a bit sick. She stood up from the stool, taking her cup. "I'm not hungry Anna. Just the coffee is enough. I'll be in the study," she said walking out of the room. Anna and Len looked at each other with concerned faces. Anna stopped what she was doing at the stove and sat down next to Len. Both said nothing; they just sat there.

In the study, Jolene sat on the couch and put on the TV. She reclined back and took sips of her coffee. She was not listening to anything on the TV; she absentmindedly rubbed her stomach, which was still feeling upset.

Her cell phone rang and she quickly looked at it hoping it would be Greg or Gus, but it was Phil. "Good morning," she said.

"Good morning, I just called to tell you that the first court day is set up for tomorrow. The DA believes this is going to be an open and shut case."

"Good, I'll be there," she said.

"I thought you would be. See you then," said Captain Wright.

She hung up the phone and went back to watching the TV, or at least trying to watch it. The rest of the morning seemed so long with nothing to do. After several hours, someone knocked at the study door. Anna walked in with a tray in her hands. "Oh Anna, I'm not sure I can eat anything. My stomach is feeling a bit queasy; it's probably nerves," Jolene said.

Anna ignored her comment and brought the tray to the table next to her. "I thought that might be the case, so I made you a bit of chicken broth that should help your stomach. I also made you some tea."

"Oh, you're so good to me. Thanks."

Anna walked out of the room, Jolene took the bowl and slowly slurped the broth then put the bowl down and took small sips of the tea. She relaxed into the couch with the cup in her hand, drinking her tea. Anna was definitely right; the broth and tea settled her stomach down.

The rest of the day passed with no call from Gus or Greg; she had already called each several times. She went to the kitchen for something to drink and found the kitchen empty so she poured herself some juice. She sat on one of the stools and slowly drank her juice. After a few minutes of sitting there Anna walked into the kitchen. "How's your stomach?" she asked.

"Much better. Thank you again for the broth and tea."

"I'm glad it helped. Are you hungry?"

"No, not really, maybe later. I think I'll go to my room."

She finished the juice and put the glass in the sink and started to rinse it. "I'll do that, you go and rest," said Anna.

Jolene smiled at her and left the kitchen. Anna noticed how weary Jolene looked——her eyes had dark circles under them and her face looked sad. Jolene walked into her room, but instead of going to bed, she sat on the couch like she did the night before. Again, she found a movie on the TV and sat back on the couch. She tried to focus her mind on the movie hoping that it would distract her from how much she missed Greg and Gus. As she thought of them, tears rolled down her face. She covered her face with her hands and more tears came down. Nothing could take away the pain and loneliness she felt without them.

She closed her eyes and continued to sob loudly. She must have fallen asleep crying because she suddenly snapped awake and hit her head on the armrest of the couch. She shook her head to clear it and went to the bathroom, brushed her teeth and got her pajamas on. She shut off the light and went to bed.

She closed her eyes, but all she saw were Greg and Gus. She tossed and turned so many times in bed that her blanket was all tangled. She untangled the blanket and settled back to try to sleep, closing her eyes again. Her weariness took over and in matter of minutes she was asleep.

Her dreams were again of Greg and Gus. She opened her eyes just as she knew Greg was going to yell at her——she knew because her mind kept repeating the words over and over. She looked at the clock on her nightstand and saw that it was only seven o'clock in the morning, but she couldn't take the chance of not waking up in time to get to court. She got up and took a quick shower and went back to the room with the towel wrapped around her body.

She went to the closet, carefully selecting an appropriate outfit for the day and got dressed. She put her makeup on then worked on her hair. She looked at herself in the wall mirror, approving of her choice of clothes. She found a purse that matched her shoes and put in her wallet and some other things including her cell phone, which she checked again for missed calls. She was disappointed when she saw there were none. She grabbed the purse and walked down to the kitchen where Anna was by herself making some coffee.

"Good morning," Jolene said.

"Good morning."

Jolene sat on a stool watching Anna start the coffee maker. Anna turned to the stove where she was already making something for breakfast. Jolene sat quietly as Anna got two cups out of the cabinet and poured coffee for them. She brought one cup to Jolene and sat next to her. Jolene took a sip of her coffee. "I love your coffee Anna," she said smiling to her.

"Thank you. I made you a bit of oatmeal that should not upset your stomach."

"Thanks, I don't know what's wrong with me lately. I think it's all the stress I'm going through. It will get better soon."

"I'm sure."

Jolene remained seated as Anna served her a bowl of oatmeal. Jolene ate slowly making sure that her stomach didn't get upset, and eventually, she was able to eat it all. By the time she was done, it was almost eight o'clock. She stood up from the stool. "I'll be in court probably most of the day. The trial starts today."

"Yes, I heard the news."

"Please have Len bring me the car," she said.

"You don't want him to drive you?" said Anna.

"No, I prefer to drive," Jolene said walking out of the kitchen.

She went to the bathroom, checked her makeup and walked out of the house. As she was closing the door, Len pulled up in the car. He parked the car and got out. "Jolene, are you sure you don't want me to drive you there?" he asked.

"Yes," she answered.

Len gave her a quick hug and a kiss on the cheek, "Be careful."

"I will."

Jolene got in the car and drove off. Arriving downtown, she saw that the area around the courthouse was crawling with news media.

She parked in the courthouse lot where she saw a large crowd of people in front of the courthouse. She moved very quietly, trying very hard to stay away from the crowd. As she passed the crowd, she saw Captain Wright coming towards her. She waved to him and he waved back. He rushed to her and gave her a hug and kiss on the cheek. "Come with me. I'll take you in."

Jolene smiled at him and followed him past the security guards and into the hall of the courthouse. Phil walked her into the courtroom where the case would be tried.

"I have to see the DA. I'll see you later."

"Okay, Phil. Thanks."

She walked all the way to the far corner and found an empty space at the last bench. She sat quietly, not talking to anyone. The court was packed and there were no empty spaces. The judge came in the courtroom and the trial started. The entire morning passed in a haze, then the judge announced a lunch break. After the judge left, the courtroom emptied out. Jolene stayed behind just sitting there. Seeing the three people who destroyed and killed her father again hurt a lot. Minutes passed before she realized that she was the only one left in the courtroom. As she turned to leave, Phil walked in.

"I thought you'd still be here. Come with me; there's a room at the end of the hall we can use to eat something," he said leading her away from the courtroom.

She followed him into a room with a small table that already had food at one end. Phil pulled out a chair for her to sit down. Jolene sat. "Thank you," she said.

Phil sat across from her. He pulled out a sandwich and a soda from the bag and handed them to her. Phil pulled out another sandwich and soda and started to eat. She did the same, eating slowly, trying not to get her stomach upset.

He kept the conversation light and didn't mention anything that happened in the courtroom. Jolene smiled at him, chatting and feeling very much at ease around him.

Phil checked his watch, "We have just about ten minutes before they open the doors again."

"Okay, can you show me where the bathroom is?" she asked.

"Okay, help me clean the table."

They stood up and quickly cleaned the table. They came out of the room and Phil showed her the way to the bathroom. When she came out, he was still there waiting for her. "You didn't have to wait," she said smiling at him.

"I know."

He walked her back to the courtroom where people were starting to file in. She found the same spot where she sat that morning and sat down. Quickly the courtroom filled up again. Minutes later, the judge came out and the courtroom went quiet. The defense lawyers started back into the case. Jolene tried to stay focused on the proceedings. Her stomach started to act up a bit, so after about two hours, she had to leave the courtroom. She ended up in the bathroom vomiting. She rinsed her mouth and put some lipstick on and went back to the courtroom. Luckily the space where she was sitting was still open.

The proceedings ran all the way to five o'clock when the judge called for the case to continue the next day. He left the courtroom and everyone quickly filed out.

Her stomach was still upset so she went straight to her car. She stayed sitting in the car for a while, trying to grasp everything that was happening.

The streets were congested with all the cars leaving the courthouse. She patiently drove, not rushing at all. She got home, parked the car and went in the house. Anna must have heard the car coming because when Jolene opened the door she was waiting for her. "Hi," Jolene said.

"Hi," said Anna reaching for her and giving her a hug. "Hungry?" she asked.

"No, my stomach is really acting up right now. I need a nice bath and some rest," she answered.

Anna tightened her hold on her and gave her a kiss on the forehead, "How about the hot tub? It'll help you relax," she said.

"Yes, that will be great," she said.

"I'll get everything ready. You go get changed," said Anna letting go of her and walking to the back hall where hot tub was located.

Jolene went up to her room, got into her swimsuit and threw a robe over it before she went back down. She saw that Anna already had the tub running so she pulled off her robe and climbed into the tub. The warmth of the water felt good on her body. Jolene got comfortable in the tub and closed her eyes for a moment. She opened her eyes startled when Anna touched her. "I'm sorry. You fell asleep," said Anna.

"It's okay," she said standing up and getting out of the tub. Anna handed her a towel. Jolene dried herself and put her robe on. Anna turned the tub off and they walked out of the room. "I made you some more broth. Go take a shower and I'll bring it to you."

"Great, thanks."

Anna went to the kitchen and Jolene walked to her room. Quickly she went in the bathroom and took a shower, then got dressed in her pajamas. She sat down on the couch and turned on the TV. Jolene heard a knock at the door. "Come in."

Anna walked in the room with a tray and settled it on the small table. She handed Jolene the bowl of broth, which Jolene started to eat right away. The broth felt good in her stomach. Anna smiled at her and left her room. Jolene continued sipping her broth, and when she finished it all, she took the cup and started sipping the tea. She finished the tea and got settled back on the couch. She turned her attention to the local news, which was reporting on the trial.

She listened to the reporters outside the courtroom. After the news segment about the trial was over, she changed the channel to a movie. She managed to stay awake for about half an hour before she fell asleep.

Jolene woke up miserable again——it seemed that she was doing that a lot these days. It was probably all the weird dreams she had been having. She looked at the time on the cable box and saw that it was past midnight. She turned the TV off and went to the bathroom to brush her teeth; she shut the light off and got in bed. She tried to sleep, but sleep didn't come.

Every time Jolene closed her eyes, the faces of Greg and Gus came into her head. Instantly, she would start to cry, which was another thing she had been doing a lot of lately. Her intention of being strong and heartless had gone out the window these past weeks. And now she felt completely awful. Nothing compared to losing Greg and Gus. She had spent so much time lying to herself, telling herself that she didn't love them, but she definitely did love them both. She loved them more than she had imagined and now she had screwed that up, too. Jolene couldn't stop crying. She covered her face with her hands and started to sob loudly. She cried so much and she was so tired that at last she fell asleep.

Chapter 22

Jolene was so tired——her sleep had been restless and her days had been very emotional. She got out of bed, took a shower and got dressed. She checked herself in the mirror and was comfortable with the clothes she had chosen. She left her room and went down to the kitchen.

Jolene sat on a stool like she did every morning for the past few weeks. Anna brought her a cup of coffee and went to finish preparing the oatmeal she had already started for her.

Jolene couldn't believe it had been more than two weeks since the trial had begun. She had met with Tim and Melissa several times. Her mother sent Tim a power of attorney letter allowing Jolene to make decisions as a full partner in the company.

It was Thursday——the week was about gone. Today was the day that the defense would deliver their closing argument and then the jury would deliberate on the verdict.

These weeks had been awful for her. She tried calling Gus and Greg for the first week, but when she didn't hear back from them, she stopped calling. Livy and Stacie called her almost every day, but they were busy at Livy's house doing some renovations and painting and they had no time to visit. That was okay with her because she was in no mood for company. Her stomach continued to be upset most of the time and she seemed to be always vomiting, and she couldn't stop crying.

Anna put the plate of oatmeal in front of her. Jolene ate just a little bit today because her nerves were definitely getting the best of her and she couldn't keep much down. She took one last sip of her coffee and stood up to go. Anna gave her a hug and kiss. Jolene held tight to her for a few seconds longer before Anna let her go. Jolene smiled at her and left the kitchen.

She went to the foyer, grabbed her purse and left the house. Len already had the car waiting for her. He gave her a kiss on her forehead and went back in the house. Jolene drove downtown and found a parking space in the court lot as she had done for the past two weeks. She walked from her car and stood at the court stairs waiting for Phil who had escorted her into the courthouse every day. She sat down on the bench and waited for the judge to come in and start the case.

Just as she started to wonder when the judge was coming out, he did. The defense lawyer proceeded to deliver his closing argument, which lasted for at least half an hour. The judge called for the jury to go and deliberate. As soon as the jury left, the judge left the courtroom, too and the courtroom emptied out. Jolene remained seated as everyone else left the room. A few minutes later, Phil came back in and sat next to her. "Hi," she said.

"Hi."

Phil stayed with her for a while. After two hours of waiting, The bailiff announced that the judge and jury were ready to come back. Phil gave her a quick hug and left the courtroom. The room immediately filled up again, and minutes later, the jury came out and then the judge. Everyone was completely quiet when the judge started to talk. The judge finished his statement then called for the lead juror to read the verdicts. He called each accuser individually by name and asked for the verdict. No one in the room even murmured while the judge continued to call out for the verdicts.

Finally the last name was called——the man who killed her father. Jolene held her breath when the juror started to read, and when she heard the verdict she let go of the breath she had been holding. Jolene left the courtroom even before the judge made his last remarks. She walked swiftly past everyone in the courthouse hall and out of the building.

She just about ran to her car. When she got to the car, she didn't even try to stop the tears from coming down. She cried for several minutes. She calmed her nerves enough to drive back home; she was shaking badly. Jolene got home and parked the car in front of the house and went in.

Jolene saw Len and Anna waiting for her in the foyer; she went to them and they wrapped her in their arms. Jolene cried a bit more while they held her. She moved away from them and tried to smile. "Thanks," was all she managed to say as she walked out to the terrace.

She walked directly to the tree house and up the ladder. The last time she was here was the day that Gus left her. She continued to cry, now harder and louder.

"Oh Dad. I did it, we did it. I kept my promise. Now you have justice," she said out loud.

Jolene cried and cried; she couldn't seem to find a way to stop. She stayed in the tree house for a long time——probably hours. All she had left were dry sobs; no more tears came out. Jolene heard Anna calling her. She opened the door and went down the ladder. Anna wrapped an arm around her shoulders and together they walked into the house through the kitchen. Anna brought her to a stool and Jolene sat down. "I made you some tea. Here, drink. It will help you."

"Thanks," said Jolene taking the cup and sipping the tea.

Anna found a bowl in the cabinet and poured the beef broth she made for her in the bowl. She brought the bowl to her. Jolene smiled at her, put the cup down and started to slowly sip the broth. Anna sat next to her watching her and softly massaging Jolene's back. Jolene continued to quietly sip her broth and Anna didn't say anything to her; there was nothing she could say that would take her sadness away.

When Jolene finished the broth, she smiled at Anna and gave her a kiss on the cheek, "Thanks." Jolene stood up, "I'm going to my room," she said walking out of the kitchen.

Anna watched her leave and tears rolled down her face. Jolene walked into her room and sat on the couch and put the TV on, just like every other day. Nothing interested her, so she just chose a random movie channel and left it there. She stared at the TV not paying attention to what was going on. She spent hours just sitting there.

Jolene opened her eyes to see that it was dark outside already. She had fallen asleep in front of the TV again. She shut off the TV, put on her pajamas, shut off the light and climbed into bed. She got herself comfortable and closed her eyes. Going to bed always seemed to make her cry these days. She missed Gus and Greg so much and it hurt her the worst when she went to bed. She fell asleep crying like she had so many nights these past weeks.

Jolene woke up feeling relief the next morning——after ten long years, justice had been done for her father. She took a long hot shower, hoping to get relief from all the aches and pains she felt in her body. She got dressed in casual clothes, happy that she wouldn't have to go to court anymore. She knew the prosecutor was asking for the maximum sentence for all three. Phil promised to call her as soon as he knew.

She combed her hair and put it in a bun. She grabbed her phone and went down to the kitchen. As she sat down next to Len, who gave her a quick squeeze of her hand, Anna came over with a cup of coffee. Jolene took the cup in her hands and took a sip. Anna rubbed her shoulders for a moment then went back to the counter where she was cutting up fruit for her.

Anna put the fruit in a bowl and brought it to Jolene with a fork. Jolene put the coffee cup down and started to eat the fruit, slowly savoring every bite. She finished the whole fruit bowl and her coffee and stood up from the stool. "I'll be in the study checking my emails," she said, walking out.

She went over to the desk in the study and opened her laptop. She went thru her emails and answered anything that needed a response and deleted all the junk. She called her boss at the modeling agency to request a transfer. Her boss told her that she would hear from the manager by the end of the weekend.

After getting closure on her father's death and realizing that Greg and Gus would not be coming back, she decided to sell the house and move away——not back to France where Gus was, but somewhere else. It would make sense for her to move either to Los Angeles or New York since the agency had offices in both cities. She was leaning toward New York.

Jolene turned off her computer. She found a book from her father's library and went to sit on the couch. She loved reading; it was one of the many things she and her father shared. She opened the book and started to read. After she had been reading for a while, her phone rang. It was Phil who gave her the good news that all three men had received the maximum sentence and would be in jail for a long time.

"Thanks Phil, bye" she said and hung up her cell phone.

She went back reading her book. She checked the time on her phone. It was dinnertime in France, so her mother most likely would be home. She dialed her number; it rang only twice before Marcia picked it up. "Hi, honey."

"Hi, Mom. I just got a call from Phil. They all got the maximum sentence."

"I know, Melissa called me just a few minutes ago. She was at the courthouse for the sentencing."

"I'm glad she called you. When is she going for a visit?" asked Jolene.

"She's coming in two weeks. I can't wait to see her. It's been a long time."

Jolene knew how much her mother missed her best friend. "That's great Mom. Listen, I'll let you go. You're probably getting ready for dinner."

"I love talking to you honey."

"I know. I'll call next week, okay?"

"Okay," said Marcia but she could sense the sadness in her daughter's voice. She knew that Gus was back in France because he had come for a visit. She never got the chance to talk alone with him, so she didn't know exactly what was happening between them. "Bye, honey."

"Bye, Mom."

Jolene hung up the phone. She needed some fresh air and a ride in the car would help. She put the book down on the table and went back to her room to change her clothes and grab her bag. She went to the kitchen and found Anna. "I'm going out for a drive. I'll grab something to eat somewhere."

Anna nodded her head and gave her a hug. Jolene got in the car and decided to drive away from downtown. She took one of the small routes out of town and drove without music, taking her time. As she drove, she remembered that this was the way to the meeting location in the woods. She took the turn onto the dirt road and took it slow. She parked the car behind some trees, far away from the place where she knew the high school kids congregated. She got out of the car and took the trail into the woods.

She walked the trail for a while until she saw the turn that led to the clearing where the shed was. She turned and walked farther into the woods. She walked for another fifteen minutes before she was in the clearing. As she came out of the woods, she could see that the shed had been demolished and was now only a pile of wood. She found a rock near the debris and sat down.

The sun hit her directly on her face. Jolene had always loved being outdoors in the warmth of the sun. She closed her eyes and sat on the rock for a while. She was so into the sun that the only thing that brought her out of this trance was her phone ringing. She pulled it out of her pocket and answered it.

"Hi, Livy."

"Hi, girl. I got your email. What's up?"

"Oh, thanks for calling me. I thought we could talk in person. I know you two are busy with the house. By the way, how are things going with the renovation?"

"Everything is good. Sure we can meet. When? Where?"

"I thought we could have dinner——Sunday afternoon around four. What do you think?"

"Sure, sounds good. See you Sunday. Bye."

"See you, bye."

Jolene hung up the phone. She looked at the time and realized she had been too long in the woods. She stood up from the rock and walked back to the woods. She walked a bit faster than before and got back to the trail in no time where she picked up the pace. She made it back to the car in half an hour. As she drove off, she passed a group of kids parked and hanging out. She took it slow going by them, and after she passed them, she speeded up a bit and before long she was on the main road.

Jolene remembered a small diner on this route, so she headed toward it and got there in twenty minutes. Inside the diner, she took a seat near the back and looked over the menu. The waitress came over with a glass of water. "Hi," said the waitress setting the water on the table.

"Hi," said Jolene back.

"Ready to order?" she asked.

"Yes, I'll take a number two and a glass of ginger ale."

"Okay, anything else?"

"No, thanks."

The waitress left with her order and Jolene took a couple of sips of her water. She got her phone out and checked for messages. A few minutes later, the waitress came back with her food. Jolene ate most of her lunch, but her stomach started to act up so she stopped eating. The waitress came back for a second time, and Jolene let her know that she was all set and was ready for the bill. The waitress came back with the bill and left it on the table.

Jolene took a couple of sips of her ginger ale in hopes that her stomach would settle. She took money out of her wallet and left it on the table with the bill. She grabbed her purse and left the diner. She started the car but didn't drive off right away; she sat back rubbing her stomach trying to get it to settle. After a few minutes of rubbing it, she felt comfortable enough to drive. She made it to the house, rushed out of the car and into the house. She ran up the stairs and into her room and directly to the bathroom.

She just made it before she had to bend down over the toilet bowl. She puked up everything she just ate at the diner and had the dry heaves for a minute longer. She rinsed her mouth and got dressed in her pajamas, taking off anything that was constricting her stomach. As she was coming out of the bathroom, she heard a knock at the door. "Come in," she said in a whisper.

Anna walked into the room, "Are you okay?" she asked.

"No, I just vomited up everything I ate," answered Jolene.

"I'll get you some tea, okay. Why don't you lie down."

"Thanks, I'm fine. I'll sit on the couch and watch TV."

"Okay, I'll be right back. I'll leave the door open."

"Okay."

She went to the couch and turned on the TV. She grabbed the quilt from the back of the couch and wrapped it around her body and got comfortable. Anna walked back with the tea on a tray. She poured a cup and handed it to her. Jolene took the cup and carefully sipped the tea. Anna stayed with her, and after a few more sips, Jolene relaxed as her stomach started to feel better. She smiled at Anna.

"Better?" Anna asked.

"Yes, thanks."

Anna smiled back at her and left her alone in her room. Jolene sat back and continued to sip the tea until it was gone. She put the cup on the tray on the table and settled back on the couch, wrapped in the quilt. She selected a movie on TV and put the remote control down. She got about an hour into the movie before she fell asleep. She woke up with a full bladder and needed to go to the bathroom.

Taking the quilt off, she went to the bathroom. She came back and tried to get comfortable again, but couldn't find any position that felt right. She shut off the TV and went to bed. She found a comfortable position and closed her eyes. Her body was tired from vomiting and she was emotionally drained, so she quickly dropped off to sleep.

When Sunday came, Jolene was excited that Livy and Stacie were coming for dinner. She talked to Anna to make sure that the dinner preparations were all set, and went back to her room for a quick shower. She found a nice dress to wear for dinner and did her makeup and hair. She took one last look at herself in the mirror before she went downstairs. Anna saw her walk into the kitchen and noticed how beautiful she looked. "Everything is fine," said Anna smiling before Jolene could ask her.

"Great, thanks. I'll be in the living room if you need me for anything."

"Okay."

Jolene went to the living room and sat on the sofa where she could see the front door. She turned the stereo on to a soft rock music station. She was nervous about seeing the girls and she hoped Livy wasn't too upset with her. Minutes passed and she heard the door opening. She got up from the sofa and went to the foyer.

Livy and Stacie walked into the house. Jolene moved quickly towards them and hugged Livy and kissed her on the cheek. Livy kissed her back and then she went to Stacie. They both gave her a big smile back. "It's so nice to see you two," she said.

"Same here," said Livy.

"Back at you, girlfriend," said Stacie.

Anna walked out to the foyer, "Hi girls," she said.

"Hi Anna," they said together.

Jolene and the girls walked into the living room. "I'll bring some refreshments," Anna said from the doorway.

"Thanks Anna."

Jolene sat on the big couch while the girls sat on the smaller couch across from her. "So how's the house?" she asked.

"Great. Can you believe Livy's father?" asked Stacie.

"Really awful."

Livy smiled, "I'm just glad that my mother came clean about it before she left," she said.

"Definitely. It was nice of her," said Jolene.

Anna came back with a tray full of beverages. She settled the tray on the table and left the room. They all reached for a drink and sipped while Livy and Stacie told Jolene more about the renovations at the house. Livy described her conversation with her mother before she moved out.

Jolene was so relaxed around them; she hadn't felt this way for weeks. They talked and laughed for another fifteen minutes when Anna came back to announce that dinner was served. They got up from the couch and walked to the dining room. Jolene sat down first and then Livy and Stacie sat across from her. They began to eat——Jolene ate slowly, just trying small bites and moving the food around her plate, trying not to get her stomach upset. The talk was animated and very enjoyable. For a little while she was able to put the memories of Gus and Greg out of her mind.

"So what do you want to talk about?" asked Livy.

Jolene laughed, "Let's finish eating first, then we can talk," she said.

Livy smiled, "You're going to make me wait?"

"C'mon, Jolene, no way," said Stacie laughing.

They all started to laugh then continued eating. When they were done with dinner, Anna brought them dessert. They all enjoyed Anna's delicious desserts, so it was gone quickly.

"Let's go to the study," said Jolene.

Anna walked in as they were walking out. "How about coffee?"

"Yes, can you bring it to the study?" asked Jolene.

"Sure," Anna said, going back to the kitchen.

Jolene listened to Livy and Stacie chatting. She admired their determination to stay together; they had been in a relationship since high school. She opened the door for them and let them go in first. She followed them in, went to the desk and sat on the chair. She signaled for them to sit on the chairs in front of the desk. Livy raised an eyebrow, obviously a bit curious. They always sat on the couch so this seemed serious. When they were seated, Jolene began, "With the situation regarding my father resolved and Greg and Gus gone…" she started to say when she was interrupted by a knock at the door.

"Come in."

Anna walked in with a tray of coffee, set it on a small table and poured it for them. She brought each a cup, straightened the tray and left the study. Jolene took a sip of her coffee then put the cup down and continued talking. "I don't know if I told you already how much I appreciate all your help with my father's case. You know I love you two."

"We love you, too," said Stacie, intrigued about where all this was going.

"You have already thanked us many times," said Livy.

Jolene was getting sad again. She was going to miss them a lot. "Jolene what's up? Just say it."

She looked up at Livy——as always she was very impatient. She smiled again and continued talking, "I have decided to sell the house."

"What?" they both said in unison.

"I accomplished what I set out to do and Gus and Greg are not coming back."

"How do you know?" asked Livy.

Jolene shook her head, "Livy they've been gone for three weeks. The last day we were together was awful. We said ugly things to each other. They're not coming back and I don't blame them."

"Jolene, give them time. You'll see," said Stacie.

Jolene moved off the chair and went to the window, looking out at the pond.

"I don't have the time to wait," she said turning and looking at Livy. "It's time to move on. Livy can you please put the house on the market?"

"Fine," Livy snapped at her.

Jolene went back to her chair and took a sip of her coffee.

"When will you be leaving? Your mother will be happy to have you back," observed Stacie.

"As soon as the house sells. I'm not going back to France though. I requested a transfer to either California or New York."

Livy's eyes almost popped out of her head, "Jolene stay with us. We have plenty of space at the house," she pleaded.

Jolene gave them a big smile. "Thank you for the offer. I can't stay here without Greg and Gus."

Livy and Stacie looked at each other but didn't say anything to her. After they talked for a while about the sale of the house it was already past nine o'clock. Stacie looked at her watch, "Wow, look at the time. We have to go, work tomorrow you know."

"I know, thank you for coming," said Jolene getting up from the chair.

The girls got up, too and all three walked out of the study. Jolene walked them to the front door where they hugged and kissed and said goodnight.

Jolene's mood changed quickly when she realized she was alone again. She locked the front door and went straight to her room, quickly changing into her pajamas and going to bed.

Livy wanted to call Greg and Gus but it was early morning in France and she knew they wouldn't be awake yet. She decided she would call them tomorrow as soon she could. Stacie and Livy drove to their house quietly, both extremely upset with Jolene's news.

Chapter 23

It was early Monday morning and Livy was already in her office. She dialed Greg's number and let the phone ring.

"Hello," answered Greg.

"Greg," said Livy.

"Livy."

"Is Gus with you?" she asked.

"Yes, let me get him. Is something wrong?" he asked.

"Get Gus, please. I just want to say this once," she said with a firm voice.

"I'm going, I'm going," he said walking to where Greg was.

"Hey Greg," he called, "I have Livy on the phone. She wants to talk with us," he said.

Greg came out of the study and Gus put the phone on speaker, "Okay, we're both here," he said.

"Hi Gus," she said a bit less tense.

"Hi Livy. What's wrong?" he asked.

"Jolene had us over for dinner last night."

"Great," said Gus.

"Yes it was nice to see her, but what she told us was not nice."

"What, Livy?" snapped Greg.

"She's putting the house up for sale. Also, she's asked for a transfer to California or New York. I'm worried about her. She looks tired and like she's lost weight."

Greg and Gus stayed quiet for a moment, absorbing what she was saying. Then Gus spoke, "Did you talk to Anna?"

"No, we didn't have time."

"It's okay, Livy. We already have plans to go back for this Wednesday. We'll take care of everything when we get back."

"You better! This is your fault——both of you——leaving her like that instead of trying to work things out."

Greg knew he overreacted to the situation, but now was not the time for regrets. No, he wanted go back and make things right. "Livy, we'll fix it, I promise."

"Good, see you soon," said Livy feeling much better than when she started the call.

Greg hung up the phone and tried to walk away from Gus. "This isn't just your fault; we both abandoned her. We'll make it up to her, okay?" Gus said embracing him and giving him a kiss.

Things only got worse for Jolene after her dinner with Livy and Stacie. She kept getting sick and her stomach was queasy all the time. Nothing but broth and tea stayed down for any length of time in her stomach——everything else she puked up. It was early Wednesday morning and she had no energy to get out of bed. She heard Anna knocking at the door. "Jolene, are you okay? You haven't eaten your breakfast."

"I'm fine Anna. I'm not hungry. Don't worry, okay?"

"Okay," Anna said, not sure what to think anymore.

She took the tray with the uneaten breakfast and went back to the kitchen. Jolene turned on her other side, hoping her stomach would stop hurting. On top of all this, she had not heard from her manager about the transfer or from Livy about the house sale. She closed her eyes and tried to go to sleep.

Anna came back at midmorning with a tray of tea and a bowl of fruit. She knocked on the door again, "I'm leaving you some fruit and tea, okay?" she said thru the door.

"Okay," was all Jolene could manage to say.

Anna went back to the kitchen where Len sat on a stool drinking juice. "She's not coming out. Len, I'm worried about her," she said.

"Honey, Jolene is a smart woman. She's probably just tired. She'll come out of it any time now."

"I'm not so sure," said Anna as she occupied herself with kitchen chores.

Jolene opened her eyes again, got out of bed and went to the bathroom. All that came out of her were dry heaves. She rinsed her mouth and went back to the bed. She must have fallen asleep again because she awoke to hear Anna knocking at the door. "Jolene, are you sure you're okay? Eat something, please," said Anna through the door.

"Leave it at the door," she answered.

Anna tried to open the door but it was locked. She shook her head and went back downstairs. She was so worried about her. She felt she needed some fresh air, so she walked out to the garden from the kitchen. She stayed there for a few minutes before going back in. She was keeping herself busy in the kitchen when she heard someone yelling hello, and she rushed to the front door. Standing in the foyer were Gus and Greg. She felt Len behind her. "It's about time," she said, starting to cry. Len embraced her from behind.

Greg and Gus left their bags on the floor and went to her, "Anna what's wrong? Is Jolene okay?" asked Greg.

"No, she's not" she said tears coming down. "The past few days she hasn't come out of her room. She's hasn't eaten anything today. Three times I brought her something to eat and she hasn't touched it."

"Have you tried talking to her?" asked Gus.

"Yes, she answered me but still didn't come out. I tried opening the door, but it's locked. She needs to eat in her condition."

"In her condition?" asked Greg.

Anna didn't say anything, but Len provided him with the answer to his question. "Anna believes that Jolene is pregnant."

"Pregnant, Gus!" Greg said looking at him.

"Anna we'll take care of her, okay," said Gus walking towards the stairs.

"Wait, the key. I remember seeing it in the desk drawer, I'll get it," said Greg rushing to the study.

In minutes he was back with a key chain with several keys.

"Do you know which one is for her room?"

"Yes," said Anna taking the key chain from him and pulling one out.

"Thanks, Anna. Fix something to eat for her. Give us some time with her okay?"

"Okay," said Anna walking from the foyer to the kitchen, Len went with her.

Greg and Gus rushed upstairs to Jolene's room. Greg unlocked the door and they walked in together. The room was totally in darkness——the light was off and the curtains were drawn.

"Greg, get the curtains," said Greg as he turned the light on. They both turned to see her curled in a ball in the middle of the bed. They only could see half her face and it was pale and she did looked thinner. Greg moved to the bed and Gus went to the other side. They climbed in on either side of her. Gus moved the blanket from her face. Jolene didn't even move——she looked so fragile.

"Gus, what have we done?" asked Greg in a whisper.

"We'll fix this, okay?" he said and then he called her name, "Jolene," he called her, putting a hand on her shoulder.

"Jolene," he called again. He looked at Greg.

"Jolene" called Greg this time next to her ear.

Jolene opened her eyes and looked around in alarm. She quickly closed her eyes again.

"Jolene, baby wake up," said Greg, still at her ear.

She opened her eyes and looked at him, then turned and looked at Gus. She just stared at them not saying anything. She didn't even move.

"Jolene, it's us," said Gus caressing her face. She leaned her face into the caress and tears fell down her cheek. "I dreamed so many times that you were back with me. I don't want to move and

I don't want to find out this is another dream," she spoke with a raw voice.

"This is not a dream, mon amour," said Gus.

"We are here, my love," said Greg.

When she heard Greg's voice, more tears came down. "Please stop crying, baby."

She didn't know what to believe. For weeks, her dreams had only been about them; she couldn't handle another disappointment. She closed her eyes and quickly opened them and they were still there. She pushed herself up and threw her arms around their necks. "You're real," she said with tears pouring down her cheeks.

"Oh baby, please stop crying," said Greg again.

Jolene let go of them and turned to face Greg; she couldn't stop crying. "I'm so sorry. I never meant to her hurt you, to hurt either one of you. I don't know why I did what I did. I'm so ashamed of myself. Please forgive me."

"I forgive you baby, but please don't cry anymore. You're breaking my heart."

"Oh, Greg. When Daniel asked me to marry him, I was stunned. I went numb. I didn't know what to say. Then he put the ring in my hand and told me to think it over. I just felt so disgusted at myself and dirty."

"Oh Jolene. We didn't know," said Gus.

Jolene looked at him and more tears ran down. "When you called me a whore I lashed out at you because I could not lash out at myself. I was so angry with myself. I'm so sorry."

"Baby, please, stop crying. Let's forget the past and move on to the future," said Greg.

"I agree with Greg. You need to brush your teeth and take a shower before Anna gets here with something for you to eat. You have her in tears," said Gus.

"I know, I will, but I don't think I can eat anything. I'm not feeling well."

"We know. It's your stomach. Anna thinks you're pregnant," said Gus caressing her face, "What do you think?" he asked her.

"I think so, too."

"Is it ours?" asked Greg.

"Yes," said Jolene looking at him.

Gus moved from the bed, "Let's get you ready, okay?" he said, pulling her off the bed to stand her up.

Jolene wobbled a bit as she tried to stand. Gus took her by the waist and helped her get steady. Greg moved behind her and took her other side. Jolene took slow steps to the bathroom with their help.

"I need to use the toilet," she said.

"Okay," said Greg helping her.

"I can do it myself. I'm fine. I'll call you if I need you."

"There's no way we're leaving you alone," said Greg firmly.

"Fine," she said pulling her pajama bottoms down. Greg got her toothbrush ready and Gus started the water. When she was done, she wobbled a bit trying to stand up and they got her steady again. Greg helped her to the sink where she brushed her teeth while Gus took his clothes off and got in the shower. Jolene finished with her teeth.

"Here, I'll take her. C'mon, honey."

Jolene walked into the stall to a completely naked Gus. She looked him over inch by inch. She always loved his lean body. A few seconds later, Greg got in the stall, too and settled behind her. Jolene tried to turn around to see him and lost her balance, but quickly they both held her up.

Now facing Greg, she got an eyeful of him, too. Greg got a washcloth and started to wash her and Gus got the shampoo. "Baby, lean your head back."

She did as he asked, holding onto Greg for balance while Gus washed her hair. They rinsed the soap and shampoo away and Greg turned the water off while Gus helped her out of the stall. He took a towel and wrapped it around his waist, then took a big one and started to dry her off. Greg got out and wrapped his lower body in a towel, too. He took another towel and helped dry her hair.

They wrapped her in the towel and helped her to get back to the room. Gus got her some clothes while Greg got underwear from the drawer. They helped her dress and quickly settled her on the couch. Greg went through the drawers and found something to wear and brought clothes to Gus. They dressed and went to sit next to her. Greg could see that she was exhausted. They heard a knock at the door. "Come in," said Greg.

Anna walked in with a tray full of all kinds of food. She put the tray on the table and went over to Jolene. Jolene looked at her. "I'm sorry; I didn't mean to make you cry. I'm fine."

"You gave me a scare," said Anna reaching for her hands and holding them.

"I would have come out eventually," said Jolene.

"Eat, okay?"

"Okay."

"We'll make sure she eats," said Gus.

Greg took the bowl of broth from the tray and started to feed her. Jolene took small sips. He stopped when she had eaten half of it and Gus handed her the cup of tea. Jolene tried to hold the cup but her hands were shaking. Gus put his hand over hers and helped her to steady the cup. She smiled and took a sip of the tea. She took a few mores sips and Gus took the cup from her.

"I want you to finish the broth first," he said while Greg went back to feeding her.

She ate all the broth and finished the tea. Greg put the empty bowl on the tray and lifted her to his lap and she placed her head on his chest. Gus sat next to Greg and rubbed her back gently. "Oh, that feels so good," she said.

"Baby, you're pale. You need some sun."

"That's a great idea. Some fresh air will do you good."

"I don't know, Greg."

"C'mon, I'll carry you," he said standing up with her in his arms. He walked out of the room as Gus walked beside them.

Greg went slowly down the stairs and they walked through the living room and out of the house. Greg walked through the garden and went to the bench across the pond. He was about to sit down when Gus stopped him, "Let me hold her."

Greg handed her to Gus and sat on the bench beside them. Gus held her tight against his body and she snuggled into his chest. "It feels so good to be in your arms. I missed being held by you both so much. The bed felt so empty without you," she said.

"We won't leave you alone ever again," said Gus kissing her forehead. They sat there talking. Gus told her about the modeling shoots he had been doing. She told them about what she heard in court and how much Phil helped her through the ordeal. She also mentioned how relieved she was when they were all found guilty.

After a couple of hours out in the sun, Jolene started to get tired and she yawned out loud. Greg and Gus looked at each other both thinking that they probably overdid it. They got up and headed back inside. As they entered the house, Anna met them. She looked at Jolene in Gus's arms, "She's asleep," she stated.

"Already," said Greg looking at her.

"Let's bring her to her room," said Gus walking upstairs. Greg followed behind him and opened the door for Gus who walked in and brought Jolene to the bed. Anna had taken the opportunity to change the bed linens while they were outside. Greg pulled the clean blanket down and Gus settled her in the middle. They didn't want to be apart from her right now, so both got comfortable on each side of her. Gus covered all three of them with the blanket and got close to her. Greg did the same on the other side. In no time, they were both fast asleep.

Jolene heard a soothing voice from far off; someone was calling her name. She opened her eyes and she saw Gus next to her. "Hi, sleepy head. It's time to eat."

"What time is it?" she asked.

"It's almost seven. Anna brought you something to eat," said Greg at her other side. She turned to him and saw a big smile on his face. She smiled back. "So get up and eat."

"Okay," she said still a bit wobbly.

She sat on the edge of the bed and stayed for a few seconds getting her bearings. After she was sure she was okay, she stood up. This time she was fine. Greg moved to go with her.

"I'll be fine. I'll call you if I need you I."

"You're sure?" he asked.

"Yes."

Jolene went to the bathroom and Gus and Greg stayed next to the door to in case she called out for them. When she came out, she found them standing by the door. "You two need to stop hovering over me," she said.

Greg and Gus both made a serious face and took her hands and led her to the couch. Greg took a plate from the tray and gave it to her, then took one for himself. Gus did the same.

Anna had put cheese and fruit on the tray for Jolene, and she put chicken and potatoes on plates for Greg and Gus. She would have loved to be able to eat what they were eating, but she knew it would make her ill. She took the fork and ate her fruit.

Greg and Gus settled back on the couch and ate, too. They made light conversation with her, keeping her distracted. The guys finished eating and went for their drinks. Greg took the empty plate from Jolene and gave her the drink. They continued to chat. Gus finished his drink and put the glass on the tray. He put his arm around her shoulders and pulled her close to him. Jolene settled in between his legs and continued to drink her juice.

Greg put his glass down, too, and got comfortable on the couch. He picked her feet up and put them on his lap and started to rub them. There was a knock at the door. Jolene tried to move away from Gus but he tightened his hold on her.

"Come in," said Greg.

Anna walked into the room and went to Jolene. "How are you feeling?" she asked.

"Better," she answered.

"Good, and you ate all the fruit. That's good."

"Thanks, Anna, everything was delicious," said Greg.

Gus nodded his head, "Definitely."

Anna gave her a kiss on the forehead and started to take the tray away. "Here," said Jolene putting the empty glass on the tray and smiling at Anna, "Thanks." Anna left the room.

Greg turned on the TV and settled back on the couch. He took the quilt from the back of the couch and covered her. Jolene settled back on Gus. He wrapped his arms around her waist and gently rubbed her stomach while Greg continued to rub her feet. She was so happy that she started to cry again.

"Baby, what's wrong?" asked Greg in an alarmed voice.

"Nothing, I'm just so happy to be with you guys. I thought I'd never see you again."

"Mon amour, we should never have left you. We'll make it up to you, promise," said Gus with a firm tone as he bent down to give her a kiss on her cheek.

"You already have by being here," she said caressing his face with her hand.

They stayed together on the couch watching the movie Greg selected. Close to the end of the movie, Greg gave Gus a tap on the arm.

"She's asleep," he whispered.

Greg took the quilt from her and Gus stood up and brought her to the bed. Greg found her pajamas, and carefully so as not to wake her up, they changed her into them. Greg covered her with the blanket while Gus stepped into the bathroom. When he came out, he already had his pajama bottoms on. He gave Greg a quick kiss on the lips and slid into bed next to Jolene. Greg took his turn in the bathroom and quickly came out in pajamas, too. He turned the light off and got in the other side of the bed. They cuddled next to her.

Chapter 24

Jolene watched in amazement at the ultrasound of the babies. All three were thrilled with the doctor's news that they were having twins. It had been two weeks since Gus and Greg had come back home. They had been wonderful to her, taking such great care of her. They insisted that she make an appointment with an obstetrician and now she was here. She was happy that Greg went back to the company; he loved working there.

She was on the examination table as the doctor turned the sound up so they could hear the heartbeats. Greg and Gus were glowing as they each held one of her hands. The doctor finished with the examination. "Get dressed. I'll be back to talk to you," the doctor said.

Jolene sat on the table while Greg found something to clean off her stomach. He got her clean and they both helped her dress. A few minutes later, the doctor knocked on the door, "Can I come in?"

"Yes," said Jolene.

The doctor came back in and sat in a chair next to Jolene who was still sitting on the bed. The doctor told them that, based on her stomach measurement and the date of her last period, she was three months pregnant. They all smiled at each other. The doctor gave her several informational pamphlets regarding pregnancy and what to expect. After she was finished telling them what they needed to know, she said goodbye. All three of them thanked her and left the office.

Jolene checked the time on her watch, it was early afternoon in France, so she decided to call her mother while Greg was driving her back home. The phone rang about three times before her mother answered. "Hi, honey," said Marcia.

"Hi, Mom. We just left the doctor's office."

"Is everything okay with the baby?" asked her mother.

"Yes, the doctor said everything is great. I have more good news: The doctor told us we're having twins!"

"Oh my, twins? That's great! Are you happy?" she asked.

Jolene could hear the happiness in her mother's voice. She was always worried that her mother would not accept her relationship with Greg and Gus, but she had been very supportive of them. "Yes, very."

"I'll let Adrien know. Jolene sweetie, I love you. I'm so happy for you."

"I love you too, Mom."

"I have to go, honey. We have a guest coming for dinner," said Marcia.

"Okay, Mom. I'll talk to you soon."

"Okay, honey. Bye."

Jolene hung up the phone and noticed that they were not going home, "Where are we going?" she asked.

"We're taking you out for lunch," said Gus.

"I don't know guys. Maybe we should go home," she said hesitantly.

"Jolene, are you embarrassed to be seen with us?" asked Greg.

Jolene turned to Greg and quickly caressed his face, "It's not that. I just don't want people to misjudge our relationship. I don't want to have people act mean towards either of you," she said.

"Oh baby, it doesn't matter what people think of our relationship. The important thing is that we're happy," said Gus behind her, caressing her arm.

"Okay."

Greg drove downtown and parked in the lot of the most popular restaurant in town. It would definitely be all over town that they were seen together. They helped her out of the car and each took one her hands and walked into the restaurant. The hostess saw them coming in. She smiled and said, "Hi, Greg."

"Hi, Tina. A table for three, please," he said.

"Sure, this way," she said leading them to a table. She put the menus on the table and told them that the waitress would be coming soon.

Jolene quietly looked over her menu while the guys talked about some of the selections. After a few minutes, the waitress came and poured water in the glasses for them.

"My name is Kim. I'll be your waitress today. Anything to drink? Are you ready to order or do you need more time?" she asked.

"We're ready, Jolene?"

"I'm ready," she said.

Greg and Gus ordered coffee and Jolene ordered tea. They also gave their food choices to the waitress and she left to put their orders in. Greg took one of her hands just as Gus took the other. She looked at them and smiled.

"I'm so happy! For the past two weeks, I woke up worrying that this was a dream and that soon I'd wake up."

"This is no dream, baby. We're real and we're going to be with you forever."

"Yes, you're stuck with us," said Gus laughing softly.

"Thank you," she said.

The waitress came back with their drinks and about five minutes later, she brought their meals. She set the plates on the table and left. Jolene started to eat, slowly taking small bites so her stomach would not get upset. Gus and Greg watched her a few seconds, then they dug into their food. The lunch was great and they had a good time. After Gus paid the bill, Greg drove them back to the house. It was already past one o'clock by the time they got home. Anna joined them in the foyer.

"Well?" she said looking at Jolene.

"Anna," said Jolene rushing to her and giving her a hug, "we're having twins."

"Twins!" said Anna hugging her back, "That's wonderful, twins, wow!" she said with a big smile on her face.

Jolene laughed out loud. Anna looked at her and noticed she was shining now. Her face was beautiful again and her smile was back. Anna let go of her and gave Greg and Gus each a kiss on the cheek. "Congratulations!"

"Thanks," they said together.

"This is great news. It's a day to celebrate and I'm going to make you a fantastic dinner. You should invite Livy and Stacie over."

"Yes, we will, thanks Anna," said Greg.

Anna danced happily to the kitchen and started to get things together for dinner. They went to the family room where Gus turned on the TV while Greg took his phone out and dialed. "Hi Livy," he said.

"Hey. What's up?"

"We want you two to join us for dinner tonight."

"Great, I know we don't have plans for the night so that will be perfect. We haven't all been together for a long time."

"I know. It will be really nice. See you around six o'clock. Is that okay?"

"Yes," she said.

"Great, see you, bye."

"Bye."

Greg hung up went and sat beside them on the couch. Gus had put a movie on already. Jolene picked up her feet and Greg slid underneath them and sat beside Gus. Gus smiled to him and wrapped an arm around his neck while Jolene was sitting across his lap. All three got comfortable and watched the movie.

Jolene stopped paying attention to the movie and looked at them for a moment. She was wondering what had been keeping her from proclaiming her love for them. Was it the situation with her father or was she just plain scared to commit? She looked up to see them staring at her.

"Are you okay?" asked Gus.

"Yes, I'm just feeling very happy. That's all."

They didn't believe her answer, but didn't push it further. She went back to watching the movie and so did they. The movie lasted two and a half hours and by the time it was over, it was close to four o'clock. Greg shut off the TV and stood up.

"We should ask Mom and Dad to come over sometime this week," he said looking at them.

Jolene stood up beside him. "Oh, Greg I'm sorry. I forget about them. Definitely, let's invite them over," she said as he pulled her into his arms. Jolene settled her head on his chest and held herself close to him.

Gus smiled and stood up, too. He reached behind Jolene and wrapped his arms around both of them. They held each other for a while. "We should get ready for dinner," said Gus. "Jolene, why don't you go first. I have to call my family and Greg needs to talk to his parents."

Jolene smiled and they let her go. She went upstairs and into her room. Meanwhile, Gus went to the study to call his family and Greg walked out to the terrace to call his father. Jolene took a quick shower and got dressed. She was coming out of her room when Gus and Greg were coming in. Each of them gave her a kiss on her lips and went to their own rooms.

She watched them go, then turned around and walked downstairs. She went to the kitchen, sat on one of the stools and watched Anna cook. After a few minutes, Len came in from outside. He went to Jolene, wrapped his arms around her and gave her a kiss on the forehead. "Congratulations," he said with big smile.

"Thank you," she said.

"Where are the guys?" he asked.

"They're getting ready for dinner."

Len sat next to her and Anna brought him a cup of coffee and a cup of tea for Jolene. She went back to preparing dinner, checking the oven, then the pots on the stove.

"Here you are," said Greg walking into the kitchen.

He sat next to her and pulled the stool close to him and wrapped his arm around her shoulders. She leaned her head on his shoulder. Anna brought him coffee. "Thank you," he said.

"Hey, can I get some, too," said Gus standing in the kitchen doorway.

Anna smiled at him and went to the coffee maker to get him his coffee. Len stood up from the stool and stretched his hand out to Gus, "Congratulations," he said, then went to Greg and shook his hand.

"Thanks," said both fathers.

Len gave Anna a kiss on the cheek and left the kitchen. Gus sat on the empty stool and Anna brought him his coffee. They all sat and sipped their drinks. When they were done, they went to the living room and all three got comfortable on the big couch. They talked about setting up one of the rooms as the nursery for the babies, and discussed some child-proofing renovations for the house.

They talked for a while then they heard the front door open. Livy and Stacie walked into the living room. Jolene stood up and went to them and all three wrapped themselves in a group hug. Livy and Stacie held her tight. After a few seconds, they loosened their hold a bit and Livy asked her, "How are you feeling?"

"Much better. The morning sickness is gone," she said.

"How was the doctor visit?" asked Stacie.

"Great. We have news for you two, come let's sit," she said.

Jolene went back to the couch and sat down between Greg and Gus. Livy and Stacie took the other couch. Livy and Stacie looked at all three on the couch and noticed that they were all beaming with happiness. "So, what's the news?" asked Livy impatiently.

"You tell her," said Jolene to Gus.

"Okay, we're having twins."

The girls looked at each and gave them a big smile.

"Twins, wow! That's fantastic!" said Livy.

"That's awesome!" said Stacie.

"Yes, we're very happy," said Greg.

They continued talking about the pregnancy and the babies. Then they told Stacie and Livy about some of their plans to renovate the house and a room for the babies. They talked for a while, everyone laughing and joking. Jolene realized how much she missed the times she spent with this group. It had been a real trial when she was alone, but now she had everyone back and she was very happy.

Back in the dining room, Anna finished with the last of the preparations for dinner. She set the napkins on the table then went out of the room. Anna walked to the living room and stood in the doorway, "Hi Livy, Stacie," she said.

"Hi Anna," said the girls.

"Great news about the pregnancy," said Livy.

"Yes, it is. Dinner is ready and the table is set."

"Great, thanks."

Anna left the room and went back to the kitchen. Greg moved Jolene's legs from his lap and stood up. He extended his hand to help her stand up. Jolene took his hand and he pulled her up. Gus stood behind her, while Livy and Stacie were already standing and slowly started to walk out of the room. The other three caught up with them and the whole group walked together to the dining room talking and laughing.

Livy and Stacie sat across from Gus and Greg with Jolene between them. This was the first time in a while that she was having dinner with the whole group. She smiled at everyone.

"What?" Stacie asked.

"I'm so happy to be together with all of you. I missed our times together."

"We did too," said Livy.

Anna walked in with the serving dishes. She set them in the middle of the table for them and left the room. Gus picked up one of the plates and started to serve the food. He passed to Jolene and soon everyone had a plateful. They fell into the old pattern of eating, talking and laughing together. Dinner was fantastic and everyone was having fun. Anna came back with a dessert for them.

They all took some of the dessert and started to eat it. Everyone was so full that no one moved from the chairs. They continued talking for a long time, enjoying their time together. Stacie looked at her watch. "Sweetie, we have to go. I have a system upgrade due this weekend, so I have to be at work early tomorrow morning," said Stacie.

"Wow, it's getting late," said Livy.

They all stood up and walked to the foyer. The girls gave each of them a hug and kiss and said goodbye. Gus and Greg took Jolene by the hand and they walked into the family room. Gus sat down and pulled her onto his lap. Greg found the TV remote control and put a movie on, then sat down on the couch. He lifted Jolene's legs onto his lap. Gus pulled the quilt from the back of the couch and wrapped it around her.

Jolene got comfortable and leaned her head on his chest. Sometime during the movie, Jolene became tired and yawned a bit. She tried to focus on the movie but after several minutes she fell asleep. Greg looked over at Gus and put his finger to his lips to signal to Gus to stay quiet. "She's asleep," he whispered.

Gus smiled at him, wrapped a hand around Greg's neck and pulled him over. He pressed his lips on his and gave him a kiss. Greg opened his lips for him and Gus quickly thrust his tongue in Greg's mouth. They kissed for some time in a wonderful dance of tongues. They stopped kissing and got back to watching the movie. After the movie was over, Greg turned the TV off and Gus stood up with Jolene in his arms and walked out of the room. Greg stood up and joined him. They walked upstairs very slowly and quietly. They got upstairs and went to her room. Greg turned down the covers and very carefully, Gus settled her in the bed. He pulled his arms from under her and softly moved away from the bed.

Greg pulled him aside and pushed him against the wall, holding his arms up and quickly devouring his lips. Gus opened his mouth for him and they continued the wild kiss they started in the living room. Greg stopped the deep kiss, but continued to give Gus soft tugs and kisses. "I want you so badly," Greg whispered nibbling on Gus's lower lip.

"Me too, but we can't. We have to wait for her," whispered Gus back, rubbing his body against Greg's.

Greg pulled away and patted his hair with his hand in frustration. Gus stroked him on the arm, "Let's get her pajamas on," he said sneaking a kiss on his neck.

Greg went and got her pajamas from the bathroom while Gus started to pull her clothes off. Greg came back and helped with the rest of the clothes. After they were done, Gus covered her with the blanket and Greg took that time to go back to the bathroom and got his pajamas on.

He came out and went to the right side of the bed and slid in next to her, curling himself around her. Gus went to the bathroom and put his pajamas on. He turned the light off and climbed into bed, curling himself next to her like Greg did, and they both went to sleep.

Jolene moaned. Greg was doing incredible things with his mouth on her pussy, and Gus was driving her body berserk sucking on her nipples.

She moaned again, "Greg," she said between her groans. Greg spread her more and started to fuck her with his tongue, in and out of her hole while, at the same time, Gus took a hold of one nipple in his mouth and pinched the other between his fingers.

"Greg," she barely murmured between all the moaning.

They were doing a delicious job setting her body on fire. Then Jolene was being pulled out of the dream; someone was shaking her.

Greg and Gus woke up surprised with Jolene's loud moans and groans. They looked at each other. "You think there's something wrong?" asked Greg.

"No, look, she's smiling," said Gus.

As Gus was speaking, Jolene called out Greg's name again.

"Greg," she said with soft whispers in a very sexy voice.

Greg lifted an eyebrow and Gus just stared at her. Gus started to shake her. Jolene opened her eyes. She stared at them with big glossy eyes.

"Are you okay?" asked Greg.

"Yes, I was having the most fantastic dream," she said.

"About us?" Gus asked.

"Yes, Greg was getting all hot and sweaty as he deliciously was eating my pussy," she said smiling at Greg.

"Yes we heard you call his name. And what about me? Was I in your dream?"

"Yes, you certainly were. You were torturing my body by sucking my nipples. It was the most erotic dream I've ever had of you guys," she said.

"Really, perhaps with can fix that," said Greg starting to slide down while Gus started to unbutton her top.

"No, wait," she said to both of them, "not now, I should have told you this a long time ago. I was so obsessed with getting revenge for my father and my pride that nothing else mattered."

"That's okay, mon amour, we understand."

"No, it was not fair to you two. I was scared to commit, to take that extra step in our relationship."

Greg and Gus were next to her, each leaning on an elbow looking at her. She smiled at them, then reached over and caressed each one's face.

"I love you so much," she said turning to Greg, "I have loved you since grammar school and you," she said turning to Gus, "I loved you the moment you set your beautiful blue eyes on me. My body felt like it was being pricked with millions of tiny pins." Tears ran down her face, "I love you both with all my heart," she said with a firm voice.

"Oh Jolene, I've been waiting for so long to hear those words. I love you, too," said Greg giving her a quick kiss on her lips.

"Moi aussi, je t'aime. You captured my heart the moment you looked at me," Gus said kissing her softly on her lips.

"Now, I think we should see about this dream of yours. What do you think Gus?"

"Definitely."

Jolene gave them a wicked smile and winked at them. Gus went back to unbuttoning her pajama top and Greg went down and started to pull her bottoms off. She watched every move they made. Gus brought his mouth to one of her nipples and quickly started nibbling and sucking on it. In the meantime, Greg opened her legs wider and settled between them. He brought a finger to her pussy lips and opened them. He slowly started to lick up and down her pussy while Gus sucked hard on her nipple.

She moaned her appreciation for what they were doing to her. Gus changed nipples and took the other one in his mouth at the same time that Greg thrust two fingers inside her while sucking hard on her clit. Jolene's body was so hot, her moans and groans were coming out very loud now. They continued their delicious assault on her body. She couldn't wait anymore, "Greg, please I want you inside me, please."

Greg stopped sucking her, "I know baby," he looked at Gus, "I want you to fuck me," he said to Gus.

Gus stopped sucking her nipple, moved to the nightstand and pulled out the lubricant tube from the drawer. He positioned himself behind Greg and lubricated his butt hole and his own dick. Greg positioned his shaft at Jolene's entrance and slowly thrust himself inside her at the same time that Gus thrust inside him. Together both guys moved in unison in and out. Their rhythm became harder and faster as they brought each other to total ecstasy.

Jolene's moans and groans became louder. She couldn't stop looking at them and she couldn't hold out any longer. In a matter of minutes, she exploded in a tremendous orgasm. Greg continued to thrust inside her as her trembling continued. A few minutes later, Greg came inside her while Gus came inside him.

They both continued pumping until the last drop of cum left their dicks and their trembling stopped. Gus pulled out of Greg and went to the bathroom to clean up, then brought two washcloths for them. He gave one to Greg who had just pulled out of Jolene. Greg started to clean her as Gus cleaned him. When they were done, they lay down next to her.

She couldn't stop smiling. Tonight they all realized that, from now on, their lives would be different, but completely happy because they all would be together. Greg wrapped his hand over her hip as he pulled her tight to his body, then Gus moved next to her with his arm wrapped around her upper body. They both surrounded her with such warmth and love. Jolene turned to Greg and caressed his face with her hand. "I love you," she said. Greg kissed her head.

Then she turned to Gus and tenderly touched his lips with her thumb, "Je t'aime," she said to him.

Gus kissed her cheek, "Je t'aime."

They all closed their eyes. When she closed her eyes she saw her father smiling at her. She smiled back, "I love you, Dad," she said in a whisper. A few minutes later, all three fell asleep in each other's arms.

THE END

33380721R00147

Made in the USA
Charleston, SC
12 September 2014